KISSING AMELIA

"How can we still be married?" Chance asked. "Your father told me he had taken care of everything. He said you didn't want anything to do with me, that you wanted me out of your life."

"And he paid you well for it," Amelia snapped.

"I did not take his money, but you won't believe me."

"You're right about that. Now let me go or I'll scream for help."

"Who do you expect to hear? My men aren't going to interfere." To still her flailing arms, he gripped her wrists and pulled her hands above her head. "And if we're married . . ."

As she let out a loud shriek, Chance did what he'd wanted to do since she'd come back into his life. What he'd wanted to do for years. He lowered his head and covered her lips with his. Her eyes grew wide. She twisted her head from side to side. But he was determined to teach her a lesson. The kiss was hard and demanding. Chance took of the sweetness stolen from him years ago. . . .

From *Saturday's Bride*, by Jean Wilson

BOOK YOUR PLACE ON OUR WEBSITE AND MAKE THE READING CONNECTION!

We've created a customized website just for our very special readers, where you can get the inside scoop on everything that's going on with Zebra, Pinnacle and Kensington books.

When you come online, you'll have the exciting opportunity to:

- View covers of upcoming books
- Read sample chapters
- Learn about our future publishing schedule (listed by publication month *and author*)
- Find out when your favorite authors will be visiting a city near you
- Search for and order backlist books from our online catalog
- Check out author bios and background information
- Send e-mail to your favorite authors
- Meet the Kensington staff online
- Join us in weekly chats with authors, readers and other guests
- Get writing guidelines
- AND MUCH MORE!

**Visit our website at
http://www.kensingtonbooks.com**

WEDDED BLISS

Judith E. French
Donna Jordan
Jean Wilson

ZEBRA BOOKS
Kensington Publishing Corp.
http://www.kensingtonbooks.com

ZEBRA BOOKS are published by

Kensington Publishing Corp.
850 Third Avenue
New York, NY 10022

All Kensington titles, imprints and distributed lines are
available at special quantity discounts for bulk purchases for
sales promotion, premiums, fund-raising, educational or
institutional use.

Special book excerpts or customized printings can also be
created to fit specific needs. For details, write or phone the
office of the Kensington Special Sales Manager: Kensington
Publishing Corp., 850 Third Avenue, New York, NY 10022.
Attn. Special Sales Department. Phone: 1-800-221-2647.

Zebra and the Z logo Reg. U.S. Pat. & TM Off.

First printing: April 2003
10 9 8 7 6 5 4 3 2 1

Printed in the United States of America

CONTENTS

MacKenzie's Bride

Judith E. French

Prologue

"With you I should love to live, with you be ready to die."

—Horace

Scotland, 1315

Lorna MacNeil reined in her shaggy pony and peered into the gathering twilight. Dark fell quickly over the Highlands in October, and the weather was turning foul. Already sleet was beginning to sting her cheeks and glisten on the feathers of her hawk, Morgance. There'd be the devil to pay for wandering off from the hunting party, but her overly protective father had to understand that she was eleven and nearly a woman grown. It was demeaning to always have Jock and Geordie guarding her, especially here, well inside the MacNeil Clan territory.

The plaintive bawling that had caught Lorna's attention earlier sounded again, this time much closer. To her left, a rain-swollen stream tumbled over black rocks, and just ahead her path was barred by a thicket too tangled for the pony to attempt. For a moment she hesitated, wondering if she should go back and summon help. But for what? If she told them she thought there was a cow in distress and she was mistaken, everyone might laugh at her.

Swiftly, she dismounted, fastened Morgance's leather tesses to her saddle, and secured the pony's reins. In two minutes, on foot, she fought through to the edge of the burn. On the far side stood a black-muzzled, Highland cow, curved ivory horns shiny with sleet, eyes rolled back in her head in panic, foam dripping from her open mouth. Her calf, born late in the summer judging by the size, struggled shoulder deep in the churning water. The little creature seemed exhausted, barely able to hold its head above the flow. Either its strength had given out in crossing or a small hoof was wedged between rocks.

Realizing that there was no time to summon aid, Lorna stripped off her mittens, hooded mantle, boots, and sleeveless jacket. Wind whipped through her woolen gown, chilling her. If she lacked courage, the calf would surely die, and winter was coming on. A chieftain as powerful as her father had many clansmen to feed, but even he would regret the needless loss of a beast that could fill the empty belly of a child. Gritting her teeth, Lorna yanked the gown over her head and waded into the burn, wearing only her stockings and shift.

The numbing cold burned as hot as any fire. By her third step, Lorna could no longer feel her legs. The current was stronger than she had believed possible, and once she slipped, plunging under and soaking herself completely before regaining her footing just as the calf lost its fight to remain above the surface of the stream.

"No!" Lorna cried. She caught hold of the animal and jerked its head up. The calf choked, bleating weakly. Lorna tried to tug it free from the bottom of the burn, but her strength was gone. Worse, her hands had gone as numb as her feet. She dashed the sleet from her eyes and tried to think, but her mind seemed as sodden as the calf's matted hair. Suddenly weary beyond belief, Lorna sagged and swallowed a mouthful of water.

"Are ye mad, lass?" a male voice bellowed. "Let go of the calf and take my hand!!"

Lorna stared in astonishment at the figure that had materialized ghostlike out of the gloaming and stood knee-deep in the burn, reaching out to her. "Nay," she protested. "I cannot—"

A hand clamped around her wrist. For an instant, she stared into the face of a dark-haired stranger, and then the icy heat of the water sucked her down and she slipped into velvet nothingness.

. . . To awaken shivering so hard she thought her bones would break.

"Hist, lassie," the youth said. "There's a shock you gave me. I thought ye—"

"Where . . . where am I?" Lorna managed between chattering teeth. She was vaguely aware of rock walls, a low thatched roof, and the earthy smell of cattle. She blinked and leaned close to the fire, reveling in the life-giving heat.

"'Tis an old house," he said. "Lucky for us, 'twas not far away from where ye went swimming." He thrust a crumbling oat cake into her hand, and she bit into it.

"Aye, lucky," she said, between bites. "And who are ye?" The boy—for he had no beard and could be no more than sixteen or seventeen for all his height—squatted on the far side of the open hearth. Lorna felt disoriented, and as confused as if she'd been spirited away to the kingdom of the Blue Men. Fingers of fear tightened on the nape of her neck, but she'd rather die than show it. "Will ye not declare your name and clan?" she demanded. "These are MacNeil lands. Have ye come apurpose to see my father?"

Her rescuer did not answer. Instead, he rose and went to where the calf stood nursing from its mother, took a handful of dry grass, and began to rub the calf's damp, shaggy hide.

"That's . . . that's the calf," she said. "Ye . . . saved it from drowning?"

"Saved ye both," he said. He grinned at her. "You're a brave wee thing, I'll give ye that. But ye've not the sense of a Michaelmas goose. 'Twas a foolish act to go in that swift water after—"

"Foolish?" Anger gave her courage. "And you, I suppose were brave to jump in after me?"

"Aye, brave as any hero in a baird's tale. I'll be surprised if they do not sing about me in the hall."

"In what hall?" She saw that he was wearing only a thigh-length homespun shirt and realized that a great kilt, presumably his, was her only garment. Lorna eyed the faded rust color of the rough plaid with suspicion. "Sweet mother of God! You're not a MacKenzie, are ye? Not one of those cattle-reiving—"

The sound of a hunting horn pierced the misty night. The boy's gaze met hers for a heartbeat, and then he grinned again and slipped into the darkness as silently as a wolf. She waited for the count of fifty, took a deep breath, then counted twice again before shouting, "A MacNeil! A MacNeil! To me! To me!"

Hoofbeats pounded outside. Lorna rose, trembling, prepared to meet whatever fate decreed, then cried out with joy as her father burst through the doorway and enfolded her in his loving arms.

One

Eleven Years Later

"You will do as you're told! This is a direct order from the king!" Beathag MacNeil cried.

Lorna released a bawling sheep and rose to face her angry stepmother. "Calum MacKenzie murdered my father," she flung back. "I'd sooner give myself to Lucifer than marry into that clan! If the Bruce wishes a bride for the MacKenzie, let him offer one of his own illegitimate daughters. Rumor is that there are enough to spare and more in the making."

"Stupid slut! You're no better than the mother who whelped you. You will wed where and when I say, or you will live to regret it." Beathag raised her open palm to slap Lorna's face.

Lorna dodged the blow and put two bleating ewes between them. "Touch me at your own peril," she warned. "Born on the wrong side of the blanket or not, I am Alexander MacNeil's daughter. I'll not be beaten under his roof."

Beathag's pocked face tightened to a mask of fury. "How dare you?" the older woman cried. "Who are you to speak so to me? Look at you! Hair stringing, gown stained with shite. You're a disgrace to this house, and I'll consider myself well rid of you, be it to a MacKenzie or a nunnery."

Lorna jerked the hem of her skirt out of her belt and brushed at the manure on her rough woolen gown. "You ordered me to the stables to help with the shearing, madam," she reminded. "And those who come into the byre must be prepared to deal with dung." When Beathag balled a fist and lunged at her again, Lorna scooped up a handful of sheep droppings and flung it onto the bodice of her stepmother's gown.

Beathag shrieked, slipped in the muck, and fell headlong into the filthy straw. "Erskine! Malcolm!" she blubbered. "Help! She's gone mad! She's attacking me!"

"Attacking you?" Lorna replied, switching from the formal French they'd been speaking into Gaelic. "Nay, lady. I fear ye be overwrought. If I wanted to do ye harm, I'd do worse than pelt ye with sheep shite." She seized the bucket of dirty water that stood in the corner of the stall and dashed it over Beathag's head. "There! That should cool ye down a bit! And if you're still eager to have Calum MacKenzie for a son-in-law, let one of your daughters wed him."

Beathag screamed again for help. Servants shouted. Pigeons flew up to the rafters. A red-faced stable lad doubled over in guffaws and fled the byre. Dogs yipped as the sheep scattered, two scrambling over the back of the prone and thrashing castle mistress. Beathag's plump French maid tried to pull her lady to her feet, but succeeded only in knocking her flat in the muck and falling on top of her.

"What the hell?" Lorna's oldest stepbrother, Erskine, burst through the doorway, his brother Malcolm treading on his boot heels. "What have you done to my mother, you crazy bitch?" he bellowed at Lorna.

"This!" Laughing, she bent to retrieve more ammunition and pelted both men royally before Erskine's knotted fist landed the first blow.

"By Satan's crimson arse! I'll nay be forced to accept a MacNeil to wife! Not if the Bruce name me traitor and put a price on my head!" Clansmen scattered as Calum MacKenzie strode into the great hall of the MacKenzie Keep and flung the king's decree onto the high table.

His mother sighed and rose to greet him in the courtly French used by the nobility. "Surely, the lady cannot be so bad," she soothed. "It would not be the first time that a MacKenzie had to bend like a willow in a March storm to hold this land. Robert has shed his dearest blood for Scotland's freedom. You cannot blame him if he goes to any means to seek peace between the clans."

"No, don't even try it," Calum said, dropping into the massive, high-backed chair beside his mother and continuing to speak in common Gaelic. "I'll nay be driven to marrying a MacNeil by a Bruce, and I'll nay be wheedled into it by a woman's wiles."

His mother waved to a serving lad carrying a pewter tray of steaming venison. "Eat, Calum," she said. "You've been in the saddle for four days. You must be starving. You need hot food and sleep. Tomorrow will be time enough to declare yourself an outlaw."

"Dinna attempt to sway me," he warned, breaking off a large chunk of bread. "I've said I'll nay have the MacNeil wench and I mean what I say."

He'd expected more support from his mother. She missed nothing, and Una MacNeil's reputation was as black as the devil's furnace. How could his mother think he would willingly bring such a faithless lass to his bed? Even her Campbell cousins swore she had the morals of a goat.

"Angus saw the lady Una at Sterling Castle," Calum grumbled. "He vows she has the face of a ewe and the disposition of—"

His mother laughed. "A poor judge of women, Angus. He has the face of a sheep himself—and the temper of a weasel."

"None have good to say about Una Campbell Mac-Neil."

She laid a hand on his forearm. Her expression was serious, but the twinkle in her blue eyes made him think she was amused by his situation. It was no secret that she had urged him to take a wife these past five years. "Robert insists you marry within a fortnight. Why not end the feud between MacNeil and MacKenzie for all time? Would that peace had been pledged between our clans before your father and Una MacNeil's added their blood and bones to the earth."

"We were not the cause of Alexander MacNeil's death. If he was poisoned, it did not happen here." Calum scowled. "Although many think otherwise, I know ye too well to believe ye'd murder a guest under your roof."

"A pity the gossips don't share your faith in my honor." She waved away the servants so that they could have a measure of privacy—no small matter where near to a hundred souls slept under this roof.

"It's been eight years since MacNeil died," Calum said. "Ha' they nothing more to gab about?"

"Eight years or eighty, the foul poisoning of Alexander MacNeil has been laid at my door. Even my confessor begs me to ask forgiveness for the crime."

"We didna start the feud," he said. "Do ye nay remember Red Niall MacNeil's attack and burning of the old tower with my great-grandmother and three of her bairns inside?"

His mother's frank gaze met his. "I forget nothing."

Calum raised a horn cup set in silver filigree and drank deeply of the fiery *usquebaugh*, the Scottish whiskey that many men called the *water of life*. Would you have me forget MacKenzie honor? Forget my father's murder?" He took another long swallow. "I'll offer the MacNeils naught but my naked sword. An eye for an eye."

"Until everyone is blind?"

He glared at her. The first gray hairs were beginning to show in her wheat brown hair and tiny lines creased the corners of her eyes, but she was still beautiful, his mother, lovely enough to turn the heads of many men ten years her junior. "Mayhap ye would care to wed Erskine?" he teased. "He is as ugly as his sisters, I've heard, but he's young and lusty."

His mother laughed. "One husband is enough for me," she said. "I wed William MacKenzie when I was fifteen and he forty. Sweet mother of God, what a shock it all was to me, fresh from a convent in Brittany. I knew nothing about being mistress of a keep and less about being a wife." She shook her head. "Your father had already buried two wives and had not an heir to carry on the MacKenzie name."

"He wasn't easy to live with, was he?" Calum said.

"Nor was I the biddable child William thought he'd wed. My temper was a match for his own."

"Then you must admit, I come by my own honestly."

"I see much of your father in you." She sipped her wine thoughtfully. "William was a good laird. He cared more for his clan than his own life." She closed her eyes for an instant, sighed, swallowed, then opened them. "When he died, I thought my world had come to an end."

"You were what?" Calum asked. "All of seventeen? Alone? Forced to take Father's place and hold this keep against the MacNeils, the English, and a handful of enemy clans."

"Not all alone. I had your father's kin."

"You led them well, Mother. Into battle once. Bards sing of your exploits."

"The Lord blessed me with a miracle. You were born, nine months and a fortnight after his body was laid in the churchyard. After that, I had a reason to be strong. You have been my whole life."

"And you both mother and father."

"Aye." Easily, she slipped from courtly French into Highland Gaelic. "And now that ye are safely grown, laddie, I'll do as I please. And I do not please to take another mon to husband. Ever."

"So ye won't wed, but ye want me to."

"Aye, Calum, I do. I want peace. I want grandchildren to spoil."

"Ye favor Robert the Bruce because he is your cousin."

"My cousin twice removed, my king, and my dearest friend. I am too old to take to the hills and live like an outlaw—which we shall have to do if you disobey Robert's command."

"If I take Una to wife, you'll have ugly grandchildren."

"Nay, my darling. Ye are far too handsome for that. Each bairn will have the face of an angel."

"With Una MacNeil for a mother?"

"She's not really a MacNeil, is she? She's Hughie Campbell's child, Alexander's stepdaughter."

"Maybe, maybe not. Una took the MacNeil name after her mother wed Alexander. Odd for a loving daughter."

"MacNeil or Campbell. It matters not. The king has ordered ye to wed her. I have faith in ye, Calum. Ye possess your father's charm. A year from now, with a wee lass or lassie bouncing on your knee, you'll wonder why ye made all the fuss."

"Child, child," Father Michael said as he anointed Lorna's bruised face and arms with healing ointment. "Have you not suffered enough?" He glanced around the rough stone tower where Lorna had been confined these past five days. "You must give in. You cannot defy Lady Beathag."

"Cannot? What I cannot do is forget what the MacKenzies did to my father, how they found him injured in the glen, carried him to their keep, and poisoned him."

"'Vengeance is mine, sayith the Lord.'"

"Have you forgotten the agonies he suffered—the hours it took for him to die?"

"It would be an act of unselfish love to go through with this marriage. To make peace between the clans." Father Michael set aside his salve and offered her more water. His wrinkled skin was almost translucent with age, his eyes clouded white, his hands twisted and trembling. Once stout and red-cheeked, the years had thinned him until his coarse priest's robe swam on his frail body.

Lorna drained the cup. Yesterday, she'd drunk rainwater that had blown in through the open tower window. Before the rain came, thirst had tormented her, but oddly, going without food hadn't. Her captors had given her no blanket, and she'd had to sleep on the bare floor. Luckily, it was June, and although her tower prison was damp, it wasn't bitterly cold.

"You have been sorely abused, child."

Lorna didn't reply. Twice, her stepmother had sent servants to beat her with switches, but worse were the taunts of her three stepsisters from outside the barred door. They had reviled her mother and father, threatened harm to those in the castle she cared for, and thrown pitchers of water onto the stair landing so that trickles of dirty liquid seeped under the door.

"I hate them, Father Michael. My stepmother and all her wicked offspring. Why did my father ever marry Beathag Campbell? We were happy before she came."

"He needed a son, and the lady had proved she was fertile."

"I hate her all the same."

"You must not hate."

"She made his last years miserable. And she has always hated me."

"Your father doted on you. He didn't want you to grow up without a woman's guiding hand. And he desperately needed a male heir."

Father Michael's angelic face shone with compassion. The fringe of hair around his bald pate was as white as frost. She did not know how many years he counted—he was older than anyone else she knew and growing frail. But he was so dear to her she could not bear to think of losing him.

"If he loved me, why did he marry such a woman and give her power over me?"

"Try not to judge him so harshly."

"She bore him no children, but hers are as wicked as she is."

"The lady may have hidden her true nature from your father at first. And, you must remember, those times were very bad. Famine, lawlessness. He needed the support of the Campbells, and Beathag brought two strong sons to help defend this keep."

"Father lived to regret his decision."

"Perhaps." Digging a packet from the folds of his worn robe, Father Michael carefully unwrapped a bit of cheese and half a broiled pigeon. "But we can do nothing about what is past. You cannot be worse off as a MacKenzie bride than you are here. You must marry someone. Yield, child. Bend those stubborn knees and make life easier for yourself."

"The king didn't even want me. He said the oldest daughter. He wanted Una. Having me take her place is Beathag's idea, although I don't know why. You would think she would want Una to have the honor. The MacKenzies are rich enough."

"Pray for guidance. If your father were alive, what would he want? To bring a lasting peace between the clans—is that not worth some sacrifice?"

"Enough!" Erskine's shout came through the door. "Away, priest."

"In a moment," Father Michael said. "Quick," he whispered. "Eat something and hide the rest. I'll come again tomorrow if they let me. And think on what I've said, child. Pray on this. It will be better for us all if you marry the MacKenzie."

Lorna pushed the food behind a broken loom. She had hardly taken two steps from the hiding place when her stepbrother flung open the door.

"Out!" he shouted at Father Michael. Behind Erskine, Lorna spied Beathag, and her three daughters, Una, Elspeth, and Annot.

"Have you come to your senses?" Una demanded shrilly. "Will you wed the MacKenzie or not?" She was a tall girl with heavy breasts and wide hips. Una's nose was hooked and as prominent as her mother's, her chin nearly nonexistent. Her only saving grace was her flaxen hair, which she wore hanging free to her waist in defiance of proper custom for a lady.

"Why me and not you?" Lorna demanded of her stepsister. "The king clearly wanted you."

"Do you think I will rot in these godforsaken Highlands?" Una flung back. "Mother will make a better match for me. She'll find me a titled Lowlander or perhaps even an English nobleman."

"Shut up, Una," Beathag snapped. "You owe no explanation to the daughter of MacNeil's whore."

Una screwed her mouth into an expression of distaste. "She's half-witted, anyone can see that. Even a witless slut would have sense enough to do as she was ordered. She'll not get another chance at marriage."

Elspeth stuck out her tongue. "Why are you so stubborn? Why can't you just do as Mother orders?"

"Maybe she doesn't want to be a wife," Erskine suggested. "Perhaps one man in her bed isn't enough."

Beathag steepled her thin, pale fingers and sniffed. "I'll have no more of your insolence, wench. Refuse me again on peril of your life."

"Yes," cried sixteen-year-old Annot, a pinch-faced reflection of her older sister. "Do it and Erskine will throw you out of the tower window."

Lorna took a step backward.

Elspeth giggled and clapped. "Out the window," she echoed. Elspeth was the worst of Beathag's litter, a horrid girl who took delight in trapping sparrows outside the kitchen door, breaking their wings, and feeding them alive to the castle cats.

"Silence, both of you," Beathag snapped. "Word has come from Keep MacKenzie. They have agreed. The wedding will take place tomorrow."

"And if I say no?" Lorna murmured.

"Then you are of no more worth to me," her step-mother replied. "Erskine may have you."

"To use as I will, Mother?" he asked.

"So long as you share her charms with your brother." Beathag chuckled. "I'd not have the two of you fight over an ungrateful slut."

"Ungrateful slut," Elspeth echoed. Lorna noticed that small gray feathers clung to the hem of her soiled skirt.

"Well?" Una asked. "Who will be the bride, sister? You or me?"

Lorna's stomach turned over. Mayhap Father Michael was right. No MacKenzie could treat her as badly as Erskine and his brutish brother. If he tried, she'd do whatever was necessary to defend herself—even if it meant his death . . . and her own.

"Well?" her stepmother asked.

Lorna gathered her courage. It was true that she did want an end to the bloodshed between the clans. Maybe sacrificing her own happiness would be a small price to pay. "I will," she said softly. "God help me, I will."

"Good." Her stepmother nodded. "You will take your vows and you will tell no one that you are not Una."

"But they will find out the truth," Lorna protested. "They will learn who I am and—"

"And it will be too late," Una said. "You will be his wife—until death do you part."

"Fitting justice for a MacKenzie," Erskine added. "He deserves no better than a baseborn whore."

Two

Forty-and-four mounted clansmen, all heavily armed with sword, bow, and sharply honed knives, guarded Calum's back as he galloped up to the ruined church on the border of MacNeil and MacKenzie lands. The holy ground had been chosen because, fearing treachery, neither clan was willing to cross onto the other's territory. Calum scorned wearing full armor to his wedding, but his right hand rested on the hilt of his broadsword. Warily, he scanned the tree line as equally armed MacNeils appeared on the far side of the chapel.

The sun barely glinted above the hills, and mist lay thick around the tumbled stone walls, muting and distorting the sounds of horses' hooves and jangling weapons. The air pressed tightly around Calum, rich with the scent of damp grass, horse sweat, and the fear that taunts men before a battle.

In preparation for Holy Mass, Calum had not eaten, and hunger did not sweeten his disposition this morning. He didn't trust the MacNeils, and he was searching for the slightest provocation to call the whole thing off. "Give me reason," he muttered under his breath. Nothing would give him more pleasure than to clash swords with Erskine Campbell before breakfast, and from the fierce look in his

men's eyes, Calum knew they were as eager for Mac-
Neil blood as he was.

His mother had wanted to accompany him and
bear witness to his wedding, but Calum had forbidden her to leave the safety of the castle walls. "I'll nay
have ye caught in an ambush," he'd said. The Mac-
Neils obviously felt the same about their women. The
bride rode between the priest and Malcolm Campbell, but Calum saw no other female in the party.
Erskine had obviously kept his mother and younger
sisters at home.

Calum glanced at the caped figure of his bride-to-be,
but the deep hood hid her face. Other men said that
Una had childbearing hips and ripe breasts, attributes
that he hoped would make up for her less-than-
attractive face. Calum favored bonny lasses as well as
the next man, but he'd learned long ago that it didn't
take fair features to give a man a good tumble between
the sheets. Few bridegrooms could expect beauty in
their marital bed. More important was a woman's intelligence, kind heart, and high morals; none of which
this lady reputedly possessed. Small wonder that he was
as foul-tempered as a speared boar.

This marriage was cursed from the start. Robert
Bruce might force him to take a faithless jade to wife,
but he could not command Calum's respect or his
love for the lady. And Una MacNeil would soon learn
who was master in MacKenzie Keep.

The priest reined in his mule and slid down. No
man moved to help the bride. Calum watched as she
dismounted while her brother Erskine remained in
the saddle. Nothing showed of the lady but the toes
of her leather boots and slender hands.

"Do ye swear on pain of damnation that this is the

oldest daughter of Alexander MacNeil?" Calum demanded, still prepared for some trick.

"I do!" Erskine Campbell glared across the ten yards that separated the two opposing groups and shouted in French. "And do you likewise swear that you are the man ordered by King Robert the Bruce to take my sister to wife?"

"Aye, I am *the MacKenzie.*" Calum drew his sword and plunged it, point first, into the earth beside an arched doorway.

Her face still in shadows, the lady stood unspeaking beside the priest.

"Do ye swear on your father's soul that ye are neither promised nor wed to another?" Calum demanded of her. The answer came so softly that he could not make out the words. "Speak up, woman!" She flinched as though he had struck her, and for an instant, he regretted the harshness of his tone.

"Aye." She would not shame herself with tears— would not allow this brute to get the best of her. From the corner of her eye, Lorna saw one muscular arm and a large hand, clean, with long, lean fingers. No small man was Calum MacKenzie. She'd heard that he was tall and powerful, a fearsome warrior, but bards turned stoat-faced heiresses into beautiful princesses and petty warlords into kings to enhance their story songs.

She'd long ago learned to trust only her own eyes and intuition when judging men. She was curious about the husband she'd been given to, but she'd not give him the satisfaction of ogling him like some lovesick dairymaid. Were he handsome as the devil himself, the MacKenzie would be repulsive to her!

"Get on with it," Erskine urged. He raised a stained

wad of cloth to his nose. "I'd not bear the stench of you MacKenzies longer than I have to."

Malcolm laughed.

Swearing, Fergus MacKenzie leaped out of the saddle, broadax gripped in his left hand, sword in his right. "I'll give ye a taste of—"

"Nay." Calum halted his cousin with a glance. "We will not soil this earth with swine's blood." Behind him, clansmen surged forward, some cursing, others hurling threats at the MacNeils.

"Father Michael!" Lorna cried. "Do something!" Tension in the air thrummed as tightly as a bowstring. Any second, her clan and the MacKenzies would fling themselves at one another. She could almost hear the screams of wounded and dying men. "Father, begin the Mass."

Nodding, the priest raised an ancient bronze cross over his head. "In the name of God, hold your peace."

Lorna dropped to her knees. Her hands were clenched into fists. A horse whinnied. A twig snapped. Harness leather creaked. "Please, God," Lorna whispered only half aloud.

Father Michael began the worship service.

Lorna's heart thudded so fiercely that she feared it would burst from her chest. So certain was she that steel would clash that Father Michael's words tumbled together in a blur.

When Calum MacKenzie knelt beside her, Lorna lowered her head and focused her attention on a worn stone at the old priest's feet. She was so frightened that she could hardly draw breath, and she wanted more than anything to turn and run. But she could not. If she fled, the sky would rain arrows, and good men would die with bad. She was a Mac-

Neil. She had come this far, and she would find the courage to see it through.

In truth, Lorna could not have said whether minutes passed or hours. When she rose from this spot, she knew that she would belong to Calum MacKenzie so long as they both lived. Her worst enemy would possess her body and would touch her with hands stained with her father's blood. Every crumb of bread that passed her lips would be by the MacKenzie chieftain's pleasure, and if he beat her or stripped her naked before his clansmen, she would have no recourse but to suffer and endure.

Small wonder that she couldn't look into his eyes, that her hands were cold and shaking when he slid a heavy ring onto her finger. *I can't do this,* she thought wildly. *I'll die before I say the words that bind me to my greatest enemy.*

But she did not die, and when Father Michael asked for her consent, her lips betrayed her. "Aye," she murmured.

"It is done," the priest said. "Go in peace, my children. And mind well the vows you have uttered here."

Calum wrenched his sword from its resting place, turned, and vaulted into the saddle. His mount, a stocky black gelding, tossed his head and snorted. "Come, wife," Calum ordered, extending a hand. "You'll ride behind me."

Lorna's stomach churned as she got to her feet. She glanced back at Erskine, but she could find no words to speak.

"Go with your lord!" Erskine shouted. "Doubtless you deserve one another."

"Una."

Calum's voice held none of the impatience she'd

heard earlier. Taking a deep breath, she turned toward him. Their gazes met, and to her surprise, he laughed.

Her eyes widened in astonishment as she recognized him. Since she'd last laid eyes on him, he had shot up a hand span in height and his shoulders seemed impossibly wide. Years of swinging a broadsword had hardened muscle to steely sinew. His legs were long, his thighs hard as oak. A thin scar traversed the plane of one chiseled cheekbone, and years of sun and Highland winds had darkened his skin to weathered bronze, but Lorna knew that high forehead with its wayward lock of seal brown hair tumbling over it, remembered well the gleam of devilment in those fathomless dark eyes.

He remembered her, too, and his tongue was as glib as ever. "Do ye not ken, Una MacNeil? Ye were the wee trout I pulled from the water."

Shocked, she stared at him, oblivious to all around them as the earth seemed to shift beneath her feet. "The calf," she stammered. "You rescued me from—"

"Aye, lass, that I did. For better or worse."

Male hands clamped around her waist and Lorna stifled a cry of protest as one of the MacKenzies seized her from behind and lifted her up behind Calum's saddle. The black horse stiffened and danced sideways. Without thinking, Lorna locked her arms around Calum's waist.

"Hold tight, lass," he ordered. "I'd nay have it said that I lost my bride on the way to her wedding supper."

Calum wheeled the horse in a tight circle, dug in his heels, and the animal shot forward, sending a spray of loose stones flying. Instantly, the MacKenzie clansmen closed ranks around them, lashing their mounts into a gallop.

Small game birds and red deer startled and scattered as Calum's company thundered past. Lorna hung on, teeth clenched, cloak streaming behind her. It took all her strength to keep from falling off as the black horse scrambled up stony slopes, sped across meadows knee-deep in purple heather, and leaped across rocky crevices. Lorna closed her eyes against the dust and pressed her face into the folds of her husband's *breacan-feile*, his belted plaid, and tried to block out the scent of the man.

Oddly, the thick wool smelled of evergreen boughs, lavender, and peat smoke, not the stale sweat, horse, and whiskey odors Lorna associated with her stepbrother Erskine. It was obvious that some woman cared enough for Calum to take great pains with his garment. And in spite of her distress, Lorna was curious enough to wonder who.

Not two hours passed before Calum slowed his horse and spoke to her. "There, lady, there is MacKenzie Keep."

The castle rose, massive and forbidding before her. Surrounded on three sides by water, the only access to the enemy fortress lay over a narrow finger of rock, spanned in three places by wooden bridges. At the edge of the mainland loomed stone watchtowers and a twenty-foot high gate of oak planks, reinforced with iron bars.

"Ye see why the MacKenzies have survived the MacNeils so long," Calum said.

Lorna looked past the dark ramparts of the castle to the wide expanse of blue-green lake surrounded by tree-covered mountains. The surface of the water gleamed as smooth and translucent as glass. "Beautiful," she murmured.

Her mind was as full of confusion as it had been when she first looked into Calum's face and recognized him as the youth who'd pulled her and the drowning calf from the burn so long ago. How could he be the MacKenzie? How could a boy who would risk his life to save a stranger's be part of treachery and murder?

"Beautiful? MacKenzie Keep? Ye think it beautiful?" Calum chuckled. "I've not heard it called that before."

"Nay," she stammered. "The loch." Doubtless he would think her as dim-witted as her stepmother did. Let him. Let them all believe she was a fool. It would be easier to deal with the MacKenzies if they did not ken the depths of her will.

"'Tis bonny, *Loch Murlainn,*" Calum said. "But deep and cold."

"Falcon Lake."

"Aye, for the birds of prey that nest along the shore. When I was a bairn, the old folks told me that monsters lived in the loch, and if I tried to swim there, they'd make breakfast of me."

She looked up, scanning the cloudless sky for sight of the hawks. "I don't believe in monsters."

"Nay, ye are wrong. 'Tis true, every word."

She fixed him with a dubious look. "Ye expect me to believe that you've seen these creatures?"

His craggy features hardened. "I didn't believe the tales either—to my sorrow. I swam there with my friends."

"And?"

"The monster ate me," he answered with a grin. "Swallowed me in one bite."

She laughed, then remembered who he was and instantly sobered. Had her wits turned to cheese that

she could be so easily charmed by a MacKenzie? She
turned away as tears welled up in her eyes. She had
only herself to rely on, and if she didn't remain wary,
her husband would soon learn that she wasn't the
bride he thought he'd taken. If and when he did,
she'd pay the penalty for her stepmother's treachery,
perhaps with her life.

To Lorna's right in a protected glen lay a small vil-
lage of thatch-roofed cottages, low stone stables, and
animal compounds. A simple church topped with a
Celtic cross stood on a rise in the center of the set-
tlement. As she watched, dogs barked, cattle lowed,
and chickens scattered as women, children, and old
men hurried to greet their returning men.

Calum raised a hand in salute, and then urged his
horse forward toward the gate. Lorna felt hostile
stares and heard the comments of the MacKenzies as
they rode past.

A gray-haired man pointed. "See her. That's the
MacNeil woman."

"Mark me, nay good will come of this," grumbled a
round-faced girl with a babe in her arms.

Lorna felt her cheeks grow hot, but she sat up
straight and kept her eyes fixed on the keep. She'd
not give these MacKenzies the satisfaction of letting
them know that she was afraid.

"Pay them no heed," Calum said. "If ye be fair with
them and with me, they will come to accept ye as lady
here."

The gate swung open and they rode through.
Lorna shivered and tried not to think of what would
happen within the castle once that iron door had
clanked shut behind her. The horse's hooves clattered on the wooden planks as they crossed the first
of the three bridges that led to the stronghold. There

was no railing and Lorna grasped Calum's middle
tighter as she stared into the water below.

"Each bridge can be pulled back to defend the keep
against attack," Calum said. "And if raiders managed to
fight their way across, they would face flaming arrows
and boiling water from the castle walls."

"Lovely."

"I will hold MacKenzie lands as my father and
grandfather and his father before him," he continued gruffly. "But I want peace between our clans, and
I will stand by my word."

Lorna swallowed, her mouth too dry to answer.

"I am not an unreasonable mon nor a fool. I doubt
that you wanted this marriage any more than I did."

Gooseflesh rose on the nape of Lorna's neck.

"Doubtless ye hold me responsible for the death of
Alexander MacNeil, the late laird."

She nodded.

"You'll nay believe me, but I swear on my mother's
soul, I had no part of that crime. I would have killed
him in battle, but not by poison, and not in my home.
Ye must look elsewhere for your murderer."

She dared not answer, could not tell him that she
thought he lied.

"Alexander's father killed my father," Calum said.
"Did ye know that? Ambushed him on MacKenzie
land."

"It was long ago. Who can say what truly happened?"

"If ye would talk of recent crimes, your brother Erskine slew my cousin Duncan on St. Swithin's Day.
Duncan was but a lad of twelve when Erskine and his
friends caught him alone and dragged him to death
behind a horse. They said he was stealing a cow, but
Duncan was a gentle lad destined for the priesthood."

"I make no excuses for Erskine. He is a Campbell

born. He has no MacNeil blood, and he is what he is." *Scum,* she wanted to cry. *Cowardly. A blot on the MacNeil household.*

"A brother to be proud of," Calum said.

Not my brother! My stepmother's son by Red Hughie Campbell. But she could not speak to defend herself. For if she admitted that she was no blood kin to Erskine, she confessed that she was an imposter—a wench born on the wrong side of the blanket, posing as a highborn heiress.

"Your brother Erskine leads the MacNeil clansmen against us," Calum stated.

She could no longer be still. "Erskine never had an original thought in his life. My . . ." The lie lay sour on her tongue. "Lady Beathag controls him and Malcolm, and through them, our clansmen."

"That may be," Calum conceded. "But ye be my wife and from this day forth, a MacKenzie. You owe me your loyalty now. I swear that I will treat ye honorably, so long as ye do not deceive me," he warned as the iron castle gate creaked open and the horse trotted through.

In the courtyard beyond the gate, dozens of people gathered. Lorna scanned the faces, wondering if she would come to know them as individuals or if the gap between MacNeil and MacKenzie was as wide and deep as Loch Murlainn.

The crowd parted to allow a brown-haired woman in fine clothing to pass through. Her complexion was creamy pink and flawless, her forehead high, her eyes a startling blue. Lorna thought the lady both beautiful and graceful. She had not heard that Calum MacKenzie had a sister, yet there was a resemblance. Surely, she was too young to be her new mother-in-law.

"My mother," Calum answered her unspoken question as a groom came to help her down. "Lady Deirdre."

Lorna's knees felt weak as her feet touched the cobblestones. "Madame," she said, giving an awkward curtsy.

The lady smiled at her son as he dismounted and gave her a hug. "Mother, this is your new daughter-in-law."

Deirdre leaned close to embrace Lorna, and Lorna caught a faint scent of lavender. "You are welcome to this house, Una MacNeil," she whispered in her ear. "Be true and you will find happiness within these walls. But betray my son by word or deed, and I vow that you will not live long to regret it."

Three

An hour later, Lorna sat beside Calum at the high table in the great hall while an endless horde of MacKenzies celebrated their marriage with food, drink, and song. Platters of venison, beef, and mutton heaped high on the linen cloth beside trays of oatcakes, wheat bread, fresh-caught trout, and poultry. Pipes skirled, kilted men danced, hounds fought for scraps of meat, and the walls echoed with raucous jests as barrels of wine, whiskey, and beer vanished down thirsty throats.

The hall of MacKenzie Keep was somewhat larger than that of Castle Storm, her own family's stronghold, but the sounds and the smells were the same. If Lorna closed her eyes, she could imagine that she was a child sitting on her father's knee, safe, warm, and loved. *If only she were . . .*

"Una."

Calum's deep voice tore her from her reverie. Lorna glanced up at him and tried to convince herself that things could be worse. Calum was not only a powerful lord, he was young and strong. He was no perfumed courtier in lace and satin; he was a Highland warrior with eyes as fierce as any gyrfalcon. A woman would have had to be blind to think him illfeatured.

She was far from blind. That made her situation all the more disturbing.

Calum was splendidly garbed for the feast in the rough Scot's fashion of his men, all doeskin boots and great kilt, with half his chest bare and a beaten copper band wrapped around one muscular upper arm. He wore no bonnet, so that his seal dark hair tumbled past his shoulders, clean and thick and sleek. If MacKenzie bore the blood of noble Normans, it did not show. He looked as savage as any Pict barbarian.

He is my husband. It is not a sin to have such thoughts.

Lorna tried to calm her thudding heart with reason. Calum MacKenzie was the mysterious lad who'd saved her from certain drowning—the one she'd daydreamed about for years after the rescue. He might be her enemy, but he had proved that he possessed courage and compassion. If he were any other man but her father's murderer, she—with neither name nor dowry—would consider herself blessed to have him.

"You've eaten nothing, daughter." The lady Dierdre spoke up from her place on Calum's far side. "Look to your bride," she chided her son. Her melodious voice rang clear as spring water.

"I have been looking at Una," Calum replied in courtly French, obviously taking his mother's comment lightly. "But I confess that my thoughts were not on my wife's lack of appetite." He bit into a breast of grouse and made a show of chewing it with deliberate slowness, all the while eyeing her mischievously.

A yellow-haired serving maid giggled and whispered to the woman beside her. Lorna heard fragments of the blonde's comment. ". . . is lusty as a bull . . . says he's hung like a . . ."

Feeling her cheeks grow warm, Lorna broke off a piece of bread and nibbled at it. Although she had never given herself to a man, she had kissed and been kissed. She was no stranger to what went on between the sexes, and she was no prude.

Sharing Calum's bed wasn't what frightened her. In all honesty, she was more than curious as to what her new husband would be like between the sheets. Intercourse was as natural a part of living as eating and sleeping, and most women she knew took pleasure from mating.

No, it was not fulfilling her wifely duties that terrified her; it was the thought that she might not be strong enough to remember the duty she owed to her clan and her beloved father's memory. She had sacrificed her own happiness for the sake of peace between the families. She would do her duty, but how could she live with herself if she came to care too much for her MacKenzie husband?

"Ye need meat for strength." Calum's gaze scorched her skin as he sliced a choice piece of rare beef and slid it onto her plate. His bare shoulder brushed her arm, and she flinched as if she had been stung.

"Atch, lass, I'll nay bite ye."

She stiffened as the morsel of bread lodged in her throat like a stone. Sitting this close to Calum made shivers run up and down her spine. How could she share his bed and remain strong enough to take revenge if she found proof that he had murdered her father?

As if her mother-in-law could see the turmoil in her mind, Dierdre said, "Accept what must be. You are man and wife. My son is a good man. And you are not the first woman to come unwilling to a marriage bed in this house. Take what happiness you can find."

The hint of a smile tugged at the corner of Calum's sensual mouth as he captured her hand in his. "Ye have nay reason to fear me if—"

"I'm not afraid," Lorna protested. In truth, she found the deep timbre of his voice so compelling that she felt light-headed. She could not have eaten the meat on her plate if her life depended on it.

He lifted a silver goblet, drank from it, and put it to her lips. All too conscious that the rim of the cup was still warm from his lips, Lorna swallowed. Gasping, her eyes welled up with moisture as the fiery usquebaugh burned a path to her belly.

"Too strong for you?" Amusement sparked in Calum's dark eyes.

Lorna reached for the goblet, but he snatched it away and held it out for a servant to refill. Calum's gaze taunted her as he offered her the brimming cup. If she refused, he would get the best of her. Lorna steadied her trembling fingers as she reached for the whiskey and drank every drop.

A cheer rang out from some of the onlookers, but Lorna felt no triumph at their praise nor ease from the warmth that spilled through her limbs. She felt as though she were still caught in the relentless current of that rain-swollen stream. She had lost her footing and could barely keep her head above water.

Calum pressed a bare leg against her thigh. She jerked back away from him. Onlookers laughed, and Calum leaned close to whisper in her ear. "I think it is time we left our guests to their own devises." He motioned to his mother. "Will you do the honors for my bride?"

His mother nodded and rose, beckoning to Una. Catcalls rose from the lower tables. Calum frowned as his cousin Fergus snickered and made a remark to the man beside him.

Calum stood, holding his temper until his mother, his new wife, and a flock of women filed from the room. Then he lunged down among the tables, seized Fergus by the shirtfront and lifted him off the bench with his left hand as he drew back his right fist. "Have ye something ye wish to say to me?" Calum demanded. "Something about my bride?"

Fergus threw up an arm to block the blow. "Atch, mon, leave off," he protested. "I said she was a Mac-Neil, and that it was a sad day for this house when we must share bread with one of them." He jerked free of Calum's grip and straightened. "Dinna say ye feel different. We all ken why ye took her. 'Twas the king we blame, not ye." Other voices called out in agreement.

"Nay, we dinna blame ye," said an older man with a tattooed face.

Calum squared his shoulders and raised his voice. "She was born Campbell, nay MacNeil. But from this day, she is a MacKenzie. Best ye all remember that."

"She's MacNeil's heiress," Fergus grumbled.

"'Tis none of her fault. Best ye'd mind your own woman, Fergus, and leave me to my lady."

"Aye," agreed Jock, another cousin, handing Calum an overflowing cup. "Calum's got no time for your ugly face, Fergus. He's something prettier waiting for him in the bower." Jock waved to the piper. "Give us a tune, Robbie!"

The piper took the cue and struck up a tune, and Calum gave Fergus a final warning glare, then returned to his seat at the high table. He'd no wish to fight with any of his cousins on his wedding day, and he could well understand their confusion. His own mind was hardly more settled.

He hadn't wanted the unknown Una MacNeil for his wife. But once he had seen her, and remembered her as the lass he'd pulled from the burn, everything changed. Being forced to marry against his will rankled, but no man could deny that she was beautiful, this daughter of his enemies. Her thick and wavy hair reminded him of autumn leaves and her eyes were as blue-green as the sea. No wonder men desired her. She was neither stupid nor meek. She intrigued him, and whatever he might think of her family, he was not sorry to take her to his bed.

Una's reputation as a light-skirt was a harder thing to accept. He had never been one to judge a lass for her past. But he would have no woman put horns on him. Now that she belonged to him, he would guard her with his life, but he would kill any other man who laid a hand on her. And if he found that she was unchaste, he would send her back to her family and demand an annulment of the marriage.

Yet, part of him hoped that the rumors were lies, that his bride was not what men said she was. If men lied about Una being ugly, couldn't they lie about her character? Hadn't untruths been spread about his own mother when gossips claimed she had poisoned Alexander MacNeil? Lies had a way of taking on a life of their own, of growing larger with every telling. Perhaps Una had dallied with another man—that did not make her a whore. More than one lass had found it easy to keep her favors at home once she was bedded by a well-endowed husband. And none had ever found reason to complain of what nature had given him.

He liked the scent and feel of women. He cared not if they were fair or dark, noble, or some shepherd lassie. He loved the kiss and tumble that came before the act and enjoyed the closeness after. And he had always found that a man received more pleasure from a wench when he gave as good as he got.

Calum drained his goblet and stood again. "Eat, drink, dance!" He grinned. "Make merry as ye will, so long as none come to disturb my marriage bed!"

Men stamped and cheered. Lassies clapped. "Go to it!" one called. "Make us proud!"

"A MacKenzie! A MacKenzie!" the piper cried and launched into a MacKenzie battle tune.

Laughing, Calum tucked a small cask of whiskey under one arm and left the great hall at a leisurely stroll. When he reached the foot of the stairs, he handed the keg to one of the armed guards standing watch. "Mind that ye dinna drink so much that ye canna fight," he warned.

"Small chance o' that ," the younger man said.

"Nay," countered the second, a giant of a man with a head as bald as an egg and thighs like tree trunks. "I've has never been that drunk."

"Raghnall and Tormod will be here to relieve ye before the food's gone," Calum assured them as he started up the twisting stone steps.

"Mind ye dinna drink so much that ye canna do ye duty!" the big man called after him.

"And if ye be needin' help, call us!" shouted the other.

Calum chuckled. Rough were his men, but they were loyal and brave. He would match their skill with sword and ax against any warriors in the Highlands. He could go to his bride with an easy heart, knowing that even on this night, the walls of MacKenzie Keep were well guarded and he need not fear the treachery of Beathag MacNeil and her devil's offspring.

* * *

"May ye be fruitful," murmured a maid as she backed from the master's bedroom.

"May ye find joy in your marriage bed, lady," said a second.

Calum's mother smiled. "Know that ye are truly welcome here, daughter. Peace between you and my son begins this night." Backing out onto the stair landing, Dierdre closed the door behind her.

Lorna shivered despite the heat from the fireplace. She pulled a linen sheet up to her neck and slid to the far side of the high bed. The women had done their best to make what was clearly a man's room suitable to receive a bride. Fur rugs were strewn around the floor and a great bouquet of heather stood in a pitcher on a round wooden table beside a bowl of figs, raisins, and nuts. Wine and cheese and sweet cakes were arranged beside two precious glass goblets on a crimson Turkey carpet.

Despite her nervousness, Lorna could not help but admire the splendid room. One wall bore a tapestry depicting Greek warriors in battle; another was hung with bows and arrows, axes, and swords. Over the fireplace mantel hung an engraved horn set in a frame of silver. Sunlight streamed through two narrow windows to further illuminate the spacious chamber. A trunk at the foot of the bed, two high-backed chairs, and an upright chest with a carved door completed the furnishings.

"A bedchamber fit for a prince," Lorna murmured. One she would have loved to call her own, if Calum's name were any other but MacKenzie. She knew she should ask for strength but she was beyond prayer. Instead, she wiggled deeper into the clean sheets and stared up at the painted ceiling beams.

A heavy rap on the door made her jump.

"Una."

Hearing her stepsister's name brought back Lorna's fears of discovery. She wondered if it would be better to tell the truth now, but that was impossible. She was wedded, but not bedded. The only other woman she'd ever heard of who'd been in that situation was Mary MacCade. And Mary had been packed away to a convent in the wilds of Sutherland, never to be heard of again. No, she could not admit her deception now. Dishonorable or not, she had to think of her own safety. Better to continue pretending to be Una until—

"Una!" The door swung open. Calum's wide shoulders filled the space. "I'm here, woman," he said, with only a slight slur in his voice to show how much he'd had to drink. "I've come to claim my prize."

Lorna opened her mouth to answer, but her breath caught in her throat. She gave a gasp and her eyes widened as Calum stripped away his *breacan-feile* and came toward the bed wearing only his boots and copper armband.

"Likely the slut will make the most of this," Erskine said to his mother. "I like it not." The two were closeted alone in a small room off Beathag's bower.

She scowled at him. "You're drunk," she replied. "We'd have been rid of the MacKenzies long before this if you'd spent more hours in the saddle and less swilling *aqua vitae.*"

"Yes, I'm drunk, and I'll be drunker before this night is out. Why did you do it? You promised Lorna to me."

"And you'll have her."

"If MacKenzie doesn't kill her first."

Beathag shrugged. "Then you'll find another whore to warm your bed. I've not noticed you sleeping alone many nights."

"That's hardly your affair, is it?"

"Everything you do is my affair, you gutless wonder. Where would you and your worthless brother be without me? Where would any of you be? Running errands for Hughie Campbell's kin?"

Erskine bellowed and lunged across the table to strike her with a coiled fist. His knee struck the bench and he sprawled facedown amid the remains of their supper. Beathag stood and dashed a pitcher of wine over his head.

"You're no better than your father," she accused. "Weak and witless, both of you."

Erskine sputtered and clasped a bloody nose. "One of these days you'll go too far, you old witch. I'll wring your skinny neck like a chicken."

She stabbed an eating knife into the web of skin between his left thumb and forefinger, pinning him to the table. Erskine howled and scrabbled to free his wounded hand.

"Mind your manners," Beathag said, stepping back away from her stool. "A witch is a dangerous enemy. And a mother with more than one son can afford to rid herself of one who does not remember his place."

"What are the two of you squabbling over now?" Una cried, sweeping into the room. She carried a small lapdog cradled in her arms. "Can you not stop squealing like a stuck pig, Erskine? You'll give me a headache."

Her brother stood clutching his bleeding hand. His face was tallow white and contorted with fury. "I'll kill her one of these days," he said. "I swear I will."

Una laughed. "We hear you." She glanced at her

mother. "He's still angry about Lorna, isn't he? He's too stupid to realize that it had to be this way."

"Exactly," Beathag replied. "Either the MacKenzies will kill the little slut when they find out she isn't you. Or they'll send her home. Either way, we'll have reason to defend our honor. To finish them once and for all. I mean to have it all, MacNeil land and MacKenzie."

"If they find out," Erskine snarled.

"Oh, there's no doubt of that," Una said. "Is there, Mother?"

"No, my children." Beathag came as close to smiling as she ever did. "None at all."

Four

Lorna could not tear her gaze away as Calum crossed to the bed. He was hard and lean and all muscle and sinew. Surely, Adam, the first man, must have looked this beautiful in the Garden of Eden. Warm sensations curled in the pit of her belly and she felt her nipples grow sensitive and taut. The whiskey had dulled her fears but not her senses, and her throat constricted with emotion.

"Please . . ." she began. She wanted to beg him to be gentle with her—to tell him that this was her first time with a man, but her dry mouth wouldn't form the words.

Calum leaned over the bed and took hold of the covering, slowly drawing it back so that her naked body was fully exposed to his searing gaze. "Ah, sweeting," he said huskily. "Ye be a bonny sight."

Lorna felt a flash of heat beneath her skin. Swallowing hard, she lowered her gaze, studying the wide chest mapped with scars of battle, over the flat belly and narrow hips to his full erection.

"Oh." She gasped and then blushed in earnest. No girl-child could grow to womanhood without seeing male organs both full and slack, but she had never found one beautiful before.

Calum's rough fingers brushed her bare shoulder.

"Skin as soft as cream," he murmured. "Ah, wife, but ye be a fair sight lying in a mon's bed." He lowered his head and found her mouth. His kiss began as tender as thistledown and then deepened as her lips molded to his. How long the kiss lasted, she could not say, but when they parted, she gasped for air and reached for him again.

Lorna felt fear mingled with anticipation as Calum knelt on the edge of the high bed. The feather tick sagged as he slid in beside her and took her in his arms. Her heart pumped fair to burst, but she did not shrink back as he drew her close and wrapped long, muscular legs around hers. Unfamiliar feelings flooded her as his chest pressed against her breast, the rock-hard tumescence of his erection against her belly and thigh.

"Lass, lass," he whispered. He enveloped her hand in his and brought it down to stroke his throbbing fullness.

She wanted to lie still as death, to offer no resistance to a husband's rights, but her MacNeil blood ran hot and lusty, and she had not the will to ignore his invitation. The whiskey burned in her veins, and the heat and scent of Calum MacKenzie weakened her resolve. Tentatively, she explored the forbidden with trembling fingertips and took secret delight in his groans of pleasure.

"Enough." He gasped. "More of that and I'll be of nay use to ye."

"I do not please you," she said innocently.

"Ye please me too much."

"Then may I touch you here?" She inched her hand up over the springy mat of curls to stroke the hard ridges of his belly. Eagerly she ran her fingers over his wide chest, massaging in small circles, savoring the contrast between soft hair and hard muscle. Calum moaned with pleasure at her touch, and the sound was tinder to her growing flame.

Calum's hands were far from still. They moved over her skin, his long fingers cupping her breasts, brushing callused thumbs over her aching nipples, and sliding down to cradle and squeeze her buttocks. His mouth and tongue were likewise engaged, kissing, teasing, sucking, nibbling at the lobe of her ear, her bare shoulders, and the sensitive skin in the hollow of her throat.

Time seemed suspended. A warm breeze wafted through the window, bearing scents and sounds of birdsong, and rippling water on the lock. Lorna let herself drift on a cloud of pleasure, refusing to think about who she was and how she had come to lie in this man's arms. For this interlude, she would only feel and be.

And when Calum's mouth closed over her nipple, rainbow shards of pleasure exploded in her loins and cascaded through her body, making her whimper and squirm and cling to him.

"Do ye like that?" he asked her thickly. Without waiting for an answer, he began to nuzzle and suckle her other breast.

She raised her head and looked into his eyes, black and storm-tossed as a loch in winter. Desire flared there in his gaze, passion, and something more . . . almost wonder. Was it possible that he felt the magic that arced between them?

He groaned and found her mouth again. His breath was clean and sweet. Their tongues touched, velvet soft. With a sigh, she yielded, taking him deep inside, reveling in the sweet, giddy sensations of the kiss.

Lean fingers slid down between her thighs, probing gently, rubbing, seeking entrance to her inner sanctum. Lorna thrust her hips to meet his touch. She was wet and slick, and the pressure of his fingers made her breath come in short gasps and her yearning grow greater with each passing second.

She had lost all control. Nothing mattered but filling this overwhelming hunger . . . nothing but coming together in this ancient mystery of man and woman.

Calum slid a knee over her and spread her legs wide. She tensed, waiting . . . knowing what would come next. But to her surprise, he lowered his head and kissed and nibbled his way up first one thigh and then the other. She moaned at the exquisite pleasure. And when she thought she could stand no more, Calum laughed and buried his face in her damp heat. Lorna cried out, knotting her fingers in the sheets, writhing with desire.

"Lass, lass," he said, rising up and claiming her breast again with his sweet mouth. "I canna wait any longer."

She gasped as his swollen shaft nudged her wet folds, then slipped inside. Her fingers dug into his shoulders as he thrust deep, deeper than she would have believed possible. For an instant, she felt a tearing pain and a fullness too great to bear, but then he withdrew and plunged again. She arched her back as pleasure conquered discomfort, and she was swept into the ancient reel of life.

Earth and sky fell away so that there was only Calum, his flesh, his power, his cries of passion. She clung to him as they tumbled up and over the brink of some bottomless chasm. Together they fell, clinging to each other, floating down and down until they came to rest in the master's bed in the high tower of MacKenzie Keep.

Lorna slept. For how long, she didn't know. When she awoke, her head lay on Calum's chest, her limbs entwined with his, and her hair tangled in damp elflocks. Golden light filled the chamber, not yet the intensity of day, but the gleaming iridescence that heralded a June sunrise in the far north of the Highlands.

Once, when she was very small, her father had taken her south with him to Edinburgh. He'd bought her a white pony with a red saddle and bridle, and she'd ridden proudly beside him. She remembered the journey seemed to go on forever, and that wherever they stopped the people were kind to her. It had been midsummer, that much she could recall. But she did not think the days so long or the nights as short, and sunrise had surely not been as glorious as this.

Strange that she had not known her station when her father lived. No one had ever called her bastard or spoke ill of her mother. All she remembered of her were a few lullabies and a fleeting image of being with her father and a beautiful woman in a high bed heaped with furs. Wind howled outside, and snow piled deep against the shutters, but the fire crackled on the heath and the room was warm. How real it seemed. She could picture her father now, brushing the lady's long red hair and laughing merrily.

"Morning, lass." Calum leaned over and kissed her.

Lorna started as Calum's greeting brought her crashing back to the present. She tried to wiggle free of his embrace, but he chuckled, kissed her once on the tip of the nose, once on the lips, and again on the crown of the head. "Please," she said. "I need—"

"On the far side of the upright chest. Push aside that curtain. There is a garderobe." When she hesitated, Calum chuckled again, rose, and strode naked as God made him to a window seat to retrieve a green velvet robe trimmed in fur. "Here," he said, offering the garment to her. "Though you've no need of modesty in this chamber."

Wrapping herself in the warm folds, Lorna slid out of bed and hurried to the privy. When she returned, Calum was at the door, calling for food and a basin of hot water. Unwilling to dress in front of him, she scurried back to bed and pulled the covers over her.

He poured himself a goblet of wine, broke an oatcake, dipped it in the crimson liquid, and ate it. "Thirsty?" he asked.

"Just water, if you please."

He poured her a drink and brought it to the bed. "It wasn't so bad, was it?"

Lorna averted her eyes as she took the cup. "No, it was good for me." She blushed. "More than good."

"I would have been gentler had I'd known you to be virgin. I'd heard—"

"That Una Campbell was free with her favors?"

"I misjudged you," he admitted. "I'll not make that mistake again."

She exhaled softly and rolled onto her back. She had not expected to like him, had never thought that he would be kind to her. "We have good reason to mistrust each other, I think," she answered.

"We can make a new start."

"Your mother said much the same." His words were what she wanted to hear, but she wondered if believing him would make her a fool . . . if making peace with her husband would be condoning her father's murder.

A knock came from the door and a stout servant entered carrying a tray laden with food. A lad followed with a kettle of steaming water. The older man cleared away last night's supper from the table and replaced it with the hot breakfast while the boy poured the water into a copper basin. Both were quick to perform their tasks and hurry away, closing the door after them.

Calum motioned to the basin. "Ye should wash while the water is hot," he said, switching from French to Gaelic. When she gave him a startled look, he went on. "Ye may as well ken my secret, wife. I have an unnatural passion for cleanliness. From April until October, I swim in the loch every day, and if I cannot, I scrub myself from head to foot."

"And ye think me dirty?" she answered.

"Nay, it was the first thing I noticed about you, as we knelt to take our vows. I couldn't see your face under the hood, but your hair was fresh washed, and your clothes bore no stench of sweat."

She could not hide her surprise. "Ye thought of such during our marriage ceremony?"

"Aye. By choice or not, we be man and wife. I had no wish to share my bed with one who smelled like a stable."

"Or me." She laughed. "I suppose you intend to watch as I bathe."

"Nay, sweeting. I intend to wash you myself."

"You—you great oaf," she sputtered. "'Tis bad enough to be spied on while I tend to my most intimate . . . What? What are ye. . ." Calum had dipped a cloth in the steaming water and was wringing it out. "Nay," she said. "You'll not—" As he started toward her, she seized his pillow and flung it at him.

Calum laughed as the pillow struck his chest. He leaped onto one side of the bed as she slid off the other. Laughing, Lorna nearly made her escape, but he grabbed the hem of her robe and yanked her back. She tripped and would have fallen if he hadn't caught her. Lorna struggled, and somehow they ended on the wolfskin rug on the floor between the bed and window, with Calum on the bottom and her astride him. "Atch, lass, do ye think to tame me with a siren's wiles?"

"I . . . 'Twas ye who started this," she protested. She tried to squirm away, but his hands closed on her waist.

"If this be a snare, it is a fine one."

The wrap, which had covered her nicely when she was upright, was hardly sufficient for the situation. In the tussle, one shoulder had slipped off so that she was only partially covered from waist to throat. Her legs, thighs, and buttocks were as naked as Calum's. He made a halfhearted attempt to scrub her face with the dripping cloth, before he left off all pretense of bathing her. He dropped the rag and tangled his fingers in her unbound hair, pulling her down so that he could look into her eyes.

"Ye be as bonny at dawn as ye were last night," he said. "It is an unexpected gift."

"Ye thought I would age, my hair grow thin, warts sprout on my chin?"

He laughed. "I'd nay be the first mon to discover such a difference."

His breath was warm on her face. His mouth beckoned, and she could not resist him. Leaning close, she brushed his lips with hers and savored the sweet taste of wine lingering there. "I should hate you, Calum MacKenzie," she whispered. "But I canna."

"Nor I hate you." His mouth molded to hers, and he caressed her bare shoulder. "Una MacKenzie, ye are a delight," he said. He nibbled at the lobe of her left ear. "Delicious," he murmured.

Lorna felt need rise in her again. Calum's skin was warm, his body hard and taut. Never had a man made her feel like this before. Never had she felt so much a woman as she did in his powerful embrace. She thrilled at the rise and fall of his chest, the touch of his hands, and the heat of his burgeoning shaft. More than anything, she wanted to give herself to him and experience the wonder as she had done the night before.

She knew that deceiving him was wrong, that she should tell him that she wasn't Una Campbell, but Lorna MacNeil. Reason struggled with desire. Once he knew the truth, he would never look at her this way again. Was it wrong to want heaven to last a few more hours?

It was impossible for her to think while Calum's hands were doing such wicked things to her . . . while he was trailing hot, damp kisses from her throat to her breasts . . . while each movement brought such delight to them both.

She would have had to be a plaster saint to be immune to his charm . . . to resist his sensual lovemaking. And she was naught but a flesh-and-blood woman. "God forgive me, but I cannot deny my nature," she murmured and gave herself fully to the joy of wedded lust.

Twice more they made love, and twice Calum

brought her to greater heights of ecstasy than she had dreamed possible. At last, exhausted, her body sheened with perspiration, she curled in his arms and fell into a sound and dreamless sleep.

"Woman!"

The chamber door crashed open, waking Lorna. She sat up in bed and rubbed her eyes. "What is it? What's wrong?"

Calum rushed into the room, his handsome face contorted with anger, his eyes as hard as flint. "Woman! What treachery is this?"

Lorna's heart sank. She froze, unable to move as he neared the bed. Her husband was fully clad in knee-high boots, shirt, and kilt. His long hair was pulled back and sword and dagger hung at his waist.

He knows, she thought. *He knows what I've done, and he's going to kill me!* She clapped her hands over her mouth to keep from screaming, and hot tears spilled down her cheeks.

"I should have known not to trust ye," he said.

"I'm . . . I'm sorry."

"Ye are not Una Campbell." He lowered his voice to a harsh whisper. "Not Alexander MacNeil's heiress, but a baseborn impostor."

When he did not draw his dagger or even lift a fist to threaten her, she scrambled from the bed and hastily pulled her shift over her nakedness. She wanted to tell him that she'd been forced to go through with the deception . . . that she'd come close to telling him the truth early this morning. But she knew that he would not believe anything she said.

Instead, she drew herself up to her full height and

looked him in the eye. "What will you do to me?" she asked. "Throw me into a dungeon to rot? Send me to a convent?"

"I am a MacKenzie. And I do not make war on women—not even deceitful ones who make a mockery of their marriage vows." He turned to a window and flung back the shutters, staring out at the vast expanse of the lock. "I will not harm a hair of your head," he said. "Ye came to me untouched. Ye will remain here as my guest for one month. If ye prove that ye do not carry my bairn in your womb, I will return ye to the MacNeils and petition the church for an end to our marriage."

"And if I am with child?"

He didn't answer her question. Rather he glared at her with narrowed eyes and said, "I don't even know your real name."

"Lorna," she replied softly. "Lorna MacNeil. Alexander was my father."

"An illegitimate daughter."

"Does it shame you to share your bed with me?" Anger made her voice sharp.

"If there is shame, it is not in your birth, but in your black heart."

"I did not . . ." She began to weep.

"Save your tears, woman. I'll not be swayed by them." His mouth thinned. "The question is—what does Beathag MacNeil want me to do with ye? What has she gained by disobeying the king's order?"

Lorna shook her head. "I don't know."

"Dinna know, or willna say?"

"I told you, I don't know." She buried her face in her hands and her shoulders trembled with the force of her sobbing.

"Leave off, I say." His voice was thick with disgust.

"How did you know who I was?"

"A message, brought by a herald this morning from Castle Storm," he answered tersely. "Congratulating me on taking Alexander MacNeil's bastard to wife."

Five

"Why?" Calum asked. "Why would they risk anger-ing the Bruce to slight me and my clan? And why would Beathag want to see her husband's illegitimate daughter married to me when her Una could have the honor? It makes nay sense." He'd had been on his way to his bedchamber to question Lorna further when his mother had stopped him on the steep and twisting stone stairs.

"Robert intended to secure peace between us and the MacNeils. Perhaps that does not suit Beathag MacNeil's plans."

"Men say she is a witch," Calum said.

"I'd worry more about an attack than a witch's spells," his mother replied. "Although I've had my own suspicions that Beathag poisoned both her first husband and Alexander. They claim Red Hughie Campbell had the misfortune to die of a fierce grip-ping of the bowels. And he was a man in the prime of his life."

Calum thought of the vital woman he'd held in his arms only a few short hours ago. In spite of his anger toward her, it was difficult to believe that she would be part of such evil. "Do ye think I need fear poison from Lorna?" he asked.

His mother twisted the heavy gold ring on her middle finger. "Who can say? Your wife has been in Beathag's power, but whether she's her stepmother's creature only time will tell us. To be safe, I would eat or drink nothing from Lorna's hand until we see if she can be trusted."

"Nay. The thought that she could do murder lodges in my belly like a hot stone. She might stab me with a dirk, but poison?" He shook his head. "I canna accept that."

"You cannot allow yourself to trust her, Calum. It would not be the first time a man's reason had been lost in the warmth of a woman's thighs."

"Ye underestimate me, Mother. Trust has nothing to do with this. I wouldn't trust Lorna MacNeil if she swore on the thighbone of St. Ninian." He stepped away, meaning to continue up the spiral staircase to his chamber, but his mother blocked his way with upraised palms.

"Think before you act. It's natural that you blame your bride for the deception, but God's mercy takes wondrous forms. Remain cautious. But when all is said and done, you may be glad that you took Lorna rather than Una to wife."

"Ye be a stubborn woman. Ye never wish to admit when you're wrong. Ye favored this marriage from the first."

"I did," she agreed.

"Had I kept my own council and thrown the Bruce's order in his face—"

"You would be an outlaw and this castle a smoking ruin."

"The MacKenzies have stood against kings' tyranny before," he reminded her hotly.

"But never such a noble king as Robert Bruce. A king that will unite a shattered Scotland and make us strong." She eyed him shrewdly. "Robert's temper is one of his few weaknesses. It is a fault you have in common."

"You would defend him, wouldn't you? And ye'd still take her part, even after she lied to me and—"

"I like her. There's no doubt she's Alexander's daughter. She has his look. And whatever our differences may have been with him, he was a brave and honorable man."

"Aye," Calum replied. "'Tis not ye that will be the laughingstock of the Highlands."

"Your pride is hurt."

"As yours should be. You'll nay have your way this time, Mother. Ye waste your time taking a fancy to her. So long as she doesna carry my son in her belly, she goes back to Castle Storm next month."

"Four weeks is a long time. Much may come to light between this day and that."

"Aye, it may," he said, stepping past her. Swearing under his breath, Calum hurried up the last two flights of stairs. As much as he valued his mother's advice, he'd not be ruled by her.

"Have I given you bad advice before?" she called after him.

"What I do with my wife is my business!"

No man in Scotland would blame him for setting Lorna MacNeil aside, Calum fumed. His mother was getting soft and womanish. Doubtless, she felt pity for the lass. He was forged of harder metal. Once he lost trust in a man or a woman, he'd never yet found reason to change his mind.

Reaching the landing, he paused, inhaled deeply, and flung open his chamber door. "Lorna!" He glanced around the empty room, strode to the drapery that covered the privy entrance. "Are ye hiding in there?" When there was no answer, he ripped aside the curtain. Empty.

Calum swung around and nearly collided with a female form.

"Sir." The chambermaid gave a squeak of distress and nearly dropped her armload of linen. "I'm sorry, sir. I didn't mean t'—"

"Where is my wife?" he bellowed.

The maid's eyes widened. Her mouth gaped fishlike. "I have n' seen her, sir."

"Since when?"

The girl reddened and backed away. "Since before noon, sir. I passed her on the stair early—"

"Find her! Go to the steward. I want my wife found. And I want her found now."

Nearly an hour passed before he had his answer. Eachann MacKenzie, one of the castle cooks, appeared in the bailey dragging a grease-smeared kitchen boy by the cuff of the neck.

"Donnee saw the lady," the cook announced. Eachann was a gray-haired barrel of a man who'd held his post since Calum was a bairn stealing sweet cakes from the kitchen. "Tell the laird, Donnee," he urged. "He'll nay bite ye. Ye saw her, right enough."

Dumbly, the barefoot lad nodded.

"Sent this one to his granny's croft for onions, I did," Eachann went on. "And he saw your lady crossing to the mainland before noon."

"No one told me?" Calum demanded. "Nobody stopped her?"

Eachann scratched his chin. "Nay, laird. I asked one of the guards meself, to learn if the laddie was speaking true. John Boyd. Ye must ken the man, one ear, thin as a pikestaff, with hair yellow as straw."

Calum nodded. "I know him."

"John claimed he asked where she was goin', and she told him ye'd given her leave, and t'was no business of his. Since he had no orders that she could not leave the keep, he dared nay stop her." The cook shrugged. "And none thought to ask why she rode awa' down the south loch road astride yer prize black gelding."

The chill wind off the loch tore the hood from Lorna's hair and made the black horse prick his ears and shift his hindquarters toward the water as Lorna tried to decide which way to go. The road, if it could be called a road, had long since dwindled to a stony path. Now, her way was blocked by a fall of rock and an old shrine. To the left, a faint trail led uphill; to her right, the tracks of a stag led perilously close to the lapping waves.

She'd not passed a cottage, seen a cow, or smelled the peat smoke from a fire in hours. And now, she began to regret that she had fled MacKenzie Keep without food or even a blanket to keep out the cold when night fell. There had been no question of her staying with Calum, not when he believed her tarred with Beathag's treachery.

What if she were with child after her wedding night? Calum might hold her prisoner until the babe was born and then put her to death. She could not remain, and she would not return to Castle Storm. Instead, she would go south to Sterling and seek the king. Her father had fought for Robert the Bruce. She would beg his protection.

Calum's question about Beathag's motive haunted her. Why had her stepmother forced her into this union and then sent a messenger to tell the MacKenzies that they'd been tricked? Clearly, Beathag wanted her out of the way, but this scheme was too elaborate. If she'd wanted her dead, a shove down the tower stairs, a knife in the dark, or a pillow over her face while she slept would have been much simpler. What did Beathag desire that was so important that she would dare the king's anger?

The horse took a few steps and snatched at a mouthful of grass. The animal was clearly hungry. Lorna could understand that. She was hungry herself, as she'd eaten nothing substantial since the day before the wedding.

"You'll need water," she murmured to the gelding. She dismounted and led the horse down the scree-strewn slope to the edge of the loch. Keeping a tight hold on the reins, Lorna knelt and quenched her own thirst while the animal drank. Then she led him close to the stump of a rowan tree and used that to scramble back into the saddle.

Retracing their route to the crumbling stone cross, Lorna urged the black up the high path away from the water. She could use the sun to find south, but she had only a vague idea of the terrain between here and Stirling. Whatever befell her, she wasn't going back. MacNeil or MacKenzie, it didn't matter. She'd suffer if she fell into the hands of either clan. Her only hope lay with her king.

As afternoon passed into evening, the hills grew steeper, the terrain more hostile. Both Lorna and her mount were weary, but she was afraid to stop without finding shelter. The temperature would drop when the light failed, but she'd not freeze in June.

What frightened her most was that she had no means
of starting a fire to keep off wolves.

As the hours passed, purple twilight spread around
her. Overhead, a few faint stars became visible over
the eastern mountains. Lorna had begun to think
that leaving MacKenzie Keep unprepared for her
journey had been the most foolish thing she'd ever
done.

Abruptly, her horse stopped short.

Lorna gasped. There, in front of the gelding,
gapped a wide fissure. The split in the rock was wider
than the horse could jump and perhaps five yards in
length. The bottom of the rift—if there was a bottom—lay swathed in darkness. Heart thudding,
Lorna backed her mount and guided the animal cautiously around the crevice. Once she reached the
crest of the low hill, Lorna let the horse pick his way
down the far side.

They'd barely reached level ground when the
black halted again, raised his head, and whinnied.
Lorna listened, wondering if the horse had heard
something she couldn't. The glen lay as silent as a
grave. She slapped the reins and kicked him into a
trot, but after only riding a short distance, she
smelled smoke.

Nervously, she slid down out of the saddle and led
the animal forward. Smoke might mean a house,
kind Highlanders who would take her in for the
night. "A house," she murmured. "Please, God, let it
be a house."

Relief flooded through her as she saw a flicker of
light and finally recognized the dim outline of a
stone cottage ahead. Then the wind changed direction and she smelled the unmistakable scent of peat
smoke. "Yes!" she said. "Yes, yes!"

As she neared the dwelling, the gelding whinnied again. This time, his call was answered by another horse. Hastily, Lorna made up a tale to tell of how she came to be here in the hills alone. She'd not give her real name, she decided. She'd use her old nurse's name, Jeanie Anderson, and she'd claim she was on her way to Sterling to find a brother. Lorna was five yards from the stone structure when a man's figure materialized from the growing darkness.

"A long way from Castle Storm, are ye not, Lorna MacNeil?"

For a second, she froze, and then lunged for the saddle in an attempt to mount. But Calum was too quick for her. He seized the black's bridle in one hand, her arm with the other.

"Nay, wife. 'Twas trouble enough coming after ye. I'll not let ye lead me on another merry chase this night." The horse nickered and rubbed against Calum's chest with his muzzle. "Good lad, good Drum," he murmured to the gelding.

"You," Lorna said, finding her voice. "How did you . . . how . . ."

"The road is long overgrown, but there's only one way through these passes, and this is the only shelter for miles." He released her and motioned toward the crumbling dwelling. "Inside, woman. I've a roast of venison cooking, and I'd as soon Drum didn't become wolf bait."

"And me? Do you mean to leave me outside to be eaten?"

"Aye, I should."

"If you wish me dead, why did you come after me?"

"You stole Drum. He's my best horse."

"Merely borrowed him. I'm no thief."

"Nay?" He uttered a sound of derision. "Strange

words from a MacNeil. Your father wasn't averse to running off with MacKenzie livestock."

"Don't speak so of my father!" She hurried ahead of Calum, torn between being glad to be found by someone and the shame of being captured by an angry husband. "Ye have no right."

"I have every right."

"My father was a good man. I loved him . . . and . . . and you killed him."

"I never harmed your father. MacKenzie men found him on our lands. He'd taken a fall from his horse and struck his head. Ye ken well that it was January and bitter. To leave him so would have been as good as murder. Instead, they brought him back to the keep and my mother tended him until he was well enough to return to Castle Storm."

"And yet he died of poison shortly after arriving home. What MacNeil would harm him?"

"That I can't say, although my mother has her suspicions." Calum tied Drum beside his own mount, closed and barred the door, and then returned to remove the black's saddle and rub him down with handfuls of dry grass.

"Who? My stepmother? Why would she murder her own husband?" Lorna shook her head as she drew near the fire to warm her hands. "Beathag's capable of it, but it wouldn't be to her advantage."

"Ye see what ye wish to see," Calum answered gruffly. Lorna's accusation troubled him. Was it possible that his mother had taken the opportunity to seek revenge for his father's death at the hands of the MacNeils? Had she given Alexander poison and then sent him home to die among his own people? Calum didn't think so, but he knew that his mother's first rule was survival. She had done what everyone said was impossible. She, a widow, barely out of her teens, had held MacKenzie Keep and their lands until he had been old enough to take his rightful place as laird.

"What do ye mean to do with me now?" Lorna asked, slipping into Gaelic.

Calum squatted on the far side of the fire pit and stared long and hard at her. How could anyone so beautiful be so devious? It had taken raw nerve to steal his horse and ride out of MacKenzie Keep in broad daylight. Yet, she hadn't returned to Castle Storm. That puzzled him. Why hadn't she?

"If ye mean to ravish my body, could ye feed me first?"

Calum flushed. "Ravish? Who said anything about ravishing ye? I'd sooner take a sea serpent to my bed than a treacherous wife."

"Where are your clansmen? Surely, ye need strong men at your back to capture a murderous monster."

He grunted and threw another chunk of peat onto the fire. "Ye have a wicked tongue on ye, woman. Did no one ever tell ye that?"

His knife lay on a flat stone beside the meat. When Lorna's gaze fell on the blade, he snatched it up. "So that ye don't get ideas about burying it in my heart," he said, slicing her off a generous portion of venison and holding it out to her.

Gingerly, she took the hot meat and began to nibble at it. "Let me go," she said. "Tell the MacNeils that wolves ate me. You can have your horse back. I'll make my way to Sterling and—"

"And tell Robert Bruce that I cast ye out?"

"He may take pity on me for my father's sake. But he never meant for ye to wed me. Una was the match he had in mind. She is the legitimate daughter."

"But no daughter of MacNeil."

"By marriage only, 'tis true, but there are no others. Beathag miscarried of several female babes, but none lived more than a few hours. My father leaves no blood heir, none so close as a cousin, to be the next laird. 'Tis why Erskine has power."

Calum dug in his knapsack and tossed Lorna an oatcake. "There's water in the wineskin." He watched her lift the container and drink, watched a single bead of water trickle down her chin to gleam like a teardrop in the firelight.

What was it about this woman that made him want to protect her? She was the daughter of his enemy, spawn of the murderous MacNeils. She'd tricked him into marriage, lied, and stolen from him. Even now, his men must be laughing at him. Yet . . . He tried to summon the anger that had driven him all day, but it was gone, lost in the relief of finding her safe and unharmed.

Memories of Lorna lying beneath him rose to taunt him . . . images of her unbound hair . . . the taste of her rose-tinted breasts . . . her soft, sweet skin. . . .

"Ye are a good man, Calum MacKenzie," she said, startling him out of his reverie. "Sorry I am to have hurt ye."

He shifted, suddenly aware of his hardening erection. "Ye could have gone back to the MacNeil stronghold," he said. "Why didn't ye?"

"There is nothing for me there," she answered so softly that it might have been the wind threading through the old thatched roof.

"And in Sterling? What will ye find there?"

"Work of some kind. I am no hand with a needle, but I am strong, and I'm not afraid to—"

"We are bound," he said. "In the eyes of God we be man and wife. Can ye walk away from that?"

"'Ye made it plain. Ye only wanted to see if I was with child. Ye said ye meant to send me back to Castle Storm."

"And if I was wrong?"

Her eyes widened.

"It may be that Beathag thought that I would kill you and give her reason to declare war on us."

"Aye," Lorna agreed. "That could be true."

"Then my setting you aside would play into her hands, would it not?"

"I suppose so, but—"

"Have I treated ye so badly, Lorna MacNeil? Was what we shared so repugnant to ye?"

She shook her head. "Nay, nay. Ye know it was not so. You treated me . . ." Tears clouded her eyes. ". . . like a bride."

He stood and reached for her hand. "The king bade me to make the peace. Should the peace not begin between man and wife?"

Her fingers were cold. They trembled in his clasp. "Ye canna pretend to trust me," she whispered. "Not after . . ."

"Or you me." He pulled her into his arms and held her tightly against him.

"I'm baseborn," she reminded him, her voice muffled in the folds of his great kilt.

"If I care not, who will dare to accuse ye?"

She raised her head and looked up at him. "If ye will treat me with honor . . . I swear . . . I swear on my father's soul that I will do the same by you."

"Then let our marriage begin in this lonely cottage." He lowered his head and kissed her full on the mouth. Her arms slipped around his neck and she clung to him. And the heat that flashed under his skin warmed him and melted the stone in his belly, until it was nothing but a bad memory.

They awoke in each other's arms. The dirt floor under Calum's back was hard and lumpy, but he didn't mind. He kissed Lorna's eyelids and the corners of her mouth and ran a hand possessively down over her hip to caress a firm buttock. "Ye are a wonder to me, my lady," he said in lilting Gaelic. "In all the Highlands, I vow, there be none to match ye." He threaded his fingers through her hair, feeling the silken texture, watching the rays of light play over the red-gold mass, and finally burying his face in it to inhale her scent.

She laughed and snuggled against him, warm, and sweet, and willing. His need was sharp; her own equally so. Kissing her breasts, he rolled her over on her back and took her quickly, filling her with his eager passion. And Lorna's cries of joy gave him as much pleasure as his own release.

Afterward, Calum rose, leaving her still wrapped in his plaid and went to the door. "I'll fetch water," he said, picking up the empty flask. "No need for ye to get up yet." He unbolted the door and hesitated long enough to retrieve his sword before stepping outside.

Dew lay thick on the cool grass, and mist cloaked the surrounding hills. Just beyond the spring, a cluster of yellow blossoms crept up a crumbling stone wall. Calum smiled, thinking how his mother loved mountain pansy. Likely it would please Lorna if he picked her a fistful.

The scrape of a horse's hoof on rock snapped him to attention. Muscles tensed, Calum spun toward the source of the sound. An arrow whizzed past his head. He dashed toward the house, but before he could cover half the distance, twenty howling MacNeils sprang up from the rocks and charged down on him with naked steel and hate in their eyes.

Six

MacNeil war cries shattered the morning stillness and tore Lorna from her bed. The clash of swords chilled her as she flung Calum's plaid around her nakedness and rushed to the open doorway. "No!" she screamed when she saw what was happening. "No!"

Sword flashing, ringed by a half-dozen mighty warriors, Calum stood his ground. In deadly silence, he thrust and parried, cut and blocked, besting one opponent after another. Shrieking MacNeil clansmen surged forward, faces contorted with battle madness, eager to take the places of their comrades who fell like ripe grain before Calum's shining blade.

The terrain ran steeply downhill to the spring, giving her a perfect view of the skirmish. To the left, astride their horses, Erskine and Malcolm sat astride their horses, gloating at Calum's hopeless struggle against overwhelming numbers. To the right waited ten more mounted troops armed with bow and steel-tipped arrows.

"No!" Lorna screamed again. She rushed forward, her bare feet flying over the rocky ground until she reached Erskine's side. "Stop them!" she cried.

"Look, brother," Erskine jeered. "MacKenzie's bride."

She seized his leg. "Stop them!"

"And spoil the sport?"

Malcolm thrust a fist into the air. "Skewer the bastard!" he shouted. "Finish him!"

Four MacNeil men sprawled on the ground. One tried to crawl away; another sat up, clutching his bleeding shoulder. Calum's body ran red, but he met each attacker, wielding his sword like some hero from a Norse saga.

"Are you mad?" Lorna cried, pounding Erskine's thigh with her fist. "His mother is a witch. She will blame you for his death."

A flicker of doubt passed over her stepbrother's pockmarked face. "Superstition."

"No, I have seen proof! There is a better way to rid yourself of him!"

"Liar."

Calum dropped to one knee and slashed a man-at-arms from breastbone to hip. A bearded MacNeil charged Calum's back, but the MacKenzie twisted and thrust upward with his sword, catching his assailant in the midsection.

"Kill him and your man root will shrivel. Your ballocks will rot like overripe fruit," Lorna cried. "I tell you, brother, Dierdre MacKenzie has the black arts."

Erskine raised a hunting horn and blew three blasts. In the space of a dozen heartbeats, the MacNeils drew back, all but one who remained in heated combat with Calum.

"What's this?" Malcolm demanded. "Finish him!" He swept his bow off his shoulder and notched a feathered arrow. "I'll do it myself."

Erskine signaled again just as Malcolm's shaft flew. The MacNeil clansman dodged out of reach of Calum's sword in the same instant the arrow tore into the MacKenzie's side.

Calum staggered back, blood seeping from the wound. He regained his balance, straightened, and snapped off the arrow shaft flush with his skin.

Erskine clapped. "Admirable, MacKenzie."

Malcolm howled with glee and reached for a second arrow.

"Don't let him," Lorna said. "Malcolm will gain the credit while you will suffer the curse. Deirdre put the spell on you, Erskine. If her son dies by your hand or at your order, you cannot escape her vengeance."

"You lie," Erskine muttered. "I should let Malcolm kill him and give you to my troops as booty."

Lorna forced herself to look up at him with calf eyes. "Why would you bring disaster upon yourself, brother, when there is a safer way? Your mother sent you to get rid of him, did she not?" Erskine didn't answer, but he didn't have to. She could read the truth in his face. "Who is master of Castle Storm? You or a woman? How long will you be ruled by Beathag?"

"Who are you to tell me what to do?" he said. "Baseborn whore. Daughter of a whore. You lay with the MacKenzie. Look at you, wrapped in his plaid."

"I did as Beathag bade me, as I was forced to do," she answered. "But I hate the MacKenzie as much as you do."

"Then what do you suggest, little whore? It has been an amusing morning. What is it that you wish me to do?"

Lorna took a deep breath. "Remember the sermon Father Michael preached on St. Columba's Day? He told us the story of Joseph and his brothers. *Joseph of the coat of many colors.*"

Erskine frowned, his bovine face struggling to follow her meaning. "Yes, I remember. What of it?"

"When Joseph's brothers wished to be rid of him

without staining their hands with his blood, they threw him down a well and left him to die."

"You speak nonsense, woman. There is no well here. A trickle of water springs from the rocks."

"There is a crevice in the earth. There!" She pointed toward the hills. "Only a short distance away." She glanced back at Calum. His body was streaked with dirt and sweat. His long hair clung to his back and shoulders. Blood ran freely from his wounds. "Throw him into that pit," she urged. "It runs deep into the earth, perhaps to the gates of hell. Throw the cursed MacKenzie laird there, brother. He will die of thirst and hunger. Slowly. And not even Father Michael could accuse you of his murder."

"Throw him into a pit to die," Erskine repeated. "Easily said. But who will take his weapon from him without killing him first?"

Lorna twisted her mouth into a smile. "Simple, brother. He is skilled with a blade, but his wits are slow. And he has a fancy for me. Tell him that you will cut my throat if he does not surrender." She averted her eyes so that her welling tears would not give her away. "Trade my life for his. He will throw down his sword easily enough. The fool thinks he loves me."

The bright morning had dissolved into a sodden night by the time Erskine's troops reached the walls of Castle Storm. The horses were spent, heads hanging, hides soaked with beating rain. Lorna shook with cold. Her hands were without feeling from the tight bonds at her wrists. Her body ached from the hours of hard riding, but she had made no complaint. She had spoken not a word to Erskine, to Malcolm, or to any of their followers on the journey home.

"What shall we do with her?" Malcolm demanded as they entered the bailey as grooms raced to take charge of their mounts.

"Lock her in the old tower," Erskine said. "Mother will want to question her in the morning."

"Don't expect me to do it," Malcolm replied. "I'm so hungry I could eat a horsehide. I'm for hot food, whiskey to warm my bones, and a wench to heat my bed."

"You and you!" Erskine shouted to the nearest men-at-arms. "Take charge of this woman. Take no shite from her. But she belongs to me. Partake of her charms and I'll hang the both of you in a crow cage until the birds peck every scrap of flesh from your bones."

The two mercenaries were strangers to Lorna, more of the hired fighting men that her stepmother had gathered around her. Grumbling, they did as Erskine bade them, escorting her up the spiral stone staircase to the highest room of the tower. They gave her nothing to eat or drink, not even a blanket to wrap herself in, but neither did they harm her by word or action.

As the door slammed shut and the iron bar dropped in place, Lorna sunk to the floor, pulled her knees to her chest, and lay her head against them. She could think of nothing but Calum . . . of the beating Erskine's men had given him . . . of the way Calum had looked at her just before her stepbrother had him thrown into the hole in the earth.

She could not blame Calum for hating her. She had given him every reason. She had played her part well, joining in the taunts of the MacNeil men, laughing at Calum's pain, bidding him good passage to hell. "I had to," she whispered into the dark. "If Erskine had guessed how I feel about you, he would have murdered you."

Mayhap he already had.

The crack was not bottomless. She had seen that by daylight. It was no more than twenty feet deep, but the sides were steep, and Calum was sorely wounded. He might have broken his neck when he fell. He might have died without ever regaining consciousness, or he might survive to suffer horribly before thirst and his injuries snuffed out his life.

"Oh, God," she cried. "Was there no other way?" Better she had seized a knife and died fighting beside Calum . . . or even thrown herself in the pit after him.

Lorna did not deceive herself, not even in the blackest hours before dawn, when rats and other vermin rustled and scratched around her. She knew that what she felt for Calum MacKenzie could not be love. How could she love her greatest enemy, a man she had only known for the time that could be counted in hours? But he had treated her with kindness, more so than any since her father had died. And Calum had offered her his protection, his passion, and his hand in marriage. Even after he knew that she had deceived him, that she was nothing but a bastard, he had treated her with compassion and honor. MacKenzie or not, Calum was a man among men, one she could imagine fathering her children and growing old beside.

"Nay, not love," she whispered in Gaelic, "but certainly respect and friendship." She shook her head. "Nay, more." Perhaps what she felt for Calum was the first sprouting of love. ". . . Like the first green shoots of primrose." She could almost picture the flower, pushing up through the winter snow. "Heralding spring," she said, "before blossoming into golden splendor."

Could she feel this way about the man who might have murdered her father? Or . . . if he hadn't, suppose his mother Dierdre had committed the crime? Calum had denied it, but she'd sensed some question in his mind. What was wrong with her that she could forget her loyalty to her father and her clan because she'd lain with a man and he had . . .

Lorna swallowed hard. What had Calum done? Given her pleasure? Soothed an ache in her heart that had hurt for so long that she had despaired of ever finding happiness again? Offered her hope?

Maybe she was wrong. Maybe it was love she felt for Calum MacKenzie. And mayhap she had destroyed the only man who would ever cherish and care for her.

But she could not believe that—she would not. She had to believe that Calum lived . . . that somehow he would be rescued . . . that in time he would realize that she had taken the only way she knew to save him. She hoped that he would—

Something furry scurried across her foot. She screamed and kicked at it. "Forgive me, hell!" she cried hoarsely. "Come for me, Calum. Scale the tower like some fairytale knight. Save me."

Her only answer was the muffled flap of wings and the squeal of a mouse as some larger creature pounced and devoured it.

By morning, the downpour had turned to a drizzle. Lorna went to a window and threw open the shutters. Outside, all the world was gray. Thick clouds shrouded the tower, wrapping Castle Storm in a cloak of invisibility. Far below, Lorna could hear the ring of the blacksmith's hammer on iron and smell the smoke of cooking fires. She could almost taste the hot bread she knew must be sliding from the bake ovens, but she could see nothing but spitting rain and white mist.

"I should have stayed in MacKenzie Keep," she murmured. "If I'd had the sense God gave a goose, I would have."

At midday, Beathag came, red-eyed, and swaddled in thick, woolen garments. Her nose was red and dripping, and her cough hacking and dry. Erskine shadowed her, but Malcolm and her girls were nowhere in sight.

"Well, what do you have to—" Beathag sneezed violently, blew her nose on a dirty rag, and continued. ". . . to say for yourself?"

Lorna waited, knowing that she wasn't expected to answer.

"How dare you interfere in my orders?" her stepmother asked. "I wanted the MacKenzie dead—his head on a pole on my castle ramparts. I said nothing about throwing him into a pit and leaving him to die."

Lorna said nothing.

"Dead is dead," Erskine said. "If I—"

"Shut your mouth!" Beathag snapped. "I'll deal with you later. What I want now is an accounting of the MacKenzie defenses. How many fighting men are in the stronghold? Did you see a postern door? Who is second in charge?"

Lorna shrugged. "How would I know those things?"

"Numbers, you stupid slut. I want numbers."

"Hundreds."

"Liar!" Beathag drew back a hand to slap her, but Lorna stepped back out of her reach. "Insolent little bitch."

"I'll make her talk." Erskine lunged for her, but she dodged his attack and kicked him hard in the side of the knee. He swore, grabbed his leg, and rushed at her again.

The room was small, no more than fourteen paces across, and one side was stacked with rotting furnishings. She tried to evade Erskine, but he caught her left wrist and twisted it behind her back. Pain shot up her shoulder. She gasped as her stepbrother wrenched her arm farther back.

Beathag smacked her hard across the face. "Tell me. Tell me what I want to know."

Lorna gritted her teeth and said nothing.

Enraged, Beathag slapped her again. "You'll not defy me! Speak, or by all that's holy, I'll have Erskine throw you from the window."

"I can think of better use for her," he said.

Blood rushed to Beathag's face, turning it a violent red. She seized two handfuls of Lorna's hair and shook her. "How many men?"

"Kill me if you wish," Lorna retorted. "I'll tell you nothing."

Erskine leaned so close that she could smell his foul breath and ran his wet tongue over her ear. "You'll tell," he said. "When my troops are through using you, you'll give up your soul."

Lorna moaned and pretended to sag to the left. When Erskine eased the pressure on her arm, she stamped hard on his right foot and slammed her elbow into his gut. When he yelped and released her elbow, she turned and slammed an open palm up under his chin.

She turned to flee, but Malcolm appeared in the doorway, blocking her escape. Erskine spun her around and struck her in the pit of the stomach.

Then the two brothers dragged her screaming to the open window and shoved her backward toward the abyss.

"Do it!" Beathag shrieked.

"Stop! Are you mad?" Father Michael's frail voice echoed through the room. "Let her go! My lady, you cannot allow—"

Malcolm let go of her arm. Lorna twisted in Erskine's grasp, but when he turned to look at the priest, she wiggled free and edged along the wall away from the window.

"Cannot?" Beathag advanced on the old man with outstretched arms. "Cannot?" She struck him full in the chest, and he gasped in pain.

"No!" Lorna said. "You're hurting him."

"Cannot?" Beathag said. "You dare to tell me—" She thrust the priest back with a second vicious blow and then a third. "I've had enough of your meddling! Enough of you!"

Lorna ducked past Erskine and ran toward her stepmother, but before she could reach her, Beathag gave Father Michael a final push and he toppled backward down the steep stairs.

Erskine swore a bloody oath.

Malcolm shoved past his mother. "You've killed him!" he shouted. "You'll burn in hell."

Beathag turned back to Lorna and sneezed again. "Serves him right," she gasped when she could speak again. "He's been a thorn in my foot long enough."

Malcolm stepped into the tower room with Father Michael in his arms. The old man's head hung slack. His eyes were closed, and blood oozed from the gash at the back of his head.

"He's still breathing, " Beathag said. "You said he was dead, you fool." Her lips had paled to tallow and she was visibly shaking. "Let her tend him, she loves him so much."

"You've gone too far, Mother," Malcolm said. "He's a man of God."

"Let him go to his God, then. Let his God feed him." She glanced around the room, eyes wild with anger or fear, Lorna couldn't decide which. "I'll be back," Beathag said. "And I swear, you'll share his grave if you don't tell me everything about MacKenzie Keep that I want to know."

Malcolm lowered Father Michael to the floor. "You shouldn't have done it," he muttered. "Crazy old man or not. He's still a priest." He glanced at Lorna. "I'll send water and bandages. You do what you can for him."

"You'll do no such thing," his mother said. "Get out of here. The sooner he is dead—the sooner the both of them are dead, the better it will be for us."

Lorna knelt beside Father Michael and touched his cheek. "Send water, Malcolm," she said. "It would be an act of mercy."

Erskine and his mother started down the steps. Malcolm looked back, started to say something, and then hurried after them.

"Water and blankets," Lorna called, but she knew none would come. "Heaven help us," she murmured. "We're on our own."

Seven

Lorna tore a strip of linen from her shift and soaked it with rainwater puddled on the wide stone windowsill. Returning to Father Michael's side, she pressed the damp cloth against the bloody swelling on the back of his head. The old man groaned and his eyelids flickered. "Shh, shh, lie still," she soothed. "Don't try to move. You're hurt."

His breathing seemed labored, and his ashen complexion frightened her. He thrashed from side to side, shuddered, and slipped into unconsciousness again.

The hours dragged by without help. When Father Michael finally opened his eyes, he seemed not to see her. He gripped her hand and tried to talk, but his voice was weak, his speech slurred. All she could understand were the words "Alexander" and "damned."

"My father?" she asked. "Are you speaking about Alexander MacNeil?"

"A MacNeil. A MacNeil," he rasped, giving the ancient battle cry to rally a clan or summon help in times of extreme danger. Father Michael's muscles twitched. He bared toothless gums, and his eyes rolled back in his head before going limp.

"God help him," she whispered. His tightly drawn skin was so pale that she would have believed him dead except for the faint hiss of his breath.

Leaving his side, Lorna flung herself at the locked door and pounded with both fists. "Help us! Somebody! Help us!" She doubted that anyone could even hear her, but she had to try. The four rooms below were used for storage, and most of the servants in the castle believed the old tower to be haunted. "No one will come," she cried in frustration. "They'll leave us here to die."

"Nay, not if I can help it."

Startled by the voice behind her, Lorna whirled to see the shadowy figure of a man's head and shoulders at the window. "Calum?" For an instant, she wondered if her mind was playing tricks on her. "Ye can't be real."

"Aye, real enough." He heaved himself up and over the wet sill into the room and swore. "No ghost would go to this much trouble for an unwilling wife."

"Calum?" Her breath caught in her throat. "Ye climbed the tower? How? How did ye—"

He put two fingers to his lips to caution silence, shrugged a coiled rope off his shoulder, and crossed the room to pull her roughly into his arms. "Did they harm ye?"

She shook her head. "A few knocks, nothing more." His sinewy arms held her in an iron grip. She could feel the power and the anger in him, but she was not afraid. Calum's rage was not for her, but for those who had dragged her here and made her a prisoner in her own home.

Lorna touched her husband's bruised face with trembling fingers. His plaid was torn and bloodstained, his great mane of black hair matted, his body bruised and streaked with mud.

Never in her life had she laid eyes on anyone more beautiful. Her joy was too great for laughter or tears.

"Your wound," she said, remembering Malcolm's shot. "In your side. I saw—"

"A bee sting. I've cut myself worse shaving." He pulled aside his plaid to show her a stained length of wool wound tightly around his waist. Fresh blood seeped through the makeshift bandage.

"Liar," she said. "I was there." She touched the injury with trembling fingers and raised her gaze to lock with his. "You climbed out of that crevice?"

"I had help. When I didn't return home last night, my cousin Fergus organized a party to come looking for me."

"But ye climbed the tower with that wound?"

"'Twas nay so bad. The stones are rough-hewn. Handholds aplenty, if a man be determined."

She shook her head in disbelief. He belonged in bed, safe behind his own castle walls. Yet, he had come here. For her. To rescue her. "How did ye know where I was?"

"I stopped one of Erskine's soldiers and asked him."

She could imagine how that interrogation had gone. She clung to Calum, unable to step from the shelter of his arms, unable to accept that anyone would put himself in such danger for her. "I thought ye would blame me," she said. "For putting you in that hole. I was afraid ye would die down there, but I couldn't—"

Tenderly, he brushed a stray lock of her hair away from her face. "I'm nay the fool ye seem to think me," he said. "Only a clever woman would think of such a scheme. And no lass who wanted me dead would drop me into that crack without cutting my throat first."

"I prayed someone would find you. That the fall wouldn't kill you."

"It knocked me senseless." He released her and turned his attention to the old man. "That's Father Michael, isn't it?"

"Yes. He's hurt badly. He tried to keep Erskine from throwing me out the window. Beathag pushed him down the stairs." She caught Calum's big hand and tugged him to where the priest lay. "It's his head. He struck it when he fell. I'm afraid he's going to die."

Calum bent down to examine the injury. When he raised his gaze to meet hers, the look in his eyes confirmed her worst fears. "His skull is split. He cannot last long."

"They left us nothing. I don't even have water to give him. Damn Beathag to a fiery hell. Father Michael is a good man. He's never hurt anyone in—"

"We canna take him with us, Lorna."

"But—" Her eyes widened in confusion. "Take him where?"

Calum motioned to the window. "I planned on leaving the same way I came in. With ye, if ye've the nerve."

"Down the outside of the tower? But your men? Surely—" She broke off. "Ye didna come alone?"

A wicked smile flashed. "Ye do think me a fool. There are six with me."

"Six?" She slid to the floor, legs folded under her. "Six," she repeated. "Ye come to Castle Storm to rescue me with only—"

"Six MacKenzies. Seven if ye count me."

"You're crazy."

"Well, I did send a lad to my mother for reinforcements."

She slipped into formal French. "To come here with half a dozen . . . you're mad as May butter."

"Aye. Furious," he answered, making a deliberate play on her words. "Erskine and his witch of a mother tricked me into marrying the wrong lass. Then they kidnap my bride, steal my horse and my sword, and try to kill me. I've reason to be angry."

"You believe that I wasn't part of Erskine's plot to murder you?"

"Ye had every chance to finish me while we slept in that cottage. I kent your worth when ye did not run back here. Only an honest lass would try to reach the King instead of her own family." He looked back at the window. "I canna leave my men for long. Are ye game?"

"To go with you?"

"To be my wife—in every way. To give me your loyalty. To stand beside me, no matter what comes."

She hesitated. She wanted to. Although she'd known him such a short time, every instinct told her that Calum MacKenzie could come to love her and she him. But lingering doubts about her father's death tugged at her conscience. And even if she could forget the duty she owed her father, how could she abandon the priest to die alone?

"I didn't murder Alexander MacNeil," Calum said, dropping to one knee and taking her hand. "I swear to ye, Lorna. I didna—"

"Poison," Father Michael said.

Lorna stared at the old priest. "Father?" His eyes were open, red-rimmed and bloodshot, but no longer dazed. "What did you say?"

"Poison," he repeated in a harsh rasp. "Alexander died . . . at his wife's . . . wife's hand. May God forgive me . . . for breaking my vow. Her confessor . . . I . . ." Father Michael drew in a long, rattling breath. "I'm dying," he said. "You must hear . . . hear me."

"No, Father!" Lorna knelt over him, clasping his face in her hands. "You'll not—"

"No time," the priest said. "If I burn in hell beside

her, Beathag Campbell will not claim this . . . this MacNeil land." His face twisted into a mockery of a smile as sweat beaded on his forehead. "I was . . . was born Angus MacNeil . . . brother to your . . . your greatgrandfather."

"Don't try to talk," she said. "You shouldn't—"

Calum's hand tightened on her shoulder. "Let him say what he must." He leaned close so that the priest could see him. "Ye ken who I am and why I'm here?"

"The MacKenzie," Father Michael said. "You are the MacKenzie. Lorna's husband. You came . . . for her. Take her. Take her before—"

"No," Lorna said. "I won't leave you. I can't."

"Go," he answered. "You heard me. Beathag. Her hands red with blood of two . . . two husbands. Poison. You must . . . must save Alexander's daughter."

"Beathag killed my father?" Lorna said. "Murdered him and put the blame on the MacKenzies?"

"Is that so hard to believe?" Calum took hold of Lorna's arm. "There's nay time, lass. We'll settle that score later. We must go."

"Why didn't you tell me before?" Lorna begged the priest.

"He's already told ye," Calum answered. "Beathag told him during Holy Confession. A priest is forbidden to reveal what he learns there."

"More . . ." Father Michael's voice became more feeble with every breath. "More, you must . . . know. At the ruins. Old church. Where you were wed." He struggled for air. "Altar . . . beneath . . . stone."

"Save your strength," Lorna begged him.

His gnarled fingers gripped her wrist. "Go to the church. Promise me. Marriage . . . lines."

"I don't understand," Lorna said. "I have my marriage lines."

"Must go," Father Michael insisted. "Beneath altar."

"Aye," Calum said. "We will do as ye ask." He pulled Lorna to her feet.

Father Michael lifted his hand and weakly made the sign of the cross in the air. "Bless you, my children. Make the peace . . . between our clans. Live and remember . . . remember me." He closed his eyes and his breath grew even more labored.

Lorna tried to pull away from Calum. "Just a little more time," she pleaded.

He shook his head. "If we stay, Beathag wins. Father Michael's death will be in vain."

She let him lead her to the spot where he'd dropped the rope, but before he could knot the end around her waist, shouting and the thudding of boots rang from the tower stairs.

"Too late," Calum said, shoving Lorna behind him and drawing his sword.

Iron grated against wood as the bolt on the outside of the door slid back. Seconds later, her stepbrother Malcolm and a man-at-arms in Campbell colors burst into the room. Calum rushed to meet them, sword blade to sword blade. So fierce was the MacKenzie's attack that he dropped Malcolm and drove the Campbell staggering back to the landing, fighting for his life. Malcolm lay motionless where he fell, arms outstretched, eyes wide in death.

More of Erskine's mercenaries crowded behind the surviving Campbell, but the spiral stairs were narrow and twisting, made to favor a single right-handed defender at the top. A backhanded slash sent the Campbell to his knees. A man swinging an ax tried to shove past him, but he slipped on his companion's blood, and the weight of his weapon threw him off balance. As he struggled to regain his footing, Calum's sword sliced down to deliver a deathblow.

Amid the chaos, Lorna heard Erskine bellowing orders. Desperate, she ran to the window and looked out. It was too dark and foggy to see the ground. Cries of alarm drifted up from the foot of the tower. Lorna thought she could smell smoke. The sound of clashing steel was unmistakable.

She turned back to see Calum fighting a mountain of a man in partial armor while two more MacNeil clansmen tried to gain the arched doorway. How long could Calum hold them back? Once they were in the room, the others would follow, and the end would be swift and merciless.

Heart pounding, Lorna glanced down at the rope, wondering if she dared attempt to make her way to the ground, but she dismissed the idea as quickly as it had come. If she refused to leave a dying friend, could she do less for the husband who had put himself in harm's way for her sake?

Retrieving Malcolm's sword, she ran to Calum's side as the fight shifted back and forth through the open doorway. When the giant forced his way into the room, Lorna crouched low and swung at the back of the man's right knee.

The mountain howled as the iron blade cut into his flesh, then recovered enough to parry Calum's blow. The two locked swords, but Calum drew a dirk from a sheath on his boot and drove the knife into the man's belly. At the same instant, the two grizzled MacNeil clansmen broke into the room. One, a man she recognized as Jock Murray, the other his brother. Both of them were her father's men, faithful followers who had guarded her when she was a child. She had trusted the pair long ago, but they had not spo-

ken to her in years. Now, Jock bore a spiked club,
Geordie an Irish curved sword.

Lorna screamed as Jock raised the war club over
his head. But instead of striking Calum, Jock used the
weight of the terrible weapon to stun the Campbell
recruit at the top of the steps.

"Alexander!" Jock shouted. "Alexander MacNeil!"

Calum whirled and would have struck at him, but
the kilted graybeard dodged out of Calum's reach.
Lorna hurled herself between them. "Don't!" she
screamed. "They're friends!"

The two MacNeils threw their shoulders against
the splintered door and slammed it shut against Erskine's forces. Panting, the man with the club braced
his back against the door and grinned. "Jock Murray
at yer service. This be me brother Geordie. Thought
ye might use some help."

"Thirty years we stood a'side Alexander MacNeil,"
Geordie said. "We'll nay see her cut doon by bloody
Campbell spawn."

"Thank you," Lorna said. "I thought no one cared
what happened to me here."

"Ptahh, lady." Jock flashed a missing front tooth.
"There's many a MacNeil looks to ye as our laird's
heir. Keeping their heads low as befits a canny mon,
but carin' all the same."

Calum was breathing hard. Sweat rolled down his
face as he pulled his knife from the dead man and
wiped it clean before returning it to his boot sheath.
"Glad I am to have ye." His gaze softened as he
looked at Lorna. "And ye, Lorna MacKenzie. Ye'll do,
lass. I'd rather have ye beside me than a hundred
mounted—"

A heavy weight slammed against the other side of
the door. The planks shuddered and groaned. "We'll

nay hold her fer long," Geordie said. "Never thought I'd meet my Maker fighting *with* a MacKenzie."

"To the window, woman," Calum pushed a heavy wooden loom against the door. "I'll lower ye—"

Another crash. Splinters of wood sprayed the room. Geordie swore and tensed his muscles for the next blow. Jock took a stand to the left of the door and readied his spiked club.

"Nay," Lorna said to Calum. "Whatever comes, we'll meet it together."

"Ye are as stubborn as my mother." He added a wooden barrel and a length of rusty chain to the barricade.

"I'll take that as a compliment."

Calum bent over Father Michael. "He's gone."

"Surrender!" Erskine shouted from the landing. "Open the door, MacKenzie, and we'll let her live."

Jock countered with an obscenity.

Calum motioned Lorna behind him and raised his sword. Lorna held her breath, waiting for the blow that would shatter the door. And in that heartbeat of silence, she heard the wail of bagpipes.

"The MacKenzies!" she cried and dashed to the open window. "Your troops!"

"Nay!" Calum said. "That's no MacKenzie piper. 'Tis—"

The iron head of an ax bit through the wood over Geordie's head. He jumped away as a second blade crashed through the door. Two more blows fell, opening a hole at a man's shoulder height.

"Guard yer lady!" Calum ordered Geordie.

The older man seized Lorna's arm and dragged her back to the window. "Ye'll get MacKenzie killed certain," he said urgently.

From the far side, a soldier thrust a burning torch

through the opening. "Bloody fools!" Jock cried. He grabbed the torch, ran across the room, and tossed it out the window.

The axes chewed steadily, widening the opening into the room. This time, when Erskine's men drove a log against the door, the hinges gave. Campbells and MacNeils spilled into the room. Calum and Jock moved cautiously back, standing shoulder to shoulder in front of Geordie and Lorna.

Her heart sank as Erskine kicked his way through the ruins of the door, a loaded crossbow gripped in his gloved hands and Beathag at his back.

Eight

"Kill her!" Beathag screamed, pointing at Lorna.

Calum saw Erskine lift the crossbow. A yelling mercenary ran straight at Calum, but he ignored him. Sidestepping the charge, Calum raised his sword, and hurled it. The blade took Erskine through the heart at the instant the metal quarrel shot from his crossbow.

Beathag shrieked as her son pitched backward.

"Lorna!" Calum shouted. He swung toward the window, dreading to see her breast pierced by the iron bolt, and hoping with all his heart and soul that he wouldn't.

Lorna dropped to her knees, red blood staining her dress.

The mercenary's sword thrust skimmed Calum's left thigh, cutting through kilt and skin, but he didn't feel it. All Calum could think of was getting to Lorna, holding her once more before she drew her last breath.

But the arrow hadn't struck her. Faithful to the last, Jock Murray had protected his laird's daughter with his own life's blood. Unhurt and weeping, Lorna, bent over the dying man, murmuring his name.

With a cry of triumph, Calum turned his attention to the man trying to kill him. Slamming a fist into his attacker's chin, Calum wrestled the sword from his hand, and knocked the cockerel flat with the iron hilt. From the corner of his eye, Calum saw Geordie battling two soldiers. Two strides put him at Geordie's side. "Mind if I join the fun?" Calum shouted over Beathag's howls of rage.

"Nay!" Geordie answered, blocking an attack from his opponent. "More than enough for the two of us."

The sound of running feet on the tower stair made Calum turn toward the doorway. Beathag was no longer there. Calum cut down the mercenary with a quick thrust and prepared to meet the new onslaught.

Lorna looked up to see her stepmother rushing at her with a long knife in her hands. She scrambled to her feet, trying to get out of Beathag's way.

"You! You did this!" the older woman screamed, lunging at her. "You killed my—"

Beathag's skirt caught on the iron quarrel protruding from Jock's chest. She staggered, lost her balance, and fell forward. Lorna grabbed for her stepmother but the tip of Beathag's knife slashed her palm. Lorna cried out as the older woman clung for an instant to the stone sill and then toppled forward into empty space.

Lorna clasped her injured hand to her side and looked back at Calum. What she saw made her eyes widen with astonishment. The fighting had suddenly ceased. Calum had dropped his sword and was embracing the filthy warrior at the head of a troop of hard-faced men.

Hesitantly, Lorna moved across the room, stopping by Calum's side.

"Luckily we saw your signal," the tall stranger said.

"Signal?" Calum asked.

"The torch. I assumed you threw it out the window to let us know where you were."

"Nay, it was—"

"Is this your cousin Fergus?" Lorna interrupted.

"Nay, lass," the tall stranger answered in Gaelic. "But a relative of sorts."

Calum's arm tightened around Lorna's shoulder. "My wife," he said, "Lorna MacKenzie. Lorna, this is Robert the Bruce, high king of Scotland."

Speechless, Lorna sank into a curtsy.

The king laughed, took her hand, and raised her up. "This is hardly the place or time for ceremony," he said, kissing her on each cheek. "I came for your wedding. I'm only glad that I didn't have to bear witness at your funerals instead."

"But how . . . why . . ." Lorna stammered. "How did you know to come—"

"I met Calum's mother on the road to Castle Storm," he explained. "Give Dierdre MacKenzie any excuse to lead an army and she's off at full cry. Not that having her son and his wife in danger wasn't good reason." The King grinned charmingly, and Lorna was struck by how much his smile looked like her husband's.

"You came to save us?" Lorna asked.

"Aye, lass," Calum answered. "It appears that he did."

The King glanced at where Erskine lay dead. "Not that you needed much rescuing," he said, "although the skirmish was exciting until the MacNeil troops realized who I was." His face grew serious. "Beathag Campbell had another son, I believe."

"Yes, sire," Lorna replied. "Malcolm. Dead as well." She pointed to her younger stepbrother's body. "There, on the floor. Beathag has only the three girls left."

"Yes," Robert Bruce said. "I shall take them back

with me to Sterling. A convent in France might be the place for them. They've no claim to Castle Storm or your inheritance. As for your father's wife—"

Lorna shook her head. "She fell from that window."

The King pursed his lips. "Hmm. Tidy. Saves trouble for us all, I suppose." He shrugged. "I'm afraid I was never fond of your stepmother. Terrible woman. Alexander only married her to protect you. To strengthen ties with the Campbells and guard your lands from the MacKenzies."

"My lands?" Lorna looked up at him in bewilderment. "Sire, I am baseborn. My father never married my mother. She was—"

"His lover?" Robert nodded. "Yes, she was the daughter of a penniless farmer, but your father did marry her. He took her to wife six days before you were born. I should know. I was witness to the ceremony."

Lorna's knees went weak. She would have fallen if Calum hadn't held on to her tightly. "Why didn't I know? Why did Beathag—"

"Alexander had no son to become laird. If it were known that his only heir was a wee lass, you would have been in too much danger. Either you would have been kidnapped and forced into marriage with some rogue or murdered. Alexander must have told Beathag the truth. I know he did. Obviously the lady knew and schemed to disinherit you and steal Castle Storm for her own brood."

"She did worse," Calum put in. "The priest here, the cleric who performed our marriage, claimed that Beathag Campbell confessed to poisoning Alexander MacNeil."

"Not only my father, but her first husband as well," Lorna said.

100   *Judith E. French*

"Then it is best the lady tried to fly from this window. I hate hanging women. Troubles my sleep."

"If you'd known Beathag better, you wouldn't care," Calum said. "She is where she belongs—with her sons in hell."

Two weeks later, Lorna stood in the King's apartments in the great palace at Sterling while a bevy of titled ladies helped her dress for the wedding. Since the first ceremony in the ruined church had been both hurried and forced, the King had insisted that she and Calum repeat their vows in his presence. "If you give your full consent, Lady MacNeil," Robert Bruce had added with a twinkle in his eye.

"With all my heart," she had assured him.

So, like some princess in a fairy tale, she'd been rescued from the witch's tower by her knight in shining armor and transformed from a nameless lass to a wealthy heiress. She and her hero had discovered proof of her parents' marriage beneath an ancient church altar, and finally, a high king had whisked her down from the Highlands to wed her true love all over again.

Today, unlike her first wedding, Lorna wore no threadbare, hand-me-down garments. Her V-necked bodice was of priceless azure silk, her robe a deeper blue velvet stitched with thread of gold and set with hundreds of seed pearls. The matching silk mantle was trimmed with ermine, and around Lorna's neck, Calum's mother had fastened a necklace of rubies set in gold. Velvet blue slippers and a pearl-encrusted headpiece completed bridal finery fit for any princess.

"You are more beautiful than he deserves," Dierdre

said, holding a highly polished silver mirror so that Lorna could see the full effect of her gown. "More beautiful than I ever was."

Lorna felt her cheeks grow warm. "Thank you, my lady. It cannot be true, but it is kind of you to say."

"It's true," Dierdre said. "Your eyes shine like stars, and your hair . . ." She tucked a stray curl into place. "Give me grandchildren with flaming hair like that."

"Grandsons as well?"

"Yes. If their hair is as red as fox, I will always be able to pick them out of a crowd of lads and know when they are up to mischief."

Lorna smiled. "The king is too good to us," she said. "Why? I know he is your cousin, but—"

"My cousin and my dear friend." Smiling, her mother-in-law waved the other ladies from the chamber. "Thank you, all. But it is time. We cannot keep the gentlemen waiting."

Lorna paced nervously, careful not to trip over the train of her robe. "It is too much," she said. "I can't understand."

"You are the MacNeil heir, my dear," Dierdre soothed. "And your marriage to my son ends a long and bloody feud. Naturally, the king would be pleased."

"But we were already wed. There was no need—"

"Robert has told me that it is in his mind to give Calum a title. He would not say what, but he promised that it would be hereditary and that I would be pleased." She chuckled. "Calum will be shocked. You must not tell him. It's to be a surprise."

"Will the King make him master of MacNeil lands?"

"No. You will keep that right. Your firstborn son will inherit the MacKenzie honors, your second, when he is of age, will be laird of Castle Storm and all that your father left to you."

"And if we have only daughters?'

Dierdre laughed. "I asked Robert about that, and he said I drove a hard bargain and I should trust his love for us. I told him to put it in writing." She shrugged. "A king is only a man, after all. They sometimes remember things differently than we do. Don't worry, if you have only girls, they shall inherit."

"He is too good to us, " Lorna said. "And I know my father was his friend. "But I still don't understand . . ."

Dierdre sighed. Quickly, she went to the door, opened it, and checked to see if there were any eavesdroppers. She came back and led the way to a window seat that looked out on a stone courtyard. "You are now as much my daughter as if you had been born of my flesh," she said quietly. "I believe that you can be trusted with a secret that I have kept many years."

"Anything, lady. I swear I will—"

"This you should know. Your children will be highborn. Who knows where your sons may look to choose a wife? In time, you may tell Calum, but not now. Wait until I am dead. I could not bear it if he judged me harshly."

"Never. He could never—"

Dierdre leaned close and whispered. "My husband died without issue and I was left alone. My cousin came to me in my darkest hour. Robert Bruce is Calum's father."

"His father? Then Calum isn't a MacKenzie?"

"He is, in every way that matters."

"The king knows?"

Dierdre nodded. "Robert has always known. He cannot claim Calum without stripping him of his MacKenzie birthright. But Robert has always loved him." Her eyes grew misty. "And me."

A knock came at the door. "My Lady MacKenzie, Lady MacNeil, the king grows impatient."

"Then we will not keep him waiting any longer, will we?" Dierdre said.

"No, we won't."

Trembling, Lorna followed her mother-in-law through the king's apartments to the chapel. At the archway, she paused and looked toward the altar. Her Highlander was waiting there for her, tall and handsome in the sunlight that spilled through the stained-glass window, splendid in his MacKenzie colors.

"Your father should be here," Robert Bruce said, taking her arm. "May I have the honor?"

"Yes, sire," she murmured. But her gaze was not on her king as they passed among the nobles of Scotland. She could see only Calum MacKenzie.

"They say the bride who weds in June is lucky," the king said to his son as they reached the altar. "I think you are the lucky one, Calum MacKenzie."

"Aye," Calum answered as he clasped her hand in his. He looked deeply into her eyes. "I love ye, lass. I swear I will love you all the days of my life."

Tears of joy spilled from her eyes so that Calum's face was wreathed in golden light. "And I you."

"Forever and forever," he promised.

And Lorna knew in the deepest corner of her soul that he would.

Simon's Bride

Donna Jordan

One

England

"Someone comes!"

The herald bellowed the announcement from his perch atop the wall. With exaggerated motions, he shielded the sun from his eyes and squinted toward the horizon and shook his head. He looked down at the waiting crowd, and with mock dismay addressed them all. "Perhaps we have gathered here for naught. It could not possibly be our new lord! The man who approaches wears no armor."

Laughter fluttered through the courtyard. "No armor? Then 'tis our lord for certain," shouted a wit. "'Tis Richard's Regret!"

The derisive name circled through the courtyard in whispers, soft murmurs, barely stifled chuckles.

Elizabeth joined in as the laughter intensified, but she soon quieted. They would all have to abandon their habit of poking jests at the new lord of Eddesley Manor. During the interval between King Richard's granting the manor to an unknown upstart of a servant, and this day, when they would at last meet the man known as Richard's Regret, they had all made merry at his name, at his circumstances. They'd even disparaged his physical appearance and prowess, which none had ever witnessed.

Richard's Regret.

She tried to recall his true name. Simon. Sir Simon, now. No surname that she'd ever heard, but most likely he would adopt the Eddesley name as his own. She was surprised to feel a little twinge of jealousy. He, who had no right to the name, would wear it forever. She, who'd been born with it, must give up the name when she wed.

She would get Rolf in return, of course. The joy of marrying the man she loved would make the loss of her ancestral name, her birthright, easy to bear.

Elizabeth could hear them approaching now. Harnesses jingled, silk banners whipped in the wind. The sounds meant the arriving party would soon reach the crest of the road's small swell, bringing them into view. Her position of honor at the keep's gate did not afford much advantage to one so small as she, so she rose to her toes and craned her neck to catch the first glimpse of her new lord.

Six knights rode in a loose semicircle. Their armor flashed beneath the sun. Their pennons snapped in the air. Their shields and plumes added dazzling color to the dancing blazes of silver. They were so resplendent that at first Elizabeth did not even notice the unarmored man who rode at the center of the group. The knights glittered like glorious, fiery jewels, surrounding an insignificant shard of granite.

Richard's Regret. Simon. Elizabeth dropped from her toes to a more comfortable stance while disappointment swept through her. Despite his dismissive name, despite the jokes and the rumors swirling about him, she had hoped he might be someone capable of restoring Eddesley to its former glories.

Someone like Rolf, the glorious, fiery knight she loved.

She sought Rolf amid those who waited in the courtyard, and spotted him almost at once. Rolf was always easy to find, standing as he did a full head above most other men, his hair golden, his teeth white and perfect, his eyes blue as the sky. He stood with his back toward her, conversing with another man. She wished he would glance her way, that his eyes would meet hers so they might share a silent moment of commiseration. Rolf, whose breeding and skills ought to entitle him to so much, instead must swear allegiance to one so insignificant.

Elizabeth's friend Joan poked her in the ribs. "Cease with mooning over yon Rolf—it is near time for your pretty speech of welcome for our new lord," Joan said with a smile.

"You do it," Elizabeth implored.

"I would. But I have nary a drop of Eddesley blood in my veins."

"I have barely more than a drop myself."

"Your drop is more than can be found in anyone else here."

Someone—she no longer remembered who—had declared that the closest kinsman of the old lord should welcome the new. Nobody had seemed to realize that she resented the newcomer more than they. Nobody seemed to understand she had reason to actually fear his arrival. She had no standing in Eddesley save for her blood relationship to the dead lord. If this new lord chose to eradicate all ties to the past, he could order her away from Eddesley. She would be cast out, homeless. Again.

Rolf knew how she feared the loss of her home. He'd given her a thousand reassurances it would never happen. And yet now, with the usurper in sight, she desperately needed to be reassured again. But Rolf did not look her way, even though he alone of all these people knew her state of mind.

Elizabeth wondered if a lowborn former servant like Simon would think he'd been dealt an insult if she simply backed away from the arch and let him take charge of his new holding unwelcomed, ungreeted. Unwanted.

The party rode closer, affording a closer look at faces grown weary from long hours of riding. She ignored the knights who formed Simon's escort. Dust coated the new lord's skin, while trickles of sweat had snaked from his forehead to his chin, creating an almost comical mask on his face, hiding his true features.

The swirling dust, the shadows cast by the knights, made it difficult to judge his size, for surely he could not be so large as he appeared.

He wore rough chausses and a tunic of the same dark brown as his horse, making it difficult to see where man ended and horse began. Like a satyr, half-man, half-horse. Satyrs, said the legends, possessed insatiable appetites—did Simon? Did he covet this place, did he hunger for something more? Elizabeth caught her breath, wondering from where such a thought had sprung.

The glittering, gleaming knights created such a spectacle around him that it was easy, at first glance, to overlook his size, his solidity, the grim determination evidenced in the strong straight slash of his mouth. An enemy chancing upon this party would no doubt target the knights, ignoring the insignificant man in their midst, and realize too late that he was equally if not more capable of slaying them all.

"It is easy to see how he was left behind," whispered Joan, proving Elizabeth's impression.

Elizabeth murmured something noncommittal. She'd laughed along with everyone else when hearing Simon's story. He'd been but a serving man, left behind after his lord was slain in the Holy Land. Nobody had missed him. Nobody even knew he'd been imprisoned until years later when he'd somehow escaped his Saracen captors.

Word of his plight found King Richard's ear. Richard had endured his own bout of imprisonment, and some said that was why he'd been so guilt-plagued to learn he'd abandoned a man to years of slavery. He'd dubbed Simon a knight and granted him this holding. Someone who'd seen the deed done had said Richard spoke in private with Simon for quite a long time, and at the end of it emerged with tears in his eyes, saying that nothing he could give Simon would be enough to pay him for his lost years.

Richard's Regret.

Looking upon Simon in the flesh, Elizabeth wondered how anyone who had met him could forget him. She knew, somehow, that any other serving man who'd endured the same would not have brought Richard Lion Heart to tears. No, this man was not Richard's Regret.

Simon. A big man, with strong features that were somehow compelling to look upon . . .

What was wrong with her! It must be the heat, far too intense for the last day of May, and the untoward excitement surrounding the arrival of their new lord, that caused her wits to scatter in so many inappropriate directions.

She clasped her hands in front of her waist, and forced her thoughts to settle.

The riders slowed as they neared the keep; she noticed it was his horse that first tightened its gait in response to a subtle shift of his hands on the reins. The knights reined in their animals to follow suit in the manner of those grown accustomed to obeying his silent commands. He kept his head steady, but as he drew closer she could see his eyes sweep the length of the front wall, as if judging the solidity of the stone. With another quick glance he took his first look at the people he would rule, granting none of them more than the most cursory inspection. Stone before people. Everyone was so busy gawking and speculating that they probably had not noticed what interested him most. It suddenly occurred to her that insignificance could be a powerful weapon in the right hands.

I, too, know how to disappear in the midst of a crowd, she thought as his glance skipped over her without pause. She wondered if he realized that here, in this place, he would not be as invisible as he was accustomed. One person, at least, recognized that a man of substance hid behind the nondescript demeanor.

He should have worn the armor.

Simon regretted the decision he'd made upon rising that morning. He ought to have known better than to follow a whimsy inspired by a sleepless night, a nervous roiling in his innards, an unexpected yearning to be welcomed into a place where he expected to find nothing but hostility.

Armed as the knights, he would have been indistinguishable from them. In appearance. Better, he'd thought, to meet his people—his people!—with no pretensions, no shining metal to pretty up the truth of what he was. A hardworking man, an honest man, a man still somewhat dazed by his good fortune, but determined to make the best of the chance he'd been given.

What a fool.

The people of Eddesley said nothing, but he heard their opinions in their poorly stifled titters, saw it in the way they tried to shield their smirks by pressing their hands against their mouths. They despised him. They'd made up their minds about him before ever coming to know him, and it would have changed nothing to appear before them resplendent as King Richard himself.

His instincts had been right. Nobody knew better than a servant that covering oneself in finery did nothing to change the man beneath the clothes, even though the nobles tried to make it so.

So be it.

Just as he had always been forced to bend to the whims of any fool with a title, so, too, would these people find themselves bowing and scraping before him, like it or not. He knew a fleeting moment of regret for what must have been a half-awake dream. He must have been insane, to think there might be a way to forge a bond with those close to him at birth, as well as those born higher, and by working together create prosperity that would benefit them all.

He relaxed in the saddle and took another, more leisurely look at the pile of stone, the mass of human chattel, handed over to him by Richard Plantagenet. Eddesley castle and keep, and the people who had been born and would die within view of its walls.

They were within a hundred yards of the gate. "Come forth to meet your lord," cried Frederick, the one knight who had shown Simon respect and courtesy from the first.

The people were massed at the gate—to form a barrier, Simon wondered, or to greet him? Nobody moved to allow the riders through. Just as Simon was considering that running down his people might be his first act as Lord of Eddesley, there was a subtle shifting in the mass of humanity. A young woman ejected from the bulk as if she'd been shot by an arrow . . . or pushed.

Simon raised his right hand and the riding party came to a halt.

She was a good fifty paces away from him. She curtsied. The hot breeze lifted the edges of her headdress to reveal rich brown hair that glinted with golden lights in the sun. She rose from her curtsy and said something. He could faintly hear a soft feminine voice, but could make out nothing of what she said.

"Speak up, or approach," he ordered.

He wondered if she had the same trouble hearing him, for she simply stood there with her hands clasped together in an attitude of prayer.

It would be no effort at all to mow her down; his horse wouldn't even miss a step.

He wondered if she was being offered to him as a gift in some misguided attempt to please the new lord. They'd chosen well. He'd always lusted after, but never was able to enjoy, females of her kind, for they seldom appeared among women of his status. She stood tall as any full-grown woman, but possessed a delicate frame like that of a woods fairy. She waved her hands as she spoke, easy graceful motions that made him think how easily a man could grasp both of her wrists in one hand, or how with both of his hands he might almost span her waist.

Women built that way often had an overabundance of hair, eyes so large and deep that it seemed you

could see into their souls, legs so long they might
rival a horse. Pretty playthings for a man's enjoyment,
and it was just as well that the nobles were saddled
with them, for they were useless when it came to
work, and worse than useless when it came to bearing
children.

He had no doubt that women like her were dangerous, in their ability to enslave a strong man with
their weakness.

From what he could see of her, she was every inch
that sort of woman.

"Step away, mistress," he said, and urged his horse
into a walk.

She backed up a step, but mainly held her
ground. Her lips worked and he knew she was talking, but even though he was closer he still could
not hear her over the sound of his horse. Perhaps
that was why he found his attention fastened so
strongly upon her lips. There, too, she fit the pat-
tern of a useless woman, with her wide, generous
mouth, and lips so full and lush that Simon could
understand how some men might become so en-
thralled that he could think of little else besides
claiming them for his own.

". . . . my cousin . . . death . . . nobody of higher
rank . . . to me to welcome . . ."

She seemed determined to stand there jabbering,
and truth to tell the few words he caught piqued his
interest. He reined his horse to a halt right in front
of her, and leaned around the horse's neck.

"What is it you want?" he demanded.

She blinked in surprise, temporarily startled
into silence. "Want?" she squeaked out at length.
"Nothing."

Perhaps she was an idiot. He spoke more gently.

"Then kindly step away from the path, mistress, so we might pass."

"I must welcome you." Her scowl told him she did not welcome the charge.

"Everybody here must do so."

"I must be the first. He was my cousin. The old lord, I mean."

A tiny curl of dread took root in Simon's middle. She filled his vision, this fairy-light creature, so delicate, so useless. He remembered his first impression, that she might be an idiot. "Your cousin was not the Lord of Eddesley." He spoke kindly, to soothe her, so she would not cry or apologize for making such a mistake.

But she merely gripped her hands more tightly together, as if she could pray her nonsense into his head. Her eyes widened with confidence and purpose.

"Aye. Jerome was my cousin."

Jerome of Eddesley might have had a hundred female cousins for all Simon knew. Richard had named only one that Simon wanted to be rid of with all haste.

"And your name is?"

"Elizabeth."

Simon uttered a one-word expletive so foul that she shrank away from him. She cringed, not in a cowardly manner, but in the way of someone who had learned that smallness, lack of substance, made one seem less threatening. Her shifting posture only caused her garment to shift and cling to slender curves, revealing her fragility, her delicacy. He had to grip the reins and tighten his legs round his horse to hold himself in the saddle rather than jump down to comfort her.

The horse, confused by Simon's tension, whinnied and spun on its rear legs. Simon brought the animal back under control, while letting forth a solid torrent of cursing so colorful he hoped nobody could understand him.

Two

Inspecting the castle took no time. Like so many others, it had been erected in haste after William's glorious conquest, with defense its primary purpose.

No creature comforts had been added in the intervening years. It remained a squat, forbidding circle of stone, intimidating from without, gloomy and damp within. Pillars and buttresses, intended as support for a second story that had never been built, made a second circle within the exterior, leaving a great round space in the center for use as a hall.

Castle residents had spaced off individual chambers by stretching ropes between the walls and pillars. They'd hung the ropes with cloth, banners, tattered old garments. Simon supposed they'd been striving for privacy, but had succeeded only in making the perimeter of the hall look like it was encircled by market booths.

Pallets and bedrolls lay strewn among the rushes, most likely where the single men slept. Dogs roamed the large, filthy space. Some watched his progress with ears alert, tails stiff. Others nosed through the bedding and the rushes, hunting for food. Squalor.

He had been cursed with a fastidious nature. The lord he'd served had been as blissfully unaware of personal cleanliness as it appeared the old lord of Ed-

desley had been. Many a night, Simon had seen his
lord to rest and then taken himself off to sleep in the
stables, where he at least stood a chance of rising
alone, without lice or other unwelcome guests having
joined him in the night.

He found only one small enclosed chamber, near
the kitchen—most likely it had served during better
days as a pantry to lock up expensive spices and special foods. Now, the door hung agape, its topmost
leather hinge frayed through. Debris clogged the
room, but some light filtered through the junk, so
Simon knew there must be an arrow slit in the wall,
which would let in some light and some air.

"Make that chamber ready for me," he ordered the
castellan who had been reluctantly guiding him
around.

"Lord Eddesley always slept with the men in the
hall," grumbled the castellan.

Simon ignored him. "Have the hinge repaired so
the door swings well."

He craved privacy. He'd never had any, save for
those nights spent in stables or alongside a stream.
He'd spent his youth lying crammed onto a pallet
with his brothers and sisters. When he'd gone into
service, he'd been glad of a private pallet even
though it was crowded into an attic with a dozen
other youths. As his lord's manservant he'd shared
more spacious quarters with two others.

While imprisoned it had been worst of all, lying
head to toe with uncounted other miserable slaves,
sweating in the hot desert nights, gasping for fresh
cool air but taking in nothing but the smell of filthy,
overworked, despairing men.

Here, where he could do as he pleased and only
what he pleased, he would have a chamber to himself.

When circumstances allowed, he would finish the second story of this decrepit shell and fashion a large, airy, well-lit chamber for himself. He'd be wed by then, but his quarters would be his alone. He would visit his wife as necessary.

His wife. No matter his feelings on the matter now, he would have to take a wife one day if he meant to take the fullest advantage of his good fortune. Someday. He pushed the distasteful thought away.

The castellan had issued orders for the repair and clearing of the chamber. Simon told him, "I shall have a look at the fields now."

Elizabeth forced lavender stems into gaps in the mortar. She crushed some of the dried flowers and leaves and let the crumbles fall to the floor, where they mingled with the fresh-laid rushes. She stepped back and cast a critical eye over the small chamber. She'd done all she could.

"What are you doing here?" Simon's demand for an explanation startled her into whirling about. The richness and deepness of his voice sent a little bolt of pleasure coursing through her.

Pleasure? More likely fear, she thought, although the sensation low in her belly held a distinctly pleasant edge to it.

She clutched one last bunch of dried lavender in front of her as if it were a shield that could deflect his effect upon her. "I did not expect you back so soon."

"There was not much to see."

She realized anew how thoroughly this man mastered his emotions. His words were neutral enough. His face betrayed no hint of anger or disappointment at the state of Eddesley manor. He revealed nothing to show whether a former servant and slave took pleasure in his new holdings, or whether he'd begun to suspect Richard the Lionheart had done him no great favor.

"My cousin was not the best steward of his land." She hadn't meant to apologize, but she felt compelled to say something.

"So I have noticed."

She pressed herself against the wall as Simon walked slowly into the chamber. She'd backed right into the stem so recently hung, further crushing it. The clean, pungent scent wafted through the newly cleared space.

"Lavender," he said.

"Aye."

He moved toward the arrow slit in the far wall, and she edged her way to the door, intent upon making her escape.

"Hold still. I despise fidgeting."

His rudeness stunned her into stillness. She had apologized for her cousin's neglect, but it seemed Simon did not intend to ask forgiveness for the appalling way he'd responded to her greeting; in fact, he'd just insulted her again!

"I meant to be away from here before you returned. I had no wish to cross your path again."

Nor I, yours, he seemed to say through the rigidity of his pose. After a brief, tense silence, he said, "I must speak with you."

"You said many things to me earlier." Her ears still rang with the harsh sounds of the curses he'd heaped upon her at the castle gate. She had no desire to stand and bear the brunt of his animosity once more.

"I regret that," he said. But he did not turn to face her and she decided he was not asking for forgiveness.

She could put little store in a halfhearted apology given by a man who kept his back to her, who stood so stiff and proud that she could only imagine the lack of remorse stamped across his features.

"There is no need for you to apologize. You may speak to me as you please." She moved toward the door, but somehow he'd spun about and crossed the intervening space so quickly that before she could step through the portal, his arm barred her way. She walked straight into him, her breasts pressing full against his forearm.

Heat, and something more, sizzled through her at the pressure of his flesh against hers, strengthening the pleasurable sensation that still lingered from the sound of his voice. She stepped away from him so quickly she almost tangled her heels in her skirts.

"What do you want?" she gasped.

He smiled, a humorless tilting of his lips. "I keep my wants to myself," he said.

Most people might have found his statement peculiar, but Elizabeth understood at once. "If nobody knows what you want, they cannot laugh if you fail to get it."

"Or use it to gain power over you."

What a strange conversation to have with someone who treated her like an enemy . . . and yet spoke so intimately. She wrapped her arms around herself as if to ward off a chill, but knew the movement was in response to this man's ability to somehow see into her very soul.

He did not appear to be as affected as she was.

"I will speak to you," he said. "With the door closed, if that laggard had it fixed as I ordered."

He touched her, just barely, by resting the fingers of one hand against her shoulder, and let the one that had been barring the door drop to press against her waist, guiding her more deeply into the chamber. Her heart hammered and all the strange sensations coursing through her heightened. She could not understand why she felt so all-atremble; most likely she feared another tongue-lashing.

He stepped away from her and tended to the door. She stared at the back of him, finding the way he was shaped to be oddly pleasing to the eye. His dark hair, long and thick, had been tied back in a queue. As he moved, it swung, drawing attention to the breadth of his shoulders and down to the narrowness of his waist and hips. His homespun tunic stretched taut across his heavily muscled upper body, and hung loosely near the waist.

He made a soft sound of approval as he pulled the door closed, reminding her he'd been inspecting the hinge while she'd been inspecting him. She felt the heat of embarrassment and was glad that with the door pulled shut the chamber was dim, quiet. Their feet had stirred the newly laid rushes, so that their sun-dried odor mingled with the lavender. She could hear him breathing.

"Why?" he asked after a long while.

"Why what?"

"Why have you sweetened the air in my chamber?"

"Oh." The question seemed so insignificant, but she did not know why she had been hoping—no, thinking, he had more important matters on his mind.

By now her eyes had adjusted to the gloom. She shot a look at him to see if he appeared ready to burst into another rage, but it was difficult to tell. The only light came from the afternoon sun slanting through the narrow arrow slit. It fell somewhere below his neck, illuminating his chest rather than his face. That was probably why his chest seemed so broad, highlighted as it was.

"Well?"

For someone who had poured out such a torrent of vituperation earlier, he seemed remarkably close-mouthed now, eking out his questions in as few words as possible.

"If I had a chamber of my own, I would like it to smell sweet and clean," she said. In the face of his continued silence, she grew bolder. "Since you would not permit me to make you welcome in the traditional way earlier, I did so with the herbs."

She did not tell him that she had obeyed an inner impulse to make at least one thing nice for him. She would have done the same for anyone, she amended, for she would have done her best to put Eddesley in a good light no matter who had appeared as the new lord.

She had not realized until Simon took possession just how much she cared about the crude castle, the verdant but unproductive acres. She'd always appreciated the shelter it afforded, always hoped she would never have to leave. But she'd never given much conscious thought to what it meant, to possess ancestral lands and know that generations of Eddesleys would possess it in turn.

She wondered if she might have cared all along, but deliberately quelled her affection, knowing Eddesley could never be hers. A woman could not hope to hold lands, save under the most exceptional circumstances, so there had never been any point in dreaming, hoping, even though Rolf had always encouraged her to do so.

Yes, Rolf must have planted that unacknowledged

yearning in her heart. Rolf, who had always whispered that by right of blood, Eddesley should be hers one day.

"You took me by surprise," said Simon. The interruption reminded her that blood did not matter, if it flowed in a woman's veins.

"I meant to be away from this chamber before you returned."

"No—not now. Earlier today."

His comment provoked the little spark in her that always threatened to turn into laughter at the most inappropriate times. She tried to quell it. "Earlier, I stood in the open beneath a bright sun, and welcomed you at the top of my voice. And yet you were taken by surprise then, and not now, when you come upon me so unexpectedly."

She thought she saw a little upward tug at the edge of his lips, as if he, too, realized the humor in what he'd said. She could not be certain in the dim light.

"I was told you were a maiden well on in years, a pauper living here at your cousin's generosity because nobody else would take you in. I expected someone very different."

"I am well on in years," she said, a little stung by the comment. "And a pauper as well."

"Your age does not appear to be greatly advanced."

"Four-and-twenty." She was glad of the uncertain light, for she knew it would hide her embarrassment. Women of her age usually had four or more children clinging to their skirts. She straightened her shoulders. "But I am not destined to be unwed for much longer."

"So you know about that, then."

It suddenly occurred to her that someone must have spoken to him about her before he'd arrived. "I am surprised you troubled yourself to learn so much about me. I do not understand, though, how you could possibly know about my impending marriage."

"Why would I not know?"

"Because it was deemed best to keep it a secret."

"There is no longer any need for secrecy. Richard merely thought it best—he has some experience with betrothals and marriages, and claimed matters were best settled directly between the man and woman."

She was having difficulty following his ramblings. Sometimes she was sure of his meaning, but other times he spoke in riddles. But one bit she understood well enough to make her heart soar. "The king approves of the marriage?"

"'Twas his idea. But, I have vowed—"

"Rolf will be pleased," she interrupted, eager to get away from him.

"Who is Rolf?"

Simon stared at her, with befuddlement writ clearly upon his features. How could he have gone from knowing so much to total confusion so easily? She backed against the wall once more, suddenly fearing that this new lord might be a madman.

"Rolf is the man I love. The man to whom I have been secretly betrothed."

"Good God." She feared he might begin cursing her again, but he tightened his jaw and took a deep breath. "I thought—the greeting, the lavender . . . you said you knew, but I think we spoke at cross-purposes."

"Know what?"

"Richard has indeed decreed you are to wed. But not to this Rolf you mention. The king has said you are to marry me."

Three

"No." Elizabeth's denial rang out with strength and determination. Inside, she felt so numb with disbelief that she could not be certain she spoke aloud, but she could hear the words echoing from the walls. "No, no, no, no."

How she had struggled, all these years, to hold her head high and smile and act delighted when one after another of her friends and relatives married and bore children. She smiled and smiled, and cooed and ahhed, while inside she'd cried at the unfairness of it. She knew she was not displeasing to the eye. She knew men enjoyed her company. And yet none had ever offered for her hand because she possessed no wealth, no enviable name. Her cousin had sometimes mocked her, calling her a useless expense in his household, one that he would one day have to stir himself to pass off to another better able to handle it.

Rolf had been the first to overlook her lack of connections and wealth. He had promised to speak to her cousin when the time was right. Neither of them could have foreseen that lazy old cousin Jerome would bestir himself at Richard's call for Crusaders. Nobody could have known that Jerome would then hie off to Italy, where he'd died ignominiously of the shits before ever striking a blow against the Saracens.

After his death, there had been no one to speak for her, and Rolf decided they should await the king's return from the Crusades. With so many nobles dying for the Cross, Rolf thought there was some slim hope that King Richard might recognize Elizabeth as her cousin's only blood kin and grant Eddesley to her. And so they had waited. Waited for years, until it seemed clear Richard had no interest at all in England, let alone in the disposition of one crumbling stone castle and its poorly tended acres. Elizabeth had despaired of the king ever giving her leave to wed at all.

And now, it appeared Richard had done so. Handed her over to this . . . this jumped-up servant as casually as he'd handed over Eddesley Manor.

Rolf's hopes, dashed into nothing.

Her heart, crushed into numbness.

How this Simon must be gloating. She roused herself out of her numbness intending to meet his smirking delight with hatred and disgust, only to find him looking upon her with an expression of such utter loathing that she had to step back from its force.

"Why, you do not want to marry me at all," she marveled.

"And so I will not." His carefully neutral expression melted into one of pure stubbornness. "I have sworn I will never again be forced to do something against my will."

He turned away from her, and she knew he regretted revealing his thoughts.

"Men do not usually find me so disgusting," she said, and immediately wished she had held silent. Her relief must have loosened her tongue. She sounded as if she were fishing for a compliment, for some reassurance of her feminine attractions, when she'd merely been surprised at the vehemence of his repudiation. Really? whispered something inside her. Perhaps her pride had been stung. This man, who had no right by blood to a woman of her status, was no more eager to wed her than any other man had ever been.

Except for Rolf.

"I do not find you disgusting, mistress," Simon said. He drew a great breath and then turned to face her. He studied her womanly curves with an intent she would have called insolence if there had been any element of lechery in it. "You are more pleasing in appearance than I was led to expect."

"Oh." Her skin warmed and tingled, from embarrassment and something more. Something about the way he stood there, awkward and uncomfortable, averting his gaze from her with obvious effort, told her compliments did not come easily to this man. She supposed servants seldom found occasion to pay a genuine compliment to their betters, and so he would have had no practice. He'd been torn from one way of life and thrust into another with no more preparation than a bull torn from his pasture and heaved into the sea, and told he must henceforth swim and eat fish.

Wallowing, with no foothold, hungering for what she could have no more—she had felt the same way when her parents had died from ague and she'd been forced to beg charity from her cousin. She knew exactly how Simon must feel. She fought now against the unwonted surge of kinship that swept through her.

"I do not want to marry you," she said. "So we are of like minds in that matter." She braced herself for another torrent of anger, which would certainly accompany her bold declaration.

Instead, he shrugged. "What you want does not matter. I have said I will not marry you."

She flinched inwardly; even though she had no desire to wed this man, his rejection still somehow stung. She must have betrayed something of what she felt, for his brow creased with concern.

"It has nothing to do with you personally," he said. "I would have been as firmly set against any woman in your place."

"You do not fancy women?" She clamped her teeth shut too late to avoid blurting out the question. What was wrong with her? Anyone chancing to overhear the conversation would think she cared that she was being rejected by Simon.

He laughed. The sound, garbled and rusty, seemed to surprise him, judging by the look of astonishment on his face. He quickly quelled his laughter. "Oh, I like women, mistress. Perhaps too much. What I don't like, and what I swore to myself I would never do again, is bending before the will of another. Not even for a king."

"I do not like being forced to do things against my will, either," she said.

He cocked his head, and looked at her with a different kind of interest, as if she'd suddenly sprouted wings. "Well, then," he said slowly, "let us work together and find a way out of this."

"You really do mean to flout the king?" Her eyes widened with disbelief. And within their sapphire depths he fancied he saw a glimmer of hope.

He knew her apparent eagerness to conspire with him should make him happy. He might, with her cooperation, be able to hold true to the vow he'd made to himself during those long years of captivity. He'd sworn that if he managed to escape prison he would never again submit his will to that of another. He wondered if Richard Plantagenet knew how close Simon had come to refusing his grant of Eddesley once Richard stipulated marriage to Elizabeth was part of the gift.

But Simon had learned another thing during captivity, and that was that until a man drew his last breath, there was hope of escape. And so he'd let his well-honed servant's demeanor present a pleasant, obliging face to the king as he'd bowed and pretended grateful acceptance of the gift. All the while his mind spun, thinking, "I will find a way out of the marriage."

He'd set his mind against Elizabeth without ever meeting her. The thought settled uncomfortably, for he'd been guilty of doing the very thing he'd deplored in the people of Eddesley.

He'd so thoroughly decided against her that he'd given the marriage no consideration whatsoever, until coming face-to-face with this enchanting slip of a girl. Until his man's urges had responded to her, and some traitorous part of his mind had come up with any number or reasons to justify why taking her to wife did not mean a capitulation to Richard's will. It made sense to marry a woman with blood ties to the manor, considering the animosity he faced from the occupants. He had to marry a woman of noble breeding anyway, if he wanted to change the course of history for his bloodline.

Even now, the devilish voice whispered he would never find another woman so appealing, so pleasing to the eye, so able to fire his loins. Children born of this woman would possess an elegant grace, a nobility of

bearing, that marriage to one of his own kind could
never produce. Richard had done him a favor in forcing this upon him. . . .

"No. I will not do it."

He didn't realize he had spoken aloud until her
lips parted and her shoulders slumped.

She thought he meant he would not defy the king.
Regret sizzled through him to see how disappointed
she had grown at thinking she would have to marry
him.

He had cautioned himself about these sorts of
things. He knew better than most how the nobility despised those of lesser blood. He'd watched his own
lord use his serving women and laugh at their hopes
of advancement. He'd listened at night while servants
themselves gossiped and disparaged their fellows who
thought they might one day escape the role their
birth had imposed. He knew that in this place, those
of noble blood hated him for being given what they
believed belonged to them, but even worse, his own
kind would hate him for his good fortune, and enjoy
nothing more than seeing him fail.

He knew that the woman Richard ordered him to
marry would hate him most of all, and he'd believed
he would hate her with equal intensity.

He'd never expected to be drawn to her, and to
feel a stab of regret that she would so eagerly seek to
escape the obligation.

"I meant no, I will not force you into marriage
against your will, either," he said. He wondered if she
would remark over the awkwardness of his explanation. He had little practice with lying. Plenty of
practice with avoiding the truth. They were two different things.

"It is very kind of you to think of my wishes," she

said. Hope sparked in her again; he could see it in the way she held herself, in the way her breath quickened.

"You could not be expected to welcome marriage to the likes of me," he said.

"I might have, if you had happened into this chamber four or five years ago." She studied him with frank interest. He felt her gaze move along his person and wondered if she compared him to the man she claimed was her secret betrothed. That man probably had slim limbs rather than the knotted, bulging legs and arms that Simon had developed in his three years of hard labor for the Saracen. Her beloved probably had hands toughened by nothing worse than leather, and probably rode a horse with the ease and grace of those born to the saddle.

Her gaze lingered on his chest and shoulders, which had grown so wide from swinging a mattock and pick, from lifting and heaving rock, that Richard's best armorer had nearly given up fitting him with his own suit of armor. As it was, Simon's armor was a combination of new and old, chain and plate, completely different from the other knights', for there had been no way to accommodate both his broad upper reaches and his taut and relatively slender midsection with large plates.

"You would have considered marrying me?" His voice sounded as gravelly as the rock shards that had splintered from the granite he'd chiseled from the earth.

"Not now," she said. It was such a tantalizing, cryptic comment, that he was immediately plagued with curiosity to know what she had endured in the past that would have made her amenable to marrying him. He would never know. She smiled, and wrapped her arms closely around her middle, as if hugging the secret to herself. "I told you, I am secretly betrothed."

"Why secretly?"

"It seemed best to keep it a secret, until we knew the fate of Eddesley. It was Rolf's idea." Her features softened, and a little smile played about her lips, at the mention of the man's name. Simon felt a wrenching ache to think she would never look like that for him.

What was wrong with him?

She seemed not to notice his effort to get his will under control. She relaxed against the wall. The movement loosened her veil, and let several long locks of silky brown hair tumble free to dangle over her shoulder. "Rolf thought King Richard might give Eddesley to me, since I was my cousin's only blood kin. He felt Richard would be more likely to do so if I remained unwed."

"Rolf sounds like a fortune hunter," Simon grated.

"He is not!" Hot color flared over her cheeks. "He feared marriage would lessen my chances, is all. I told him from the first that there was next to no chance, but he would not allow me to forfeit even the slightest hope."

She had come to her Rolf's defenses like a she lion defending her cub.

She loved the man, it was clear. And perhaps Simon wronged him in believing the man's insistence upon secrecy had more to do with hedging his bets than gaining an advantage for the woman he loved.

"It matters not," Simon said. "Your secret betrothal may make things easy for us. You and Rolf need only marry at once, in secret. I cannot believe that Richard Lionheart will worry overmuch about whether or not we have wed, but if he sends inquiries later, you can claim the marriage took place before I arrived. By then nobody will give the matter any serious thought."

She smiled, wrenching his heart once more. "We need only to beseech the priest to marry us in secret."

"You may tell him to ask me directly, if he questions the need for secrecy," said Simon.

He turned away from her, and tugged a sprig of lavender from its niche in the wall. "We are done with each other, then."

"Yes, I suppose we are."

But as soon as she said that, he didn't want to be done, not at all. "How will you tell him?"

"I will make an offering of flowers for the altar, and then I will say—"

"Not the priest. Your Rolf. How will you tell him the waiting is at an end?"

She made a soft sound that slammed into him with the effect of an ocean wave, for he could imagine her making such sounds under other circumstances. The wordless sound of utter delight a woman sometimes makes in the throes of passion. He could not stop himself from turning to see how her features changed with the sound, for he knew he would never have another chance.

She did not disappoint him. She was suffused with such joy, such delight, that it fairly glowed from her. He felt an improper, an unwanted, stirring in his loins.

"Well?" he rasped. "What will you say?"

"Perhaps his name, my lord," she said, a little breathless, a little dreamy. "But I fear I may be so overcome with happiness, I might not be able to say anything at all. I may just . . ."

"Just . . ." he prompted.

"Just run to him and catch his face between my

hands and implore him to look into my eyes. Surely my joy will shine so brightly he will know without the words being said."

"Men are creatures who require specific words."

With a little trilling laugh she stepped close, lifted her hands, and rested their cool length on either side of Simon's jaw. "Can you not hear me without words, my lord? Can you look at me, and not realize how happy you have made me this day?"

He turned rigid as stone, all over, while she smiled up at him. Her eyes sparkled with merriment, mischief, and delight. She wasn't seeing him at all, he knew. In her mind's eye, she was touching and seeing her Rolf, imagining her Rolf's reactions to her good news.

If Simon wanted her, if Elizabeth wanted him, they could look at each other this way every day for the rest of their lives. . . .

He jerked his head, breaking her light hold. Her hands felt so soft, so delicate, sliding against the harsh stubble of his cheeks. Perhaps it was that small discomfort that roused her from her giddiness, for she backed away and flushed a flaming red, staring at her hands as if they'd betrayed her in some manner.

"Your method may well work," Simon said through a throat still tight with desire. He felt the compulsion to ease her embarrassment, as well as the urgent need to be rid of her, to have her safely cleaved to Rolf before he began listening to the devil's whispers in his head. "And I thank you for the lavender," he added, as if the pleasant scent meant more to him than did her walking out of this chamber into the arms of another man.

"Oh, 'twas nothing." She would not meet his gaze again. She wrapped her arms round her waist and hurried away. Simon walked to the arrow slit in the wall and braced an arm on either side while he stared without seeing through the hole in the stone wall.

He heard the scrape of the door over the rushes as she opened it, heard the door close, sealing him inside with the privacy he had so craved. The small chamber seemed to ring with emptiness, with only himself inside.

Can you look at me, and not realize how happy you have made me this day, my lord?

The chill from the stone eventually seeped through his skin and eventually cooled the heat raging through him. He grew aware of the waning light outside, and that he still held a lavender sprig clutched in his fist.

He dropped the lavender sprig to the floor and stirred it with the toe of his boot into the rushes. The clean, sweet scents freshened the air even more. She would provide such gentle touches in her own home soon, for another man.

He ground the lavender into dust.

And then he lifted his head, and angled his jaw upward, the way a knight did when he'd struck a telling blow. He had succeeded. He had flouted the king and would not be forced into marriage against his will.

He had won.

Four

She couldn't find Rolf. She had to find him. Not only to tell him that their long wait was at an end, but to dispel the strange sensations that were fluttering through her; sensations unlike any she'd ever known, brought about by the voice, the scent, the touch of another man.

Simon. She felt almost breathless at remembering the stirrings she'd felt in her most secret places when she'd touched him, when her breast had pressed into his arm. No, the breathlessness and quivering were just from hurrying, she told herself. Her eagerness to find Rolf was what had made her so flustered.

She found all the castle's knights, save Rolf, gathered in the hall, awaiting their new lord. To a man they stood dressed in their best, some appearing nervous, some resigned to whatever fate would deal them. Simon had passed through the hall before finding her in his chamber, so he must have known his men were waiting for him—and yet he had lingered with her.

Only to be sure you understood he does not want you, she scolded herself. Her hands tingled as if in rebuke, reminding her of how it had felt to cradle his face between her hands, to feel the warmth of his skin, the roughness of his beard, to see the stark hunger in his eyes.

She should not be feeling such sensations while thinking of any man but her beloved.

"Rolf!" she whimpered the name. She picked up her skirts and ran.

He was not in the stables, where he could sometimes be found tending his horse.

He was not in the kitchens, where he often stopped to cajole the cook into spooning out a special treat for him.

"Have you seen Rolf?" she asked at each cluster of people. People seemed to be whispering as she approached, and resumed their whispering when she darted off in search of her beloved.

She found him at last at the far end of the orchard, where he lay sprawled on the ground, his back resting against an unpruned apple tree. An empty wineskin lay near his feet, while two others, only half full, lay within reach of either hand.

His face bore the ruddy complexion of a man who was wine-flown. His golden hair was tousled, stringy with sweat, with bits of leaf and bark clinging to the ends. He blinked up at her, his eyes bleary and red-rimmed.

"Ah, there you are, my prize," he murmured. "My hope, my treasure."

"Oh, Rolf." Even his familiar endearments could not lessen her disappointment at finding him so befuddled. The excitement she had felt, the thrill of knowing they would soon become man and wife, had waned with every moment she'd spent searching for him. Now, she could barely summon up a shred of her happiness.

She'd been so confident, telling Simon that Rolf would know without words what had happened, what would happen. Now, she prayed Rolf could not read her thoughts, for they were disloyal and . . . and angry.

Why, on this of all days, when she needed so desperately to rely on Rolf's love and strength, had he withdrawn to the wineskins? Over the long years of their courtship, Joan and others had planted within Elizabeth a niggling worry she'd never before allowed to flourish. Rolf had a tendency to turn to wine when matters did not go his way on the tourney field. She had always told herself that his escape into oblivion did not make him a drunkard, since under usual circumstances he drank no more than the other knights.

But today, the other knights were not wine-flown. And today there had been no contest or tourney loss to send Rolf in search of oblivion.

Not unless he'd considered Eddesley manor a prize, only to see it handed to another this day.

"At least I got this." Heedless of Elizabeth's agitation, Rolf groped for one of the half-filled skins and held it aloft. "Filched them straight from the stores. From now on I shall be forced to ask permission. From a base-born clod."

He fixed her with a woebegone and yet angry expression that told her he blamed her, that it was her fault that Rolf would be bound to do Simon's bidding.

"It matters naught," she said. She knelt in the dirt, and tried to gently disengage the wineskin, but Rolf held tight.

She settled for resting her fingers against his cheek, a sad imitation of the touch she'd shown Simon. Once again she had to quell the disloyal response of her body to the memory of touching Simon. This was the face of her beloved, she told herself—cool, for he had been at rest, and smooth of cheek, for fair-haired men like Rolf ofttimes sported scanty beards.

Yet her hand could not forget the heat, the roughness, of Simon. And so she broke the touch and tucked her hand away, tangling it in a fold of her gown. She rubbed it hard against her thigh, as if she could scrape off the feel of a man . . . but which one?

"There is no need for secrecy any longer, Rolf. Simon knows all about us. I told him everything, and he approves. He wants us to run off and marry immediately and pretend we have been wed for some time."

"Oh he does, does he?" Rolf jerked his head away from her touch, and then lifted the wineskin and drank deeply. "Must do as Simon decrees. Must give him everything and leave me with nothing."

His words struck her heart like arrow bolts.

"Do not say that, beloved. We have each other."

Rolf laughed, an ugly, humorless sound that chilled Elizabeth to her soul. He made no apology for his hurtful words. He drank once more.

Fortune hunter, Simon had called Rolf, without ever having met him.

If he truly loved you, he'd marry you in an instant without worrying about the disposition of Eddesley, Joan had often commented.

Joan had stopped criticizing Rolf, and would say nothing now if Elizabeth confided her confusion over this encounter to her—but she might raise a brow and let a knowing smirk cross her face. And if Simon met Rolf at this moment, his opinion would only gain strength. If *she* met Rolf for the first time now, she would think the same about him. Joan had never liked Rolf much, but had always been vague about her reasons for disliking him. Had Elizabeth been so overwhelmed by at last receiving some male attention that she'd been blinded to his true motives?

No. Elizabeth shook that disloyal thought away. Rolf loved her. He'd sworn so again and again. When flown with wine he often said and did things he regretted later, and this was no different. Tomorrow, he would be wincing from the headache, would be shielding his eyes from the sunlight, but would be begging her forgiveness for anything he'd said or done that might have offended her.

She rose. There was no sense in talking to him now, in his condition, and something within her shuddered at the notion of going before the priest with Rolf in this state and asking to be married. They had waited this long; another day or so would not matter.

She turned to practical matters. Everyone knew that the wife of a knight often had to suggest social strategies to men who were trained to fight rather than keep a sharp eye open for their opportunities to advance in status.

"All of your fellow knights are gathered in the hall to state their allegiance to the new lord, Rolf. You should make yourself presentable and join them. You must earn a place in Simon's good graces."

Rolf laughed again. He made a parody of a bow from where he sat, leaning a little forward, and bending from the waist in such a wobbly manner that she feared he might fall over on his side. But he didn't.

Nor did he rise and make an attempt to brush himself clean for presentation to his new lord. He scowled at her and waved her away, and then pulled the wineskins close to him on either side the way a beggar might gather his possessions to protect them from thieves.

* * *

Simon leaned back in his overlarge chair, with his hands folded low on his lap, with his eyes half closed. He hoped he fooled them all into thinking he sought a brief nap after gorging on dinner.

He had not gorged; truth to tell, the food had been barely palatable.

His feigned oblivion accomplished what he had desired—those around him relaxed, and revealed something of their true natures.

The six knights who had accompanied him congregated in their own small, sullen group, away from the men who had served the old lord. Simon could tell from his knights' glowering countenances, by their motions, that they heartily disliked their new home. Keeping them happy would be a challenge. Richard Plantagenet had handed them over to Simon, but had made no provision for their upkeep, and had offered no advice on how to ensure they liked their new home. Like any man of title, Simon would be bound to keep a number of knights armed and ready for battle on the king's command.

The other castle folk appeared happy enough, with no obvious malcontents. They joked and laughed, and a few tossed scraps to the floor for the dogs. None seemed to be appalled by the filth, by the near-inedibility of the food they'd just eaten.

Which of these men held Elizabeth's affections?

Simon continued to study the room through half-closed eyes, judging, casting aside. That one too old. That one too fat. That one too weak around the chin. That one eyeing a slender boy rather than a serving girl. Not a one of them looked worthy to take her to wife.

Elizabeth had not come to table. Perhaps she and her knight had already run off to do as Simon had bid. Perhaps even at this moment she lay clasped in another man's embrace, sealing the vows of marriage.

He sat up with a start and a muttered curse, his deception forgotten in the surge of anger that overcame him at thinking of Elizabeth in her wedding bed with another man.

Someone leaned close and whispered into his ear. "Putrid fare, eh, my lord?"

It was Frederick, the merriest of his new knights, who accepted any charge with a nod and a smile. Simon welcomed the interruption, which offered an explanation for his sudden bolting up and cursing.

"I have had worse," said Simon, "but not much worse."

"They say 'tis a cousin of the old lord who tries to manage the household, but she lacks the authority to provoke the cook into doing her best."

So Elizabeth turned her hand toward managing the household. Her attention to his chamber—the sun-dried rushes, the heady lavender—had been nothing specially aimed at him, then. She would have done the same for anyone. He did not understand the disappointment that shafted through him.

At that moment Elizabeth stepped from behind one of the curtained partitions that ringed the hall. She let the cloth fall back into place, keeping her space enclosed, private. Simon sat up straighter, and his heart commenced an erratic pounding. She would not be dressed as she was if she'd spent the day getting married. She wore a smock over her gown, and a cap instead of a veil, as if she'd been working alongside the cook in the preparation of the horrible food. The task was below one of her station, but at the moment he was supremely delighted to know she'd been playing scullion rather than virgin bride.

Was she a virgin?

The disgusting food must have poisoned his brain, for there could be no rational reason for the paths his thoughts were taking. He had no good reason to speculate on the state of the maidenhead of a woman who belonged to another man.

Was she a virgin?

She did not join the others at table. She stood with one hand gripping the edge of her cloth, as if it were a real door and she longed to duck back behind its cover. Her other hand twisted in the apron tied at her waist, while she appeared to search the crowd for someone, something. She never looked in Simon's direction. After a long while, her shoulders slumped, and she lifted the edge of her apron to wipe her face; Simon couldn't help thinking she wiped away a tear.

He wished she would join them now; particularly that she would take her place next to the man who owned her heart. Simon reluctantly acknowledged to himself that he'd been consumed with curiosity about the man ever since Elizabeth had mentioned him. He was curious beyond all reason to know which of those average men surrounding him held her heart in such thrall that she would turn so soft and yearning at the mere thought of him.

Simon studied the men again. Now that she had appeared in the hall, surely the one she loved would betray himself with an expression of utter besotted-ness. But none of the men appeared to be watching her with any special interest or affection.

Maybe Rolf lolled abed behind the cloth, and she stood there to ensure he would not be disturbed. Maybe they'd wed, consummated, and he'd sent her back to work—such was the way among Simon's own kind, he knew.

She lifted the edge of her smock to her eyes again, and this time Simon knew she did indeed wipe away tears. She would not be crying if she'd married her Rolf. She stood still and yet an aura of dejection surrounded her, and he had to grip the arms of his chair to keep from racing across the hall to comfort her.

He would have to speak to her again. If they were to carry out their plan of pretending she had been secretly wed, she would have to do a better job of appearing with Rolf as a couple rather than looking so starkly alone.

"Ah, there's the wench now," said Frederick, turning to Simon. Simon wondered what he'd betrayed upon his features, for Frederick stared at him with an odd, speculating look, and then darted his glance toward Elizabeth, as if he'd realized how thoroughly Simon's thoughts had dwelled upon her.

Simon stiffened, taking insult at Frederick's referring to Elizabeth as a wench, though he had no reason. He knew, too, that he had to deflect Frederick's curiosity. "The lady Elizabeth. I have met her. I did not realize she had assumed responsibility for the entire household."

"I suppose someone had to do it," Frederick said with the offhanded manner of someone who had no interest in the subject. "You will want to take her to task over her ineptitude, I should imagine."

"I will talk to her," Simon said.

"I will hail her for you."

"Not here," Simon forestalled him. "What I have to say to her is best said in private."

"Aye." Frederick nodded. "She is blood-related to the old lord. Best not to rebuke her in public." He

motioned to a young page who ignored him until
Frederick let loose with a piercing whistle. At that, the
page sighed and heaved himself away from the wall,
and then sauntered lazily toward them.

When the boy drew close enough, Frederick
caught him by the ear and pulled him to his toes.
"You will, in future, respond to a summons with more
alacrity, will you not?"

The lad grimaced with pain, but to his credit did
not cry out. "Aye, my lord."

Frederick let loose of him. "Hurry yonder to Mistress Elizabeth and tell her your liege wishes to speak
to her in private."

"In my chamber," said Simon.

"In his chamber."

The boy dashed away, nearly tripping over his feet in
his eagerness to do Frederick's bidding. He skidded to
a halt next to Elizabeth, and then rose to his toes to
whisper in her ear. Her brow creased, and then she
scanned the room in search of Simon. Simon stared
back, outwardly unperturbed while within him something happened—his heart commenced pounding, his
blood rushing with fevered heat. She nodded, and his
blood pounded even harder.

In private. In his chamber. He would be alone with
her once more.

Five

Candlelight treated her kindly, Simon thought as he watched Elizabeth walk into his chamber. She had discarded her cap, giving him his first look at the full glory of her hair. She wore it pulled straight back from her face, and anchored it somehow at the back of her head, from where it cascaded down in a rich, silken fall of golden brown that shimmered in the candlelight. She had washed her face; in her hurry to answer his summons, she had not stopped to dry away the wetness, so the candle glow played against tiny droplets of water glistening atop dewy soft skin, casting shadows that accented the high crest of her cheekbones, and lent an attractive shadowing to the curves of her face.

She had also discarded her apron, so if there was any dirt or foul odors from the rotten victuals she'd handled in the kitchen, he could not tell. The burning beeswax combined with his fresh rushes and lavender, and the secret, delightful scent of woman in an intoxicating blend. A man could spend endless hours inhaling that scent, caught in a spell as profound as that cast by the opium smoked by the Infidel.

Yet, he had seen all manner of kitchen wenches lit by nothing more than candlelight, and none moved with such grace, or stirred his loins, as did this female.

Curse his man's body! It paid no heed to his mind, which had sworn he would not be tricked or tempted into doing anything against his will. He did not want to marry this woman just because Richard had decreed he must. His mind was so set upon not having her—how did it happen that his body ignored his will and tormented him so?

He laughed a little to himself, bitterly, knowing that none other than Satan could be behind his physical dilemma. The girl was not that beautiful.

Except, perhaps, in candlelight.

He pretended to study a mortar joint between two stones, but even that failed to sway his body, since it seemed determined to turn into its own version of stone, in certain areas.

"I know the dinner did not please you," Elizabeth said. She did not sound the least bit apologetic, which he knew should annoy the lord of a manor. Instead, her calm announcement let him glance up at her with a bit of admiration tempering his lust. She had a bit of spirit.

"I did not call you here to speak of matters that should be handled by the castellan."

"He is a lazy scoundrel who has never worried much about his duties, even in my cousin's day."

"Then he shall be replaced. You are not to enter the kitchens again, save to give orders."

She said nothing, but quirked a brow, and a small smile played about her lips. He fancied he could hear her say, "Then you shall starve," as plain as if she'd spoken aloud.

"What is it?" she asked, cocking her head in question.

"What is what?" he countered, feeling like a dunce.

"You smiled—I saw it. 'Twas just as though you'd

somehow heard the most improper remark I stifled before saying."

Her eyes danced with merriment and a little confusion; she, too, had sensed the eerie connection in seeming to hear words between them that had not been spoken.

"There was a man," he said, slowly, and somewhat incredulously, for he could not believe he was about to speak of such a thing to her. "Where I spent those years under the rule of the Infidel . . ." He might have stopped there, should have stopped there, save for the warm concern he read in her eyes.

Tell me, he fancied she said. But she had not moved her lips. And then she did, asking, "Was he your friend?"

The question set him aback. "I suppose so, even though we could never openly speak to each other."

Tell me, he read again in her eyes.

"Our masters were harsh overseers who would not tolerate one breath of air wasted on anything other than work. And there were so few of us who spoke the same tongue—most of the poor devils were Saracen themselves, or Africans, or Chinese. The Saracens did their best to keep apart any who could understand each other."

"How cruel," she whispered.

"Save at night—they piled us all in a vast room, head to toe, and sometimes we could hear one another if the desert winds blew right, and we were close enough together."

"What did you say to each other?"

Simon found himself unable to speak of the man who'd most likely saved his sanity just then. He deliberately pretended to misunderstand the thrust of Elizabeth's interest.

"Each man eventually took his turn at telling how he'd come to be captured."

He sensed her curiosity about his own capture. "I was taken from the field. I'd fallen alongside my lord. We'd fought together and taken blows from the same warrior. But mine, while stunning me into darkness, was not fatal."

"The other Crusaders must have thought you dead," she said. "That's why they left you behind."

He shrugged. It was done. "Most men had been captured straight from their tents. The Saracens knew how to move in utter silence. We practiced in the night, some of us, until we mastered the skill as well."

"You gave up sleep to learn. And it must have been extremely dangerous to practice such a thing."

He wondered how a noble, pampered woman could have understood the sacrifice of giving up even five minutes of sleep after toiling all day beneath the relentless sun, knowing that another day followed. Wondered how anybody who had not endured the terrors of imprisonment could understand the price that would have been paid if a guard had caught them practicing stealth.

"It cannot be easy to move without making a sound."

"It takes every scrap of strength and cunning." He felt sweat spring to his forehead, remembering.

"Would you show me?"

"No."

She looked about to question why.

"It is not something I will ever do again," he said, forestalling her, "unless the most important thing in my life is at stake." Her mouth opened into a small O, her lovely eyes darkened with sympathy, but she did not ask him again.

But perhaps he should have allowed her to explore that path of interest, for now that it was closed she seized once again upon her earlier questions. "The man who was your friend—he must have spoken during the night of more than how he'd been captured."

"There is nothing for men who have lost all hope to talk about save the past."

Memories assailed him, memories he had sworn he'd buried so deep in his mind that they could never again rear their treacherous heads. But there they were, so raw and bleeding that he knew he had never healed from the invisible wounds inflicted upon him in that awful place. He might never heal. Best to keep those memories locked away where they could not hurt him . . . and yet it was as if now that he'd allowed that memory to blossom again in his mind, it would not be forced back into its place.

"His name was John," said Simon. "We few English liked it best when he would talk at night, even though . . ."

"Even though what?" Elizabeth prompted.

Simon hesitated. Every fiber of his male pride demanded he keep to himself how he'd sometimes thought he would die of the sense of isolation, the loneliness, the despair. And yet his wayward tongue would not be stilled.

"Bad enough to waste the prime years of one's life toiling for the Saracens. Bad enough to suspect deep in your heart that the years would stretch ahead endlessly, with just enough food to sustain the body, just enough water to keep from keeling over beneath the sun, just enough strength to keep from sickening to a merciful death. What John told us let us know we were being robbed of something even more precious."

"What?"

"He told us about a special bond he had with his wife. ''Tis as though we are joined at the mind as well as the body,' he would say, his voice raw with agony and yearning. 'I have known true love and could die a happy man with just her memory in my heart, but I would give whatever God asked to hold her once more in my arms.' You cannot know how a man would feel to learn true love was the one thing he might find regardless of his station in life, and that it would be forever denied to us."

"Did he make it home with you?"

Simon could not answer.

"Oh, Simon," said Elizabeth. Tears shimmered in her eyes, as well as something more—he fancied he saw within her a hint of the aching hunger that had gripped him when John would tell his tale. "I did not know there could be such a bond, either. If it could exist, then her suffering equaled his own."

"*If* it could exist?" He could not believe she had said such a thing. "Do you not share such a bond with your Rolf?"

"I am never sure what Rolf might be thinking," she said quietly. "Especially of late."

And yet Simon knew he had read her thoughts as clearly as if she'd spoken aloud. And he would swear she had read his.

That did not mean, though, that he felt anything like love for her. He sometimes fancied he could sense whatever mischief his horse might be planning, after all, and dogs could sometimes tell just what you wanted them to do without your issuing a command.

He had never wanted to kiss his dog, though, or pull his horse into the circle of his arms and whisper that maybe, maybe John and his lady wife were not the only two in the world who could find such a connection.

And yet suddenly, unexpectedly, without him consciously directing his legs to move or his arms to wrap about her, she was there in his arms. Her face was tipped up to his. Her eyes were wide with trepidation, her lips parted and quivering slightly. He did not know if he had moved toward her, or if she had moved toward him, but somehow they had come together.

"Do you not know when he wishes to kiss you?" His voice was a raw rasp of hunger.

"Of course I do!" Then she flushed, and looked abashed. "He always asks first."

"I would not ask," he said. Or he thought he said; he was not sure, for no sooner did the thought occur than his lips claimed hers in a demanding kiss that threatened to steal every ounce of willpower from his soul.

"Does he kiss you like that?" Simon asked, trying with all his will to draw away from her but not succeeding in doing more than breaking the kiss.

"No."

"How do you kiss him?"

"Like this." She pursed her lips into a chaste pucker and rose to her toes to plant a virgin's kiss on his cheek. But somewhere, somehow, her aim fell short, and his head turned in such a way that their lips found each other again. The tight bud of her pucker loosened beneath his tender assault and flowered into something wild and sweet. Something he had never dreamed to find. Something that a man could spend his life exploring, all the while thanking God that he'd been forced against his will to do what turned out to be the best thing that had ever happened to him.

No.

He did not know from where he summoned the strength, but somehow he ended the kiss. Somehow he stepped away from her, and turned away so that she could not see the state he was in, although he had been so closely pressed against her that she could not have failed to notice his arousal.

"If you would kiss your Rolf the way I have just showed you, then he will be the one hunting down the priest, not you."

"You kissed me . . . just to teach me the right way to do it?"

He didn't answer her. He wished he could lie, but he knew she would be able to tell. "I should not have to show you. You should be wed and . . . and beyond this by now."

"I have not managed to arrange matters yet."

"Your beloved"—his voice caught on the word— "ought to be arranging matters, not you. Perhaps he speaks with the priest at this moment. I did not notice him at table."

"Rolf is not with the priest."

"Nor did he present himself to me along with the other men of the castle." Simon's anger toward the man suddenly found a rational target, and provided a useful outlet for the emotions surging through him. He let anger take precedence. "He insults me by failing to appear, and he insults you by failing to pursue the chance I have given to you both. I did impress upon you, my lady, the need for haste in this matter."

"Aye, you did." She leaned back against the wall, looking exhausted beyond what a few hours in the kitchen would cause, looking disheveled and delectable and thoroughly kissed. He ached to take her back into his arms. "I beg your mercy, my lord. This day has taken a toll on us, all of us. In different ways. It has not been the sort of day I would like to look back upon as my wedding day."

He wanted to say, *You need never beg from me.*

He wanted to say, *Your Rolf is a fool for not rushing straightaway to a priest, before I change my mind . . .*

To his horror, he realized he'd said part of it aloud. "Your Rolf is a fool."

"He may be." She nodded with resigned acceptance. "But then, the idea of marrying me does send men scrambling for a way out. After all, you would yourself defy a king rather than marry me."

She aimed for the door the moment she uttered that witless observation. She missed her target, half blinded by something—the dim flickering candlelight, no doubt. But he stopped her by calling her name, and she paused at once, lest he reach out to catch her and she did not think she could survive being touched by him again. Not without bursting into flames, so hot did he make her blood flow.

But he touched her anyway. He caught her by the elbow, and she fancied his hold trembled—or perhaps it was merely her own shaking that caused it to seem so. He held her, not with a tight grip meant to punish, but rather somehow supporting her weight with his palm below her elbow, with his fingers curled round the fleshiest part of her forearm.

"I told you my lack of interest in marriage is nothing personal," he said. She had not mistaken the trembling; she heard it in his voice, sensed the tightness of his throat in the way he forced the words from himself.

"I am beginning to suspect Rolf's interest in marriage is nothing personal, either," she bit out before she could stop herself. She closed her eyes and mentally berated herself. Her lips still tingled from Simon's kisses; her flesh seemed to surge toward his. She'd never realized that a man's passions could turn a woman so weak, so willing. Make her lose hold of her control and reveal everything to him—look at her, standing there jabbering and letting him know how deeply his earlier insinuations had wound themselves into her heart, making her doubt the motives of her knight.

My treasure, Rolf called her. *My hope, my prize.* All terms of endearment that had gladdened her heart until this day, when Rolf had mumbled them in drunken mocking tones that hinted he might have always meant something else. *My treasure, my hope, my prize*—as if she were a valuable asset to be won, something to relieve him of the need to earn a living, and not a woman at all.

Simon called her nothing but her given name, and yet the sound made her feel as if she were melting inside.

"Elizabeth." Simon's hold upon her firmed, lending his strength, as if he'd somehow sensed she needed it.

She shook him away, though she yearned to turn into him, to feel those strong arms wrap round her and draw her close. She could not forget the sorrow, the pain radiating from him when he'd told that little bit about his life in the Saracen prison. It had taken every ounce of her self-control to hold herself aloof, to stand apart from him when she wanted to take him into her arms and tell him he never had to be alone, never feel so isolated, ever again. To tell him that she understood what it was like to find oneself alone in the midst of a

crowd, to tell him that there were times she felt she
might faint from the need to be held by another
human being.

Rolf would hold her, sometimes, but never for
long, and never without her asking to be embraced.
He claimed being so close without hope of consum-
mating his lust took too great a toll on a man who
needed to keep his strength honed for tourney or
battle.

She knew somehow that Simon would not be-
grudge her the comfort of being held.

She wondered, as she had never done before,
whether servants . . . and slaves . . . grew up as bereft
of human touch as she had.

"Thank you for guiding me over that rough spot in
the stone," she said, deliberately casting his hold
upon her in a false light, deliberately keeping her
voice low and even to hide from him the inappropri-
ateness of her thoughts.

His hand dropped from her elbow as if he'd suddenly realized he touched a newly forged horseshoe.
"I am pleased to be of assistance, my lady."

She glanced over her shoulder and saw that he'd
crossed his arms. She could not see the hand that had
held her with such care.

"I pray that by this hour tomorrow, Rolf and I will
be wed and you need not worry over carrying out the
king's decree," she said.

He said nothing. He stood silent for so long that
she began moving away toward the hall when he
stopped her with a command.

"If you are not wed by the morrow, I will have you
come to me here and tell me why."

She could imagine nothing more humiliating than
to have Rolf refuse to marry her, except for the mor-

tification of reporting that failure to yet another man who did not want her.

"I daresay Rolf and I will be gone from this place by this time tomorrow."

"It would be best."

"For all concerned," she agreed, and then she hurried away before he could stop her again.

Stop her? Had he really meant to stop her those other times? He'd done nothing more than lend a strengthening touch, nothing more than speak her name as it had never been spoken before. It was not so much Simon who had stopped her, but her own treacherous body. She'd been the one to stop, as if in doing so she might find the sense of belonging, the purpose that came from being wanted, that she had always craved.

Six

His own pallet, his own chamber, his own *castle,* by God, and Simon had not been able to sleep.

He could not close his eyes without being tormented by the memory of holding Elizabeth in his arms, of claiming her lips with his own, of tasting her and breathing air warmed by her. He could not lie with his eyes open waiting for sleep to take him, for the moonlight shafting through the arrow slit made shadows dance in the corners, and his mind shaped them into the form he could not obliterate from his mind.

And yet, despite his agitation, he felt unusually light in spirit, as if in telling her things he'd sworn to keep secret until his grave, he'd been unburdened.

When the subtle shift in light told him dawn approached, he gave up the pretense of resting and rose, knowing he greeted the day in the foulest possible mood.

Servants trembled when their masters emerged from their chambers in such moods. Today would mark his first time of terrorizing his people with his temper.

He found the castellan, still lying rolled in his pallet in the hall. He kicked him awake.

"My—my lord?" The castellan sat up, grimacing as he rubbed his backside.

"You should be about early in the morning, seeing to the comfort of the people. If I must rouse you again, my foot will not stop pummeling you until your sorry carcass lies outside these castle walls."

The castellan leaped to his feet, mumbling promises that Simon did not bother to hear, could not hear, for his mind kept chanting *Is she standing with him now before the priest? Will she soon lie in her marriage bed?*

He stormed next into the kitchens, drawn by foul odors rather than appetizing smells. A fat old hag sat upon a stool near the fire, snoring, her back resting snugly in a nook, her chin pressed hard into the pillow of her overblown breasts. Simon hooked one foot under a leg of her stool and pulled, jerking her awake. She flailed for balance, gasping in distress.

"Find as many wenches as needed to scrub this pigsty clean from top to bottom," he ordered, motioning with his hand to include the full kitchen—floor and ceiling as well as walls. "The food you serve will henceforth be tasty and nourishing. Meals will be ready on time. Heed me well. If the fare does not please me today, I shall replace you with another who can meet my demands, and you shall find yourself picking rocks in the fields."

She mumbled something.

"What say you, wench?"

"I say, the Lady Elizabeth will hear about your treatment of me." She glared at him with unapologetic belligerence.

Simon understood her antagonism; few would resent him more than the servants who envied his good fortune. Even so, he would have dismissed her on the spot, except her calling of Elizabeth's name had started up the chanting again. *Are they standing now before the priest? Will she soon lie in her marriage bed?*

He had to leave the castle, he realized. He would
fetch some of his knights and ride out now, inspect
his lands more thoroughly, breathe fresh, clean air,
and fill his mind with the sight of frolicking sheep,
rooting pigs, grazing cows. He would ride until exhaustion drove out all thoughts of Elizabeth of
Eddesley. By the time he returned, she would be wed,
and she would be gone.

The people were stirring in the hall when he
strode back through. His shouting at the castellan
and cook had roused even the sluggards, who yawned
and blinked their dismay at greeting the sun so early
in the day.

He recognized from the night before all the men
stretching and rising from the pallets on the floor. He
also recognized those who had stepped outside the
scanty privacy they'd rigged in the partitions at the
perimeter. Some of the makeshift chambers were still
drawn closed against the light, including the one
where he knew Elizabeth had claimed a small area for
herself. She must have slept so well that even the
noise made by those greeting the day did not make
her stir. Or did she lie within its meager shelter with
her new husband?

Perhaps she and Rolf were behind the cloth walls
at that very moment, celebrating their first morning as man and wife, in the way of a newly married
couple.

"Frederick! Thomas! James!" Simon bellowed out
the names of three of his knights. "Accompany me."

He headed straight for the outside, knowing that if
he remained within the castle for one more moment,
he would tear aside those concealing lengths of
cloths for himself to see if she lay inside, wrapped in
the arms of another man.

* * *

Elizabeth lay atop her pallet, exhausted. She'd slept not at all the night before, and though she could hear the castle folk stirring, she had no stomach for leaving the dimness of her shelter, revealing her fatigue-darkened eyes, her drawn features, for all to see and speculate upon.

They would suspect that a problem had flared between herself and Rolf, and they would be partially right. They would never guess, though, that her sleeplessness stemmed from thoughts of another man entirely. It was Simon, not Rolf, who had been in her mind's eye whenever she tried to close her eyes. It was the memory of Simon's lips upon hers, Simon's arms clasped around her, Simon's heat seeming to penetrate through her very skin to turn her soft as butter inside, melting.

He, obviously, had not been as affected. She heard him ordering his men about and heard them all leave the castle well before anybody had ever stirred from Eddesley before. He'd slept so well he greeted the day before it dawned.

And why shouldn't he sleep well? He'd admitted that the kisses that troubled her so had meant nothing to him, that he'd merely been teaching her the way a man liked to be kissed. He'd proven it by being the first to step away—oh, how the flush of embarrassment heated her face to remember that!—and then he'd sent her away into the arms of another.

Yes, he'd kissed her and ordered her into Rolf's arms, where he expected her to employ the kissing skills Simon had taught her. She shivered, but not from the cold. She ought to be seeking Rolf out at this very moment. How many other sleepless nights had she spent, yearning for the day when Rolf would make her his wife? Now, that day was at hand, and she wished . . . she wished . . .

She wished she were marrying someone more like Simon. Perhaps, even Simon himself, since she'd never met another man quite like him.

She sat bolt upright, unable to credit thinking such an outrageous thought.

Simon did not love her. Simon did not want her. He was thwarting the will of a king to push her into Rolf's arms. Rolf had scorned the notion that they needed only each other to find happiness. She might never find herself in a place where she was truly wanted.

She had to find Rolf. She had to say the things to him that Simon told her men wanted to hear; had to kiss him the way Simon had shown her men wanted to be kissed.

Women liked to be kissed that way, too, she realized. Could she live the rest of her life with kisses that did not stir her so? Rolf's kisses had never made her quiver, never made her tremble and ache for something more.

She pushed that thought away. Disloyal. Rolf loved her. He respected her, and would never do anything to rouse such inappropriate lustings within her, since they could not pursue those lusts before marriage. Simon did not know how to cosset a gentle-born lady. Rolf understood. He had loved her for years. By now he would be over whatever disappointment had sent him searching for wine, and together they would rush to the priest and beg him to make them man and wife.

She would make herself look beautiful today, for this would be her wedding day.

She rose. She discarded her night rail and chose her most becoming gown. She fussed with her hair for a while and then topped it with her least thread-bare headdress.

She noticed while she was dressing the enameled cup that her cousin had given her during a rare moment of generosity. She'd kept it hidden in her shelter lest he realize how she'd valued the gift and demand it back from her.

The cup was of no use to her. It was sized for a man's hand, making it far too heavy when full, and it held a portion of wine or ale far too large for a woman of her size to drink.

She could offer it to Rolf as a wedding gift.

But . . . Simon might have the greater need of such a cup. Her cousin had taken most of his finer things when he'd left for the Crusades, and the few trinkets he'd left behind had disappeared during his absence. There was little of value or quality left to brighten Simon's quarters. She would just take her cup into his chamber, where he would be sure to find it. Perhaps he might use it, and once in a while, think kindly of her. Perhaps, even though he wanted nothing to do with her, the gift might allow him to remember her with a touch of fondness.

Two of the old lord's knights had invited themselves along for this morning's expedition, and Simon was soon glad of their presence. They showed him his new holdings' strengths and weaknesses from a fighting man's point of view, and he knew they had changed their opinion of him for the better when he voiced his appreciation and promised to make changes based on their recommendations.

They were approaching what one of the knights had advised was the farthest boundary of Eddesley when they spotted a man, weaving uncertainly, walking toward them.

"Good God!" exclaimed a knight. "So that's where Rolf has been keeping himself since yesterday."

"Rolf?"

Simon's interest sharpened. He sat higher in his saddle, straining for his first look at the man Elizabeth loved.

Exhilaration, and disappointment, swept through him. Exhilaration because Rolf's presence here meant he had not yet taken Elizabeth before the priest. Disappointment, for Elizabeth's beloved was of a type Simon recognized instantly. He was handsome enough to turn a woman's head. Simon was not so affected and recognized the weakness in the chin, the vague discontent in the eyes, the indolence of movement. Such a man would join in the cries for honor and revenge, but would find an excuse to stay behind when the fighting force rode out. He'd charm his way into an invitation to stay as a guest, and then stay beyond the bounds of decency, until he found a new shelter where he might live for free for another month or two.

There had been men of this ilk in every household Simon had ever stayed. The servants despised them, even when their lords had yet failed to recognize the parasites they nurtured within their households.

From all accounts, Jerome of Eddesley had been the perfect host for Rolf—too lax to notice the lack of value in feeding and housing such a man, and too lazy to bestir himself to send him away. And in the meantime, he'd allowed his ward to lose her heart to the rogue.

I am a better man than either of them, even without the title and lands of Eddesley behind me, Simon realized.

Elizabeth would have no proper life with this man as her husband. He'd seen that, too—the dewy-eyed young brides, enraptured with their new husbands, but growing impatient over the years when their fortunes did not improve, until eventually they realized the truth about the men they had married and turned sour and bitter.

Elizabeth, four or five years from now, with that intoxicating smile turned down, with the light in her eyes dimmed by disappointment . . . better should Simon marry her and save her from that sad fate.

He cast the thought aside. It was merely the devil at work again. If he let the devil have his say, then Satan would no doubt conjure a thousand reasons why he ought to do as Richard had decreed and marry Elizabeth of Eddesley.

"Matters are improving for me," Rolf called out, a cheerful grin crossing his features. Simon could see what Elizabeth saw—a man of pleasant, truth to tell, handsome features, tall, lithe in his movements. "Who will let me ride pillion?" Rolf asked.

"Climb up behind me," said one of the knights, somewhat resignedly, as if he'd allowed the privilege more than once before.

"In a moment." Simon raised his hand to hold them all in their places. "I wish to speak in private to yon Rolf."

He nudged his horse in the ribs and it bolted forward. Simon idly pondered running down the man, but pulled up well before reaching Rolf. He then thought about addressing him from atop the horse, knowing from experience the submissive pose it necessarily enforced upon the man on the ground. But something within him wanted to meet Rolf eye-to-eye, up close, with no obvious trappings of power between them.

But why? he wondered, even as he dismounted. As lord of Eddesley, he did have the responsibility of assuring himself of Rolf's suitability as Elizabeth's husband. He would do the same for every Eddesley maid who would seek his permission to wed. Responsibility did not explain the fury that was heating his blood, the urge he felt to gather his hand into a fist and smash it right into Rolf's smiling face.

For the man was smiling, his handsome face creased with a rogue's canny blend of goodwill, regret, and apology. He bowed at the waist when Simon stood before him.

"You must be the new lord. I cannot begin to tell you how sorry I am to have missed your first meetings with your knights." Simon's anger sparked, and he noted Rolf offered no explanation for his absence. Such charm exuded from him that Simon thought a woman might be willing to overlook the matted hair, the red-rimmed eyes, the signs of dissipation making his face look older than its years. Rolf would not age well.

If he lived.

Simon let the man wait in silence while he conquered his rage. He studied Rolf's soiled garments. "Wine," he said when he could trust himself to speak. "Horse dung, mud, woods trash. Is this how men of your status dress for their weddings?"

"Weddings?" Rolf appeared thoroughly befuddled.

"The Lady Elizabeth says you have been waiting for years to marry her."

"Elizabeth?"

Simon hoped the man was not so simpleminded as

he sounded. But just then understanding dawned over Rolf's face. "Ah, yes!" He rubbed his eyes, and his rueful smile deepened. "She did come upon me in the orchard last eve. She mentioned something about marrying soon. I was in no condition to discuss the matter. She will be most displeased with me, but she will get over it. She always does."

"So you will marry her. At once."

A hint of cunning lit the man's eyes. "If you would indulge me, my lord, I would know why you are so interested in my marriage."

"I am lord of this manor. Every detail interests me."

"Of course."

Simon waited, cursing himself. He knew he'd given away too much by blurting out so much about weddings and Elizabeth. He could tell Rolf had recognized his weakness. . . .

Weakness? What weakness?

His weakness where Elizabeth was concerned, he realized. There was no longer any point in denying that he felt . . . something . . . for the woman.

"These are hard times for a man to embark on marriage," Rolf said. But there was no woebegone expression to back up his words—merely a speculative gleam in his eyes.

"Aye. A wife, children, all make demands upon the money pouch."

"We have time."

"You may not have as much time as you think," Simon muttered.

Rolf apparently was too absorbed in his own thoughts to notice Simon's warning. "We need only find the right patron. Might it be you, my lord?"

Simon tamped down his loathing lest he reach for his sword and rip the man asunder. "I will stand patron to those who earn their keep with their skills and loyalty. So far, you have not impressed me as possessing much of either quality."

He couldn't stomach talking any longer to the man. Besides, he had to somehow warn Elizabeth. For all he knew, she might at this very moment be pleading with the priest to marry her in secret to this opportunist. And he, Simon, had goaded her into doing it. He had to stop her.

It was not a task to be shouldered gladly, for the bearer of bad tidings was often held in contempt. So why did he feel such a thrill, so much eagerness, to race his horse as fast as it could run and tell Elizabeth that marrying Rolf would be a terrible mistake?

Anyone who could feel the pounding of his heart, the racing of his blood, might think he was in love with the woman himself, and glad of the chance to shatter her illusions about her false prince.

He did not love Elizabeth, he told himself. He merely felt . . . responsible. If he had not forced the issue, Rolf might well have drifted away on his own account, in search of a wealthier bride, breaking Elizabeth's heart without any help from Simon at all.

He mounted his horse and reined it around, spurred it toward the waiting knights. "After me, back to Eddesley," he called. His knights fell in, save for the fellow who had promised to let Rolf ride pillion.

"Aye, my lord," said the knight. "I shall follow after as soon as Rolf boosts up behind—"

"He walks," Simon said.

Seven

Elizabeth frowned at the chair she'd dragged into Simon's chamber, and then tugged it a few inches to the left. Better. She sank into it with a tired, satisfied sigh and let herself relax.

But not for long. Her eyes had begun drifting closed when she heard a commotion in the hall. Simon had at long last returned from wherever he'd gone that morning. Her heart quickened its pace—not from excitement at having him home again, she told herself, but as a warning to flee his chamber before she was caught sitting here, in the deepening dark.

She couldn't seem to chase the pleasant languor from her limbs, though, so she settled back into the chair again. She knew the ways of men. He would wait in the hall, taking ale and sampling the food the cook had grumbled and toiled over all the day long. Elizabeth would have a long while yet to sit here in the dark, gathering her thoughts, and deciding what to tell him.

After all, it was peaceful here, in the dark, with the privacy enveloping her like a soft, warm shawl.

Simon had kissed her in this very place the night before. Her skin tingled, first hot, then cold, then hot again.

She shook her head, not wanting to remember. But she'd had difficulty dismissing the memories all the day long. No matter where she forced her thoughts, they were determined to return to Simon. If she succeeded in wiping away the image of his lips coming toward hers, she would only be plagued by thinking of the way Simon had held her by the arm, lending his strength, asking nothing from her in return.

He had not even asked for the kisses. He'd simply taken them, and she'd given in to his silent demand all too willingly—he could have had more.

She gripped the arms of the chair until her fingers ached, and with the help of the pain eventually wiped her head clean of memories. She closed her eyes and breathed as deeply and quickly as someone who had run the length of the tourney field. The chamber smelled clean and fresh, partly from the rushes and lavender she'd strewn here herself, but also from soap and rainwater. Simon's scent.

She gritted her teeth and berated herself for letting her thoughts drift that way yet again, and then realized she had a good reason for noticing Simon's scent. Last night, when she'd found Rolf in the orchard, a veritable stench had wafted from him. He'd drunk so much wine that the smell of it reeked from his skin. During her sleepless night, she'd noticed he had not returned to the castle. If he'd followed his usual habits, he'd no doubt stumbled face-first into his horse's stall—and slept there.

That explained why she had not tracked him down this day to urge him to see the priest. She could not ask the priest's leniency over the matter of banns with Rolf in such a state. She would explain to Simon that she required another day to bring about her marriage to Rolf; surely he would understand.

He would. She knew, somehow, that Simon would always understand her. She snuggled more deeply into the chair, glad that she'd dragged it into the chamber for him. Just as he seemed to understand her, she could see into his heart—she knew he would appreciate the chair, and she knew he would know she was responsible when he noticed the small bits and furnishings she'd scrounged from the castle for his use.

When she'd slipped into his chamber earlier in the day to leave the cup as a gift, she'd noticed how little he'd done to enhance the chamber on his own. The chamber held only a narrow sleeping pallet. His belongings, surprisingly meager, were stacked neatly at the head of the pallet in the manner of a soldier accustomed to sleeping guard over what he owned.

Simon had not been a soldier, only a manservant to a knight. He must have picked up the habit from his lord.

He'd picked up other finer habits as well, she mused. He exercised excruciating care with his speech, and possessed social manners that equaled or bettered those of most of the knights in Eddesley. Truth to tell, his manners and speech were finer, by far, than those evidenced by her late cousin. Finer even than Rolf's, who seemed to have forgotten his gentle birth completely these past days.

She stirred in the chair, discomfited by the direction of her thoughts. She had known Rolf long enough to understand he would suffer these bouts after overindulging in wine. He always regained his noble nature, his proud bearing. Once he did, it would be quite laughable to remember how she'd sat here comparing Rolf to an upstart serving man, and found the serving man to be the more . . . attractive of the two. It wasn't fair to compare them now, when Rolf was at his worst.

But, she realized suddenly, Simon was not at his best, either. He'd been thrust into a new situation, where it seemed every man hated him, where it seemed every woman mocked him. They all waited for the missteps he was sure to make—but he had made none. And he would not, she knew it as surely as she knew Rolf's wine-flow oblivions would occur again and again.

Could it be that Simon was a better man than Rolf?

She might have laughed aloud as proof of her fidelity to Rolf, except that a tiny movement of air warned her she was no longer alone. She did not even have time to draw a breath, to scream, before a strong hand gripped her forehead and tilted back her head to expose her throat. Moonlight glinted off the blade of a knife as it hovered right before her eyes.

The grip upon her head tightened, and then changed, with the fingers seeming to tremble slightly as they stroked along her crown. She squeaked, "Simon! 'Tis only me." But by then the knife had wavered and moved away, and he had already let loose of her.

Somehow, she had known he was her assailant. Somehow, he had known it was her.

"I . . . I had been hoping to see a demonstration of your skill in moving without making a sound," she said, in a weak attempt to explain away her presence in his chamber.

"Your ears need sharpening," he said. "I knew I would take whoever sat here by surprise, and made no effort at all to disguise my approach."

"Oh, I forgot—you move in silence only when the

most important things in your life are at stake. I am
not so important." She laughed, a little shakily. "Let
loose of me, so you might see if this chair suits you."

He loosened his grip. She hoped she had diverted
his attention away from the way she had spoken his
name with the familiarity, with the welcoming warmth,
of a wife who had sat waiting for her husband.

Elizabeth shot to her feet, and Simon let her slip
through his hands. He was appalled to realize how
he'd held the knife to her throat; but never had he
expected she would be sitting in his private chamber,
in the dark.

His hands shook. He tried telling himself it was
from his near decapitation of her, but that would be
a lie. He had known the instant he'd touched her
that it was she—something in his flesh had called out
in joyous recognition. The trembling extended beyond his hands, as well, turning him taut and hard
and ready to claim what he'd found here among his
true belongings.

"Wait here." He strode blindly from the chamber,
drawn like a moth to a flaming torch hung upon a
pillar. He snatched it from its anchor. He'd not gone
in search of a torch but it gave him a logical excuse
for the time he'd needed to gather himself in hand.

She was still there when he returned to his chamber. He sought a bracket in the wall to hang the
torch, and again his hand trembled—this time from
knowing she could have fled but she had stayed. Because he had asked her to stay . . . or because she had
wanted to stay?

"I did not expect to find you here tonight," he said.
He found the bracket and fastened the torch in

place, and then studied her in the flickering light. She lifted a hand to her hair. She wasn't wearing a headdress, and she touched her hair with the nervous motion of someone who'd suddenly found themselves standing stark naked.

"Your hair is beautiful," he said.

"So is yours," she blurted in answer.

"Mine?" He'd never given his hair a moment's thought, except to be glad, in the way of men, that it seemed determined to continue sprouting from his head.

"It's quite thick," she said. "And long." He worried for a moment that she might have begun to describe another part of his anatomy, which fit the description at the moment. "I see gray sprinkled throughout," she said, putting an end to that worry. "How old are you, my lord?"

It was the first time he could ever recall anyone asking about his age. "Near as I can reckon, a half year past thirty," he said.

"Truly so young?" She clapped a hand over her mouth as if she suddenly realized she'd insulted him.

Instead, he smiled. "Are you the same woman who just recently claimed to be old, at a mere twenty-four?"

She smiled back at him.

He could stand there all night looking at her, Simon realized. The torch flame cast dancing shadows over her features, but caught the sparkle in her eyes and teased golden flashes from her hair. It must have been the uncertain light that made him think she looked at him with the same avidity, as if her very soul . . . hungered.

"You must be hungry, my lord," she said, seeming to eerily read his thoughts.

"No!" he all but shouted the denial, and knew he'd erred when she cocked her head at him.

"You did not pause in the hall for your supper."

"Ah, what I would find there would not assuage my appetite," he muttered.

She laughed, but something about the sound heightened the tension in the chamber, rather than relieved it. She always seemed to read his thoughts so well; perhaps she'd divined the hidden meaning to his outwardly innocent words. He prayed she had not, and deliberately reverted to the role he'd assigned himself with her.

"Your husband will ofttimes arrive home with fierce appetites. You must assure your Rolf that you are able to satisfy them."

She moved a step closer to him. "I assure you, my lord, if he would just let me know how to sate his hunger, I would do my best to see him satisfied."

Simon felt a heat unlike any he had ever known take root in his middle and flame through his blood. He wished he knew more about women—noblewomen, specifically. A woman of his own class would understand there was a ribald meaning behind such bantering. But did Elizabeth?

She stood there, not looking the least confused. She looked . . . as hungry as he felt. Her lush lips were parted slightly. Her hair hung over her shoulders, and he could tell she trembled by the slight movement of the curling tendrils as they bounced near her waist.

"And what would you say if your husband said, 'I see nothing on this table that pleases me'?" he managed to grate out through a throat gone tight with desire.

"I would say, 'Why, all that is yours cannot be found on the table, my lord.'" She almost whispered. She drew a deep breath, and then he knew she understood, for her trembling increased, and the hunger in her eyes darkened with trepidation. "I would urge him to sample the fare from wherever he chose to feast."

He needed no further invitation. He reached and caught her slim shoulders between his hands. He pulled her toward him, crushed her against his chest, and buried his face in the thick softness of her hair.

She tilted her head back, granting him the freedom to wander the smooth column of her neck with his lips. She made exquisite, wordless sounds that echoed the cries of his heart. He needed but one arm to support her slight weight. He let his other hand roam free, to caress the long, smooth line from her hip to her breast, to trace the diameter of each soft mound, and then to claim the peak with a clasp that declared his possession.

He wanted her. He wanted her more than he'd ever wanted anything in his life.

Somehow, he knew not how, he backed up against the chair and inelegantly fell back into its embrace, drawing her with him. She wriggled on his lap, causing him to gasp at the feel of her round, firm bottom against his most sensitive parts, but in the end her wriggling had a purpose, for she somehow settled against him in a way that allowed his hands full access to her front. The torchlight flickered, granting him the most beautiful sight he'd ever seen, Elizabeth of Eddesley lying willingly in his arms.

Her clothes were a hindrance. He found ribbons and tucks and dispensed with them all until she lay bare to the waist. Her breaths were shallow gasps, not so harsh as his own, but vibrant with passion.

He touched the upper edge of her belly, and thought nothing could be so exquisitely soft until his hand reached higher and found the fullness of her breast. She gasped and arched. Her eyes opened and her gaze found his, and the delight and wonder he read in her eyes caused him to harden more. He lowered his head and his questing lips captured the tip of her breast. Gently, he drew it into his mouth, coaxing it past his teeth, encircling the quivering, hardened little tip with his tongue.

She made a sweet sound, a sound unique to women, wordlessly imploring him for more. He obliged and again she arched, but this time he could feel an inner quivering that he knew was beyond her control.

"Simon!" She called his name in a way that inflamed him, something between a muffled scream and a moan. "What are you doing to me?"

She'd cried out the question in the throes of passion, but it doused his fires as thoroughly as if the words tumbled from the mouth of a nun.

What was he doing, making love to a woman who loved another man?

No sooner had that question occurred to him than his head was filled with taunts from a thousand demons. Had she somehow learned the truth about Rolf this day and turned to Simon as second best?

He had to know.

"Elizabeth—why are you in my chamber?"

She grew still, more still than the sudden silence that seemed to freeze them into stone.

But the burning hiss of the torch, the muted din of the folk in the hall, soon penetrated the silence. Elizabeth wriggled again, this time to remove herself from his embrace. She gained her feet, not very steadily, and whirled away so that the smooth curve of her back faced him. She tugged and pulled at her gown, working furiously to cover herself.

"I did not intend for this to happen, my lord," she said as she pulled her garment back into place.

"Nor did I," he whispered.

She might not have heard him, for her breath was coming in harsh rasps, and he fancied he caught the sound of hard swallowing, as if she choked back tears. He wanted to go to her, comfort her, tear the blasted gown back off—but even more, he wanted to know the truth about her feelings for him.

"I came to ask you for more time," she choked out, crushing his hopes and shriveling his desire. "I was not able to settle matters with Rolf today."

"You should not be the one to arrange matters." The heat of passion shifted into a raging inferno of anger. "He should have clasped you to his breast and run off with you long ago, when there was no lord here to grant him permission or say him nay. I would have, if . . ."

If I had known how much I wanted you.

He stopped himself before revealing his weakness, but she finished the sentence herself.

"You would have stolen me away from here if you wanted me," she said. "Without a word, without a sound. If you wanted me."

This time the bond that held them together so tenuously had failed altogether. He felt empty, and alone, with it severed.

She left him, proving that she, too, knew how to escape in silence.

Elizabeth wished she could die from shame, that she could shrivel up into a husk and simply blow away in the wind.

Simon did not want her.

She realized, then, that she'd been hoping, praying, that the way he'd kissed her yesterday, the way he'd touched her and loved her just now, meant he might have changed his mind. Somehow, in the space of a single day, she had fallen out of love with one man and fallen into love with another. She loved Simon. The quivering in her body, the way she yearned even now to fling herself into his arms and beg him to consider her as a wife, told her that she loved Simon.

He did not love her.

The realization pummeled her with a weakness so debilitating that she had to brace a hand against the wall to keep from sinking to the floor in dejection. She gathered the shreds of her pride, and forced herself to stand tall. What had come over her, flirting with this man, thrilling to his interest in her, as if she were a wife welcoming home her husband at the end of a day?

She carried Eddesley blood in her veins—only a drop, but more than this man ever would. She must remember it always. No matter that he did not want her—she did not want him!

She wanted her old satisfaction and peace of mind back. She wanted to be in love again with Rolf, her golden, smiling, affable Rolf. He had not turned into the sullen, scowling, petulant Rolf until this man had shown up. She wanted to be someone's prize, someone's treasure, someone's hope, and not a means to a manor or a plaything to pass an hour before dinner.

She had not realized the depth of her wanton nature until Simon made free with her body. Everything awful that had happened, that would happen, was his fault. Simon's fault.

She should hate him. Instead, she loved him. In destroying all her illusions, he had freed something fine and bold within her. She had never realized she could be so strong.

Eight

Elizabeth sighed with relief when she spotted her friend Joan heading toward the listings field. She hurried to catch up. They often watched the tourney practice together. No one would think it amiss to see her approaching the field with Joan, and they might mistake the anxiousness quickening her step for excitement.

No one would suspect she knew the tourney field was the last place she could think to look for Rolf.

She'd searched for Rolf after running away from Simon the night before. She'd checked all their usual meeting places, asked what questions she could without betraying her anxiousness. Someone, one of the knights, mentioned seeing him earlier in the day and had said something about him taking a long walk—the other knights had laughed, but nobody enlightened her with more information. She'd thought that maybe they meant Rolf had deserted her and run off from his duties at Eddesley.

And she'd felt relieved.

She'd taken refuge in her makeshift chamber, where she'd cowered beneath her wolf pelt, shivering, reliving over and over again the ecstasy she'd found in Simon's arms, and the heartache at realizing his kisses, his embraces, meant nothing to him.

The long sleepless night accomplished one thing: She knew for a certainty that she did not want to marry Rolf. She could not marry him, knowing how susceptible she was to another man's embrace, another man's loving.

But neither could she remain at Eddesley and watch Simon take another woman to wife. She had to leave this place. Loveless, homeless, but her pride would see her through. It always had.

Still, she sought Rolf. He, too, seemed unhappy now that Simon was lord; perhaps the two of them could strike out for someplace new, traveling as friends, and try to find happiness elsewhere.

And she had to explore the faint hope that perhaps she did still love Rolf. She had loved him, after all, up until the minute Simon had taken to kissing her. Maybe there was some weakness in a woman that made her believe herself in love with whichever man kissed her, which was why men were always keeping women locked away from temptation. Perhaps, once she and Rolf were together again, her heart would lose this aching sadness that had filled it since she'd fallen in love with Simon, and return once more to the light, carefree gaiety of loving Rolf.

Her relief at seeing Rolf astride his horse, holding one glove in his teeth while he tugged and pulled the other onto his hand, was so great that she all but collapsed against Joan. The weakness in her limbs must mean she did love him, she told herself. She grew weak in the limbs when Simon kissed her, after all. Her quaking knees proved it; she loved Rolf.

Liar, scolded her conscience.

"He—he cuts a fine figure," she said, to cover her agitation.

"Surprisingly so," Joan agreed, with so much enthusiasm that Elizabeth had to look at her. Joan usually had nothing good to say about Rolf and so seldom said anything at all, for Elizabeth had warned her that her constant criticisms were putting a strain on their friendship. It seemed she did not mean this compliment for Rolf, either, for Joan's attention rested upon another man who sat his horse at the opposite end of the field.

Simon. Even though they stood too far away to make out his features, Elizabeth instantly knew the set of his shoulders, the strength of his torso. Her heart quickened at the sight of him, in a different way from the way she'd reacted to finding Rolf. Her lips tingled with remembered kisses; God forgive her, but her breasts throbbed and her nipples peaked as if they were reaching for him.

He'd cast aside his usual homespun garments in favor of something more lordly, chausses and a tunic in a dark forest green.

"Those garments match his eyes," Joan said. Elizabeth bit her lip to keep from blurting out that no woman but she ought to be noticing Simon's eyes.

She wondered if Simon had ever noticed her eyes, or hair, or form, and found them as pleasing as she found him.

She had to stop this.

"I spoke of Rolf," Elizabeth said, turning resolutely back toward the man she had until recently believed to be her beloved. Rolf did indeed look fine, as always. The wind teased his thick, golden hair. His garments fit him to perfection. His horse sidled with eagerness to list and he controlled it with masterful legs and hands. He showed no sign of the terrible state he'd been in when last she'd seen him.

No sign of where he'd spent the past two nights.

And to her distress, she felt no real curiosity within her to wonder where he'd been. She should wonder, if she loved him.

"I doubt he'll join the practice," Joan said, still fixed upon their new lord. "I daresay 'twould be humiliating to find himself tossed into the dirt by one of his own men, so soon after taking command."

Elizabeth recalled the strength in Simon's arms, the taut perfection of his body. A man who had fought alongside his lord, who had escaped the Saracen Infidels, a man who had risen from servant to lord.

She did not care how Rolf had passed the nights, but she ached to know how Simon had spent the night after she'd left him.

Unbidden came the memory of his telling her of the way he'd passed nights in captivity, listening with an aching heart while another man told of the joys of finding true love. She banished the memory.

"You should not underestimate him, Joan."

Joan leaned back and fixed her with a look of astonishment. "Elizabeth, he is naught but a servant. Any knight worth his salt could unseat him in an instant."

"Perhaps we should all stop thinking of him as he was, and remind ourselves of what he is today," Elizabeth murmured. She was puzzled by her need to keep to herself the information she knew about Simon, to guard his secrets as a new mother might watch over her infant, so precious did the knowledge seem to her.

Neither had she confided to Joan the king's decree that she and Simon were to marry, or Simon's distaste for doing so. Not because she was embarrassed about being rejected yet again—God alone knew Joan had held her often enough in earlier years while she wept bitter tears over men's unwillingness to look beyond her lack of fortune. But Simon had told her it must be a secret, and keep it secret she would, even from her only, truest friend.

Odd, to find herself holding her vow to Simon so close to heart when he cared nothing for her.

There was no reason, however, why she could not tell Joan that Simon had given her permission to marry Rolf at once. No reason at all, save for an all-consuming reluctance that caused her to hold her tongue on the matter.

"I knew he would not join them," said Joan, dragging Elizabeth's attention back to the listing field. The men had commenced their exercises, staging mock jousts, mock hand-to-hand skirmishes afoot with squires and men-at-arms. Elizabeth watched Rolf first dash this way and then that along the length of the field, and she spotted something that two days earlier would have caused a heaviness to settle round her heart.

Rolf was not wearing her favor.

Joan did not seem to notice, and indeed it was more common than not for a knight to handle his practices without a lady's favor. But Rolf had always made an ostentatious show of fastening her scarf to his sleeve. *My prize, my hope, my treasure,* he would say, giving the scrap of silk a pat, and her a blazingly bright smile.

Perhaps he had lost her scarf, during his nights of drunken melancholy, and had spent all this past un-accounted-for time searching for it.

She tugged absently at the kerchief tucked in her waistband. She ought to run it down to the field and hand it over to Rolf now, and let him fasten it to his

sleeve. Show Simon that someone did indeed want
her. She tried to summon enthusiasm for doing it,
but it was a muted thing, not enough to make her stir.
A voice in her mind warned her that doing such a
thing would be nothing but an act of desperation,
and that to Simon she might appear pathetically
needy of Rolf's affections.

Besides, she didn't want Rolf wearing her colors
anymore.

The past few years of her life had been wasted, as
devoid of purpose as had been Simon's. She'd been
in a prison of her own making.

Joan let out a raucous cheer, and Elizabeth noticed
through tear-dampened lashes that the knight Joan
favored—one of the new men who had arrived with
Simon—had knocked the pole from Rolf's hand.

"Oh, sorry," Joan said, not sounding the least bit
apologetic.

"No need to apologize," said Elizabeth. It was as
though these tears that distorted her sight somehow
made it easier to see things she'd not noticed before.
Rolf rode well enough, but did not handle his lance
or his shield with as much command as most of the
other men. "They are only practicing," she said. "And
besides, Rolf is not one of the best."

"I never thought to hear such from your lips." Joan
seemed shocked—and pleased.

"He wins often enough," Elizabeth defended Rolf
while she acknowledged that he possibly did not win
enough. Trinkets, usually, or once in a while a small
silver cup. Never the top prizes, though he swore they
would all be his one day. But if his skills did not improve, if his luck did not change, he won merely
enough to support himself. He might be able to support a wife, providing they remained at Eddesley and

served Simon. She shivered at the thought. If they did wed and leave Eddesley, they would have to beg bed and bread from relatives, from tourney hosts, lest they be reduced to sleeping alongside the roads . . . and when children came, as they must. . . .

She had never worried about these things before.

And with a start she realized it was because Rolf had always silenced her doubts with a kiss, or with a confident assertion that her cousin would see that his kinswoman did not suffer.

My prize, my hope, my treasure. She wished she could curse Simon for causing her to cast doubt upon the source of Rolf's affections for her, but in the bright light of the sun, with no splash of her color upon her knight's sleeve, the truth lay plain to see.

Lay, literally, for Rolf lay sprawled in the dust as Joan clapped for her knight who had unseated him.

Elizabeth ought to rush to Rolf's side and assure herself of his well-being. Instead, she sought Simon at the far end of the field and fancied he watched her. He glanced from her toward the fallen Rolf, and back to her again, and then with a nod and a movement of his shoulders urged his horse into a turn and cantered back to the manor.

Joan had raced toward the rail, where she cast daisies toward her knight. Rolf slowly rose to his feet, brushing his garments clean, but laughing and joking in good humor about his spill. Simon's horse kicked up clouds of dust on its way back to its stable. Elizabeth stood alone in the center of it all. Alone. More alone than she had never felt before.

She loved a mediocrity.

Each strike of Simon's horse's hooves against the

earth drummed the truth into his head. Elizabeth loved a man who simply did not deserve her. He had asked the knights who had lived for years at Eddesley to rank the pool of fighting men, and to a man they had reluctantly ranked this Rolf near the bottom. As Simon had suspected, Rolf possessed below-average skills, no cunning, enough intelligence to portray himself as charming but not enough to let him win by guile or wit. A mediocrity.

Simon had gone to the practice field to watch the man in action, for fear that he'd let his opinion matter more than the truth. But his instincts, and the reports of his men, had been perfectly on target.

And yet Elizabeth loved Rolf, she loved him . . . she proved it with her presence at his practice, as if she could not bear to let him out of her sight for even such a mundane chore. She proved it with the way she'd gone pale and all but fainted when he'd been unhorsed.

So what if she did? It was of no matter to him, save that it shed some light on the man's reluctance to wed the girl. Perhaps Rolf was too stupid to realize what a treasure was his for the taking, or too stubborn to marry her because he hadn't gotten his way about her inheriting Eddesley.

Stupid. Stubborn. Might those words described another man. A man such as Simon himself?

With a curse, he goaded his horse into a full gallop as if he could outrun the truth that suddenly blossomed in his mind.

He loved Elizabeth. He wanted her more than he wanted anything on this earth, and yet he was clinging with stubborn stupidity to the notion that he would not marry her just because Richard had told him to do it.

A treasure was his for the taking.

And then, it was as if the strangest sensation settled around his heart. She was his, already. No matter that she had run away from him—he had provoked her into it with his stupid, stubborn insistence that she marry Rolf. No woman who wanted to marry another would surrender her will to him as Elizabeth had done. She had curved her body to his, shuddered with the inner joy that only a woman who loved a man could experience—and only when she was given that pleasure by a man who loved her.

He loved Elizabeth.

He knew what he had to do.

Nine

Rolf, charming to the last, accepted Elizabeth's breaking of their secret betrothal with a smile and a wink. He'd just as charmingly declined her offer to travel as friends to a new place.

"I think I shall fare all right here, once you are away," he said somewhat enigmatically, and with complete selfishness.

He'd never loved her.

No true knight would allow a lady to travel without an escort. No man who loved a woman would allow her to take up such a dangerous mission on her own.

She had to wonder if she'd ever loved Rolf, or if her feelings were as false as his. She felt no agony at their parting, no heartache at realizing how little he cared—instead she felt more of an abiding relief that she'd discovered the truth before taking vows with him.

Elizabeth returned for the last time to her tiny, cloth-walled enclosure. She pulled down the length of wool that covered the back wall, and piled her few belongings atop it. She gathered the corners together and made a small bundle. She'd find a stick in the woods and carry her bundle at the end of it, over her shoulder, like a Gypsy, as she left behind the only place that could remotely be called her home.

Simon would stop her, if he knew. Even though he did not love her, he would not allow her to travel alone. Although he had not been born to the rank, he was more of a knight than any man she knew.

She would have to steal away in the night, the way Simon had escaped his prison. He'd done so to save his life, and she must do so to save hers.

Simon. Just thinking about him was enough to tighten her throat and make her eyes sting with tears. She loved him. He had saved her from a drab and loveless future with Rolf, but in another way had condemned her to a drab and loveless future of a different sort, for she knew she could never find happiness in another man's arms.

Her candle guttered out. The other makeshift chambers around her were already silent and dark. Some noise still came from the hall, but it was the sound of men drinking the dregs of their ale, and settling into their pallets for the night. Soon all the castle would be abed, and she would steal away. She didn't dare risk it until all were asleep, for someone would be sure to question why she was leaving in the middle of the night. She would not be able to bear the humiliation of admitting she was leaving because she could no longer bear being unwanted.

She sat on the floor, upon the rushes, with her back braced against the uncurtained wall. She would close her eyes and snatch a few minutes of rest, for her journey would be long and difficult. She did not know where she would go, only that she must be far away from the castle by morning.

Not that it mattered much. She doubted anyone would miss her, and she did not expect anyone to follow after her.

She settled back and felt the rough rock through

the back of her gown—her last contact with her ancestral home. Once she was gone, there would be no more Eddesley blood upon Eddesley land. Her eyes stung despite being closed; a tear trickled down her cheek.

She lifted her hand to wipe it away, but before her fingers could brush the wetness from her skin another hand clamped hers against her mouth, using her own hand to silence her.

She recognized him at once. Simon. Her heart hammered so hard in her chest that even if he had not covered her lips, she would not be able to speak.

His strong arm encircled her from behind her back to tuck under her knees. He lifted her. With quick, sure movements, he carried her through the cloth wall, stole soundlessly along the perimeter of the hall, drawing not a single bit of attention from the people bedding down all over the floor.

He moved with utter silence. He moved with the skill he had risked his life to learn, a skill that he had sworn he would only use when the most important thing in his life was at stake.

And he did it while carrying her in his arms.

He took Elizabeth to the small abandoned cottage he'd found in his wild, solitary ride that afternoon. Part of the roof had caved in, but the slipping thatch had only settled into the dwelling, making a small, slanted-roof cave of the interior.

Moonlight streamed through the window, the open door, the gaps in the ruined roof. It illuminated Elizabeth as he set her upon her feet, gilding her with silvery white light, like an ethereal bride.

She stared at him, her eyes wide, looking so in-

credibly beautiful in the moonlight that he felt a
pang of doubt. Could one so exquisite as she want
him? He dared to believe he read hunger in her expression, that her lips trembled with suppressed
excitement rather than fear.

He waved at their humble surroundings. "This is
the sort of place where God set me down upon this
earth. Through His grace and the goodwill of King
Richard, I have done better. But even so, here is
where it feels right to speak my heart."

"What does your heart tell you, Simon?"

"It tells me I love you. Elizabeth—do you think you
can love me?"

She moved toward him. She lifted her hands and
slid them gently around either side of his face. "Can
you not look at me, and tell what I feel, my lord?"

He read joy, he read delight in the radiant smile.
His heart skittered and slammed. He lowered his
head and found her lips ready to meet his. He wanted
nothing more than to claim them, but he paused.
"Tell me, Elizabeth. We men require specific words."

"I love you, Simon."

The words inflamed him as nothing ever had. He
pulled her hard into his arms and kissed her, and
without breaking the kiss he lifted her into his arms
again. In some distant part of his mind he remembered where the falling thatch had split apart, the
darkened outer layer giving way to a torrent of clean,
soft reeds. He took her there; he lay her there and
knelt next to her. He loosened the ribbons at her
neck. She pulled at the hem of his tunic. Soon they
were both bared to the moonlight, to each other's
eyes.

He pressed close to her, to lend her his warmth if
she should feel chilled on this soft June night. But he

found skin as hot as his own, and he knew the trembling was not from the cold. He braced himself above her; she felt so small beneath him, so fragile. Her breasts pressed against his, soft and yielding, save for the hardened points of her nipples that roused a sensation that seemed to pierce straight into his heart. She ran her hands along his sides from waist to shoulders, then across, and then down again to settle at the small of his back.

Simon tore his mouth away from hers, hungering to taste all of her. Her forehead, the downy softness of her cheek, the smooth sweep from her throat to her shoulders. And then lower, brushing his lips and tongue over the rising swell of each breast, and slowly, hotly, drawing in the tips that had tormented him so pleasurably until she moaned with pleasure. With his fingers he found the softness, the wetness between her thighs and gently coaxed her open for him. He gently probed and let her wetness ease passage for first one finger, then another.

She writhed, she moaned, she cried out his name, all nearly driving him insane. His fingers told him she would feel pain when he claimed her and so he restrained himself.

They would have a lifetime to assuage this hunger.

Elizabeth shivered and burned.

Simon did impossibly wonderful things to her with his hands, and when she thought she might swoon from the pleasure, he shifted above her. She threaded her fingers into his hair, thrilling to the movement of his head between her hands and the hot silk of his tongue against her breasts, her belly, her. . . .

"Simon!"

She almost reared away from the floor when he moved even lower, his lips and tongue moving with excruciating purpose over the mound of her womanhood and then even lower, causing her to gasp out, cry his name again, when his tongue teased and tormented the soft hidden folds that nobody but she had ever touched. She tried to roll away, and then rolled into him instead, pressing, welcoming. His tongue, his fingers, drove all sense from her head; she writhed and abandoned herself completely to the pleasure coursing through her.

He lifted himself over her, and her legs wrapped around him as if they'd been fashioned for this purpose and no other. She felt him, incredibly hot, amazingly silky at the tip, and yet hard as wood probing her cleft. He looked down at her with passion-clouded eyes.

"It will hurt, Elizabeth. I am sorry."

"Do not be sorry, Simon. It is what I want."

"You are what I want," he said, and then he found with his shaft the place he had made ready with his fingers.

She cried out, because there was a sudden sharp stab of pain, but it was a fleeting thing. Simon held himself still, cradling her, raining soft, warm kisses all along her face and throat until her body relaxed and forgot the pain. In the stillness she could feel him inside her, throbbing, and then gently, ever so gently beginning to move. And then fast, and harder, and then so masterfully and completely did he possess her, that she could not tell where she ended and he began.

Even so, it was not close enough. She wanted more of him. She wrapped herself around him, her arms encircling his wide, muscled shoulders, her legs clamping round his smooth waist. When he moved, she moved with him, for she suddenly lacked the breath to make motions of her own. Something had happened inside, making her pant and whimper and urge him to move even more deeply within her.

She could tell when he abandoned restraint, for he cried out and moved and surged. And she would have told him not to worry, that there was no pain and she was all right, except she couldn't speak, for she felt as if she'd splintered into a thousand crystal shards, glittering and gleaming and dazzling, rivaling the stars in the sky for purity and brightness.

Simon cried out her name and she was filled with a glorious warmth and heat. They held each other while shudders coursed through them both, while their spirits soared and their hearts healed of wounds neither had ever acknowledged.

Elizabeth held him in her arms. Simon held her in his. Their hearts eventually settled into a normal rhythm, in concert. Their breathing slowed and grew regular. She loved being entwined with him this way, loved breathing in his scent and feeling his possession of her body.

As her senses returned, she noticed the moonlight spilling over their bed of reeds, noticed the daub and wattle walls surrounding them. A servant's home, a place where a woman of her breeding ought never set foot, except to offer succor to the sick.

She angled her head to plant a kiss on top of the dark head resting against her breast. She breathed in the scent of soap and rainwater. Simon. She tangled her fingers in his hair. He tightened his arms around her.

At last, she had found where she belonged.

* * *

"Most improper." The priest scowled, and rubbed his hand over his head until the scanty wisps of hair stood straight out. They'd roused him from his bed, but Simon noted that the man apparently slept in his robes, which would save them from waiting for him to dress.

"Now," Simon ordered.

The priest sighed. "I know you are a, er, newcomer to the ways of the nobles. A proper wedding should take place in full day, with your people present to witness and cheer."

Elizabeth tightened the arm she had wrapped around his waist and rested her head against his shoulder. He loved holding her like this, but there were other, more intimate embraces he was eager to employ.

"Now," Simon repeated.

"Very well." The priest sighed. "You are the lord, after all. If you are sure this is what you want . . ."

"This is exactly what I want," said Simon.

Saturday's Bride

Jean Wilson

One

Monday for health, Tuesday for wealth, Wednesday best of all.
Thursday for losses, Friday for crosses, Saturday for no luck at all.

Wed in May and you'll rue the day.

"Molly, ye had best hurry," chided Callie Moran. "'Tis bad enough you chose to wed on Saturday in the month of May, ye don't want to be late for yer own wedding." Under her breath, Molly Montgomery's great-aunt mumbled something in Gaelic, then said aloud, "I still think ye're too young for that Warren Moneypenny."

The young woman laughed. "Aunt Callie, you worry too much. Doesn't she, Aunt Amelia?"

Amelia Swanson smiled. She ignored her aunt's words as nothing but superstition. As far as she was concerned, Saturday was no different from any other day of the week. Callie and her mother had come from Ireland as girls, and her aunt continued to live by Irish sayings and fables. Callie was not only Amelia's aunt, but her best friend and confidante.

Amelia turned from the balcony where she'd

watched the citizens of Mayfield approach the church at the other end of town. A rented carriage waited in front of the large white house, ready to drive Molly to the church. In honor of the celebration of the wedding of the year, flowers decorated the horses' bridles, and ribbons streamed from their tails. Amelia shook her head. The festive conveyance looked totally out of place in the small Texas town. However, Molly had insisted, and as usual, Amelia had given in to her beloved niece's desires.

"You run on to the church, Callie," Amelia said. "I'll help Molly dress. Tell the driver she'll be down shortly."

On a "Hump," Callie marched into the hallway and down the stairs. "Now don't ye be late, too."

Molly glanced at Amelia in the mirror. A tiny smile tilted her lips. "You look very pretty, Auntie," she said. "That new green gown is very flattering." At thirty-one, Amelia was too old to blush. She was far from pretty, but the emerald silk complimented her auburn hair and green eyes. And Amelia loved bright colors. As a banker, she generally wore white shirtwaists and black skirts. In a "man's position" she shied away from colorful gowns and jewelry. But for the special occasion she had chosen the stylish attire.

Returning the younger woman's smile, Amelia adjusted the veil around Molly's soft wheat-colored hair. "You surely are the most beautiful bride in Mayfield's history. Your parents would have been very proud." The blue eyes that should have been shining with happiness seemed a bit sad. Amelia supposed her niece missed her own mother, who had died in a train accident ten years earlier. "Honey, are you having second thoughts about marrying Warren? If you are, we can call everything off right now."

"Of course I'm happy, Aunt Amelia. This is the wedding of my dreams." Molly continued to fiddle with her veil as if she had all the time in the world.

Amelia studied her niece. She and Callie had spoiled the girl, but with Molly's sweet nature, it was easy to do. They wanted nothing but the best for Molly. She hoped that Warren Moneypenny was the right man.

A noise from the doorway drew Amelia's gaze. "Callie, we'll be there in a minute," she called. When she glanced back, she saw it wasn't Callie. A man pressed against the wall, lurking in the shadows.

She gasped, and rushed to the door. Before she could close it, the man slapped his hand against the panel. "Please, Miss Amelia, I just want to talk to Molly."

Amelia squared her shoulders and stared at Billy Sinclair. She hadn't seen the young man in nearly a year, not since the evening he'd left Molly crying in the parlor. Soon afterward, Warren began courting Molly, and before Amelia knew what was happening, they were planning a wedding. Like Callie, Amelia agreed she was too young, but headstrong Molly couldn't be talked out of the wedding. And Warren was a better match than Billy. At least he had a future at the bank.

"Go away, Billy. Molly is already late for the church." She caught the young man by the arm. The solid muscles under his faded shirt tightened. He was tall and strong, with the same black hair and blue eyes as his older brother. Billy looked so much like Chance, her heart clenched every time she stared into his midnight eyes—the picture of Chance fourteen years earlier.

Molly swung her gaze back to the cheval mirror. "I

don't see where we have anything to talk about, Billy Sinclair. You said you wanted to go to Colorado and look for gold. Well, go. I'm not keeping you here."

"Please, Molly. Hear me out," he pleaded.

"All right." Molly sighed. "Aunt Amelia, will you leave us alone for a few minutes? Run on down to the church. Tell Warren I'll be there directly."

"Honey, are you sure?" Amelia knew that Molly was safe with Billy. Although the man was wild as an untamed stallion, he looked as forlorn as a newborn colt lost on the range. Molly nodded.

Reluctantly, Amelia started down the hallway, leaving the door open. Whispers followed her to the stairway, then there was silence. By the time she reached the foyer, more, slightly louder words came from above. Then more silence. Amelia refused to leave until she was certain Billy was gone, and Molly was on her way to the church.

The clock in the hallway chimed—two-fifteen. They were already fifteen minutes late, and Molly still hadn't come down. Amelia lifted the hem of her slender skirt and hurried up the stairs. "Molly, you really must hurry," she called out from the landing. No answer. Amelia continued to the open doorway of Molly's room, only to find it empty.

Her heart skipped a beat. The long white lace veil hung on the bedpost, and the bouquet lay wilting on the quilt. For a moment, Amelia simply stared. The valise Molly had packed for her honeymoon was missing from the floor by the door. She called out again. "Molly, where are you?" Fear clutched at her chest. Where could Molly be?

The curtains fluttered in the open window, stirred by the afternoon breeze. Amelia glanced out toward the rear yard. Two horses were tethered near the white picket fence. As she watched, Billy lifted Molly onto the saddle of her gray mare. Then he tied her valise to the horn of his saddle and leaped onto his big black stallion. Before Amelia could call out for them to stop, the young couple was on the way down the back road out of town. Billy let out a loud, "Yahoo!" as they disappeared from view.

Her hand covered her lips; she sank onto the bed. My Lord, what was happening? Had Billy abducted her niece, or had Molly gone with him willingly? Shadows of the past shifted across her mind. Was history repeating itself? Was Saturday truly an unlucky day? She could only blame herself if anything happened to Molly. She should never have left Billy alone with her niece.

Her thoughts in turmoil, Amelia staggered down the stairs. Someone rapped on the front door. She flung it open and found the driver she'd hired to drive the flower-and-ribbon-bedecked carriage to the church.

"Ma'am. Are you all ready? A boy just came from the church. He says they's awaitin' for the bride." Shamus returned his battered top hat to his balding head.

Amelia bit her lip and stared up the road where Billy and Molly had disappeared. There was no way she could catch their fast horses with the buggy and horses that she had rented from Shamus for the day. Lifting her skirts, she rushed to the conveyance. "Take me to the church, Shamus, and hurry."

The older man looked over her shoulder. "Where's Miss Molly? I'm supposed to drive her to the church."

"She isn't coming." Quickly, she climbed into the worn leather seat of the open carriage. "Hurry, Shamus. The church."

To her dismay, Shamus seemed in no hurry. Amelia had to get to the church and enlist help in finding her niece. She couldn't allow Molly to make the same mistake she had. With luck, she may be able to locate the young couple and avert disaster.

She gripped her stomach, closed her eyes, and prayed that the dreaded motion sickness wouldn't immobilize her. She'd suffered the malady since childhood, and it never seemed to get better. Fortunately, she reached the church before the queasiness set in. As soon as Shamus stopped the carriage, she stepped down and ran into the church.

From the foyer she heard the murmur of voices as heads craned toward the door. Preacher Elijah Brown stood in front of the altar, frowning over his Bible. Even from the distance across the pews, she noted the sheen of perspiration on his forehead. Beside him, Warren Moneypenny waited in a new frock coat and black trousers, undoubtedly paid for from the raise in salary he had wheedled out of Amelia on the occasion of marrying her niece. His brown hair was freshly trimmed, as was the small mustache that covered his thin upper lip. In anticipation of his marrying into the family, she had also appointed him assistant manager of her bank.

When she'd first hired him as a teller at Mayfield Bank and Trust, the bank Amelia had inherited from her father, he'd briefly called on Amelia. He soon found Amelia was no longer a dew-eyed maiden taken in by sweet words. When his suit didn't work, Warren had turned his attention to eighteen-year-old Molly. Having recently been rejected by Billy, Molly was vulnerable and susceptible to a handsome man's attentions. Now Warren was left at the altar, jilted and alone. At least he still had his job at the bank.

Seated at the organ, Miss Nellie Potter spotted Amelia, and struck up a chord on the organ. The strands of the "Wedding March" echoed through the church. All heads swung toward Amelia. For just a second, she wondered how it would feel to be a bride and walk down the aisle with Chance Sinclair waiting eagerly for her. Chance? Amelia shoved that impossible thought from her head. That was as likely as her taking off and flying above the church like a bird. And just as stupid.

Picking up her pace, she hurried to the front of the church. With a hand, she signaled the organist to stop playing. The music faded away, and the audience began to grumble. She cleared her throat, and looked out at friends and neighbors, most of whom she had known all her life.

"Ladies and gentlemen, I'm afraid there won't be a wedding here today," Amelia announced, her voice quivering slightly. Gasps rang through the church, and Warren caught her arm. From the front pew, Callie flashed an all-too familiar "I warned you" glare.

"What's wrong?" Warren asked, anger and concern mixed in his eyes. "Is Molly ill? I must go to her."

Amelia covered his hand with hers. "Wait, I'll explain everything in a minute."

Questions flew at her from the pews. "Where's Molly?" "What's wrong?" "What happened?"

Again, Amelia held up her hands. "Molly is fine." She swallowed down her trepidation. "The wedding has been postponed. I know many of you have come a long way, so feel free to enjoy the cake and punch on the lawn. Thank you for coming."

"Amelia, I demand to know what happened? Why isn't Molly here?" Warren tightened his grip on her arm.

Amelia glanced at the crowd that was beginning to gather around her. "Callie, will you lead everybody out to the lawn. No use letting all that food go to waste." They had spent days baking and decorating cakes for the wedding.

Callie questioned Amelia with her eyes, but did as she was bid, and urged the people from the church. Her narrowed eyes reminded Amelia of her prediction of a disastrous Saturday wedding.

"Pastor Brown, may we go to your office to talk?" Amelia had no desire to air her dirty laundry in front of the whole town.

The kindly minister nodded. "Certainly, Miss Amelia. If there's anything I can do to help, just let me know."

Inside the office, Warren folded his arms across his chest. "Now, will you tell me why Molly called off the wedding?"

Taking a deep breath to gather her thoughts, Amelia plunged ahead with the truth. "Molly is gone."

"Gone? Where? I'll go find her."

"I don't know. She's with Billy Sinclair."

"That hooligan? He abducted her. I knew he was no good. We'll get up a posse and hunt them down before he hurts her." He took a step toward the door.

She stopped him before he reached the door. "No. Billy won't hurt her. I don't want to call in the law just yet."

He glared down at her. "What do you mean? Your niece has been kidnapped. He'll probably demand a fortune in ransom."

"And I'll handle it. I don't want the law involved. I would like to keep this between us. If word gets out that she's with Billy, it will cause a scandal. I don't want that and I'm sure you don't either. They're probably on their way to Castroville. You go that way and see what you can find." She hoped for Molly's sake it was the right decision. "I'm certain she'll come to her senses and be back by this evening." She didn't mention that Molly had taken her valise with her.

Warren hesitated, staring out the window. "I don't know. The sheriff would know more about tracking them than I."

"Sheriff Powell is out of town taking a prisoner to Austin. And I don't want a posse stirring up trouble." They were wasting time arguing. She gave him a gentle shove. "Just go to the livery and rent a buggy." When he hesitated, she gave him another push. "Tell them to charge the rental to me."

With a reluctant nod, he strolled from the office. He seemed in no hurry to find his absent bride.

"Miss Amelia," the pastor asked softly, "is there anything I can do to help?"

She shook her head. "I'm not sure anybody can help."

"What about Billy's brother? Surely Chance would know where his brother would go."

On a sigh, Amelia shook her head. Chance was the last person she could ask to help. Over the past years, they had rarely spoken and she wasn't about to ask him for a favor. Unfortunately, there was little a lone woman could do. And Billy might have taken Molly to their ranch.

Swallowing her pride, she headed to the door and the decorated carriage waiting to take her to face her destiny.

Two

Chance Sinclair strolled out of the barn, using his sleeve to swipe away the sweat and grime from his face. He ran his hand over a week's worth of whiskers. After days spent seeing nothing but cattle and surly cowboys, he was ready for a hot bath, clean clothes, and a good meal. A willing woman from Violet's place would top off his evening. A small grin tugged at the corners of his mouth. More likely, he'd spend the night in the clutches of that card shark and be lucky to break out even.

Half the cowboys he'd hired for spring roundup had already returned to the bunkhouse to get ready for their night in town. A few unfortunates would stay out on the range watching the cattle. In another week, he hoped to have rounded up and branded all the stray calves. Looked like he was in for a pretty good year.

He glanced toward the road leading to the ranch house. A wagon barreled down the narrow lane, throwing up a cyclone of dust in its wake. He shaded his eyes and stared. As it drew nearer, he recognized the driver by the tall top hat he wore. Shamus McNab had a strange sense of style. The other occupant, a woman, rode with her face buried in the skirts of her green dress.

The buggy stopped at his porch. Chance shook his

head in wonder. What was a buggy draped in ribbons and flowers doing here? Even the horses' manes and tails were tied with satin streamers. After slowly climbing to the ground, Shamus offered a hand to the woman.

For a second, Chance's heart stopped beating. Amelia Swanson. Even with her face hidden, he would know her anywhere. What the hell could she want with him? The thought almost made him laugh. She'd already proved she didn't want anything to do with him. Taking his time, he sauntered toward the strange-looking carriage.

By the time he reached the porch, the woman had lifted her head. Wide green eyes stared at him from a milk white face. He lifted a hand to help her down, but quickly recovered his senses. Safely tucking his fingers into the pocket of his worn jeans, he rocked back on his heels. Shamus helped her to the ground.

"Out slumming today, Duchess?" He couldn't resist taunting her with the name her father had bestowed on her as a child. A name she hated.

She cringed. Her face paled further. For a second, he was sorry he'd chosen to harass her. Quickly, she recovered. A frown turned down the corners of her mouth. She faced him boldly, like a fighter taking on an opponent. "Mr. Sinclair, I am looking for your brother. Where is he?"

Unknowingly, she'd hit on a sore spot. When he'd wanted Billy to help on the range, his reckless young brother had informed Chance he had more important business to take care of. "Why? What's he done now?" Billy had been in and out of trouble since their paw had died. Chance was sick and tired of continually bailing out his younger sibling.

Amelia took a step toward him. A good eight

inches shorter than he, she tilted her head to stare
into his eyes. Fire burned like hot emeralds in her
gaze. "Your brother kidnapped my niece."

"He what?"

She jabbed her finger into his chest. "You heard me.
Now where is he? Are you hiding that . . . criminal?"

"Watch out, Duchess. You'll get that white glove
dirty by touching a filthy, no-account cowboy." An-
grily, he tossed back the words her father had thrown
at him fourteen years ago. "Billy isn't here. And neither is Molly."

She jerked back as if he'd slapped her. Her gaze
left his face and she studied the ranch. "Do you have
any idea where he might have taken her?"

His gaze followed hers to the barns, corrals, wood
shed, bunkhouse—all neat and orderly. White and
pink blossoms covered the fruit trees, and tall oaks
shaded the porch. He had done a lot of work to improve the ranch in the ten years since he'd returned
home. Chance was proud of his accomplishments.

"What makes you think Billy kidnapped Molly?"
His brother was wild and reckless, but the younger
man was nuts about Amelia's niece.

"I saw them ride away together."

"That doesn't prove anything. She could have simply gone off with him on a lark."

"On her wedding day?" she ground between her
teeth.

Chance jerked back a step. "You mean she ran off
with my brother and left the groom at the altar?" The
humor of the situation struck him. He began to
laugh. "If that don't beat all."

"I see nothing funny. She could be in danger."

He sobered. "Like you were in danger? Are you trying to run her life like your father ran yours?"

"It isn't anything like that. I just don't want her to make a mistake—"

"Like you did?"

Amelia fisted her hands. "This is not about me—or you. It is about Molly and Billy."

He pulled his hat from his head and beat the dust on the legs of his denims. "Look, Amelia. I don't know where they are. But I know Billy would never hurt Molly. He's crazy about her."

"Crazy is right."

Chance took a deep steadying breath. "I warned Billy about getting involved with Molly. Obviously, he didn't take my advice. What do you expect me to do about it?"

"You have to find them."

"*I* have to find them?" He settled the hat back on his head. "Duchess, I'm in the middle of spring roundup. I don't have time to go off on a wild-goose chase because a Sinclair isn't good enough for a Swanson."

She planted her fists on her hips. Her green dress pulled taut across her chest. "I don't want the law to go after them. Or a posse. Somebody could get hurt. I do not want a scandal."

His gaze dropped to the front of her dress and the womanly fullness she'd lacked all those years ago. She looked good, like a gaily wrapped Christmas present to a little child. The pretty young girl had matured into a stunning woman. Unwanted desire twisted in his gut. "Duchess, is this about what you want? Or what Molly wants?"

"Molly is too young to know what she wants."

He didn't want to remind her that she was younger than Molly when they had run off together. However, he had to admit she was right. It had been a huge mistake. For both of them. Getting involved with her would be another mistake he had no intention of making. "Sorry, I'm busy. Let the groom go after his bride."

"Warren went to Castroville. I need somebody to head toward San Antonio. There's no telling how far they could have gotten by now."

"I told you I don't have time." And he didn't want any part of her scheme.

"Have it your way. I'll go instead." Her chin held high, she stalked away. She halted in front of the flower-bedecked buggy. As she reached up to climb aboard, she staggered like a drunken cowboy on a Saturday night. Chance caught her arm to steady her. Immediately, she shrugged him off. "Shamus, can you drive me to San Antonio?"

The old man scratched the thick stubble at his jaw. "Now, Miss Amelia, I reckon I could, but you only rented this fine carriage for one day. It's kind of late. If we go to San Antonio, we'll have to spend the night in La Casa. That means we won't get there till tomorrow. And we won't get home till Monday."

"I'll pay double for the extra days."

Chance's conscience prickled. He couldn't let Amelia go off with the old man. "Never mind, Shamus. Take Miss Amelia back to town. I'll find my brother."

She spun to face him. Relief softened her eyes. "I want to go, too."

This time he stood his ground. "Amelia, I can go faster alone."

"Molly is my niece. She may need me."

He recognized the stubborn look that had not changed over the years. "What about your motion sickness? You're still a little green around the gills."

"I've weathered worse. And I'll do it for Molly."

"Oh, hell. Have your own way. Give me a few minutes to wash and change." Chance gritted his teeth as he marched around the house. Under his breath, he cursed his brother for his foolish actions. What was he getting himself into? That was all he needed—to get involved with Amelia again. It had taken years to get over her rejection. This time she wasn't going to get near his heart. No, sir. He intended to protect it like the gold in that vault in her bank.

Amelia sent Shamus back to town with word for Callie not to worry. She would send a telegram when she found Molly. Only as the wagon rolled away did she realize what she had done. She covered her mouth with her gloved hand. Her heart dropped to her stomach, still churning after the ride from town. How could she put herself in this position? Was she out of her mind?

Not only was she going to spend hours riding in a bumpy wagon, she would do it with Chance Sinclair at her side. Chance, the man who had deceived her so long ago. The man who had broken her young heart and shattered her life. He had claimed to love her, but proved he loved her father's money more. She touched her hand to her chest, pressing the cold gold of the chain around her neck to the area near her heart.

On a sigh, Amelia started toward the shelter of the porch, but stopped in her tracks when she spotted Chance at the water pump. As she watched, he removed his shirt. Her heart skipped a beat. He stretched, flexing the muscles in his back and arms. Tingles settled in her stomach at the sight of his strong male body. He bent at the waist and stuck his

head under the pump. Water splattered over his dark
hair, rolling down the corded muscles at his neck and
shoulders. His careful, graceful movements fasci-
nated Amelia as he washed away the day's dirt. He
straightened and wiped his face and hair with a towel.

Amelia couldn't tear her gaze away from his near-
naked body. Heat surfaced to her face. Only once
before had she seen a man in this state of disha-
bille—the night she had spent in Chance's arms. The
wiry youth she'd once loved had matured into a wide-
shouldered, muscular man. Shiny drops of water
gathered in the dark hair on his wide chest. She remembered rubbing her cheek into that hair, and
tickling him in his ribs. Holding her breath, she
watched the droplets roll down his flat stomach to his
navel and then into the waist of his low-slung jeans.
She bit her lip to control the soft moan that rumbled
from her chest to her throat. Time and hard work
had sculpted Chance into a beautiful specimen of
manhood.

He dropped the towel from his face. Across the
short distance his gaze locked with hers. A crooked
grin tugged at one corner of his mouth. He'd caught
her staring at him—a half-clothed man. Spurred by
her embarrassment, she turned on her heel. A deep
chuckle followed her to the shade of the front porch.
Amelia fanned her scorched skin with a lace-edged
handkerchief and struggled to calm her racing pulse.
She was much too old for such youthful fantasies.

By the time Chance sauntered out the front door,
Amelia had managed to get her emotions under control. Barely. A clean chambray shirt covered his broad
chest with a blue kerchief tied carelessly around his
throat. He stopped inches from her. "I'll be ready as
soon as I hitch up the wagon."

He hadn't bothered to shave. With several days' growth of beard shadowing his jaw, he looked as darkly dangerous as the heroes in the romantic novels she kept hidden in her room. The books were Amelia's secret addiction.

Her gaze dropped to the holstered gun low on his hip and the rifle in his hand. "Do you think firearms are necessary?"

He shrugged, drawing the shirt tight across his shoulders. "Never know what kind of critter we might run into on the road." At the edge of the porch, he turned back to her. "And I might decide to shoot my brother for the trouble he's causing me."

"Unless I shoot him first," she said.

A few minutes later, Chance drove a wagon pulled by two horses up to the porch. Amelia cringed at the sight of the rickety buckboard. Chance glared at her from under the brim of a gray Stetson. "Duchess, you sure you want to go through with this? I can have one of the boys drive you to town. And I'll let you know if I find Molly."

Amelia set her mind. "I'm sure." She only prayed that she could hold the motion sickness at bay. It would be humiliating to embarrass herself in front of Chance of all people.

In one graceful motion, he jumped down from the wagon. Ignoring his offer of help, Amelia climbed onto the high, narrow seat. With her emotions in turmoil, she didn't want him to touch her. Lord only knew what she would do if he did. She tucked her skirt around her legs and adjusted the pins to hold her wide-brimmed hat in place.

Chance snapped the lines and the horses trotted off. Amelia gripped the seat with both hands. She gritted her teeth against the rocking, swaying motion.

So far, so good, she thought as they wound along the narrow lane that led to the main road. With a deep breath, she managed to calm the rumble in her stomach. However, she couldn't ignore the tingles caused by the man at her side. With every sway of the wagon, his shoulder brushed against hers, making her aware of the warmth of his strong body.

She glanced to the side from under the brim of her hat. His gaze was on the road, his mouth pulled into a grim line. Chance's boyish good looks had changed and hardened. Tiny lines crinkled at the corners of his eyes, and his once-straight nose was slightly off-center. She wondered if it had been broken. Even the dark whiskers covering his strong jaw didn't take away from his looks. She had always considered him the handsomest man she'd ever known.

Lost in her musings, Amelia was caught off guard when the wagon hit a deep rut. She tumbled sideways against Chance. She gripped his arm for balance. He covered her fingers with his. "You okay, Amelia?" he asked, concern in his deep voice.

Sensation sizzled up her arm. Aware that she continued to dig her fingers into his arm, she jerked her hand free. "Yes, yes, I'm fine." She again gripped the edge of the seat. "Doesn't this thing have any springs?"

He chuckled softly. "Duchess, this isn't a fine carriage like your father used to have. It's a farm wagon. I use it to carry supplies and deliver hay to the cattle. I can still take you back to town if you're uncomfortable."

"That won't be necessary. I told you I'm going to find Molly." Uncomfortable wasn't the word for how she felt. Physically, she'd been able to control her troublesome ailment. Her emotions were a different matter. The last time she had ridden in a wagon with

Chance—fourteen long years before—he had kept his arm around her as she snuggled her face into his shoulder. And she hadn't been the least bit sick all the way to San Antonio.

With an effort, she shoved those disastrous thoughts back to the corner of her heart where she kept them safely hidden away. Only in the dark of night, when she was alone in her bed, did she dare remember that devastating day. The day she had run away with Chance. The day he had shattered her heart into a million pieces.

"What are you going to do if . . . when we find them?" He shook the lines and the horses picked up speed.

"I intend to talk some sense into my niece. And I expect you to do the same with your brother."

"I already tried, for all the good it did."

"Maybe together we can convince them to come home." Together. The word brought back even more bittersweet memories for Amelia. She and Chance had planned to spend their lives together. Now, she was a thirty-one-year old spinster with only memories to keep her warm at night. And her novels for company.

Chance had never married, but nobody knew how many times she'd watched from her bedroom window and seen him enter Miss Violet's Pleasure Palace on Saturday nights. Then, on Sunday mornings while on her way to church, she saw him swagger out. He had never failed to tip his hat and wish her "Good day." He didn't know that his dalliance ruined not only her day, but her week as well.

They rode in silence with the sun slowly dipping in the west. At twilight, they reached La Casa. Amelia was grateful when Chance stopped the wagon in front of the marshal's office. This time she didn't object when he set his hands on her waist to help her down. His grip was strong, his hands warm. Unwarranted tingles surged through her. For a long moment he stared into her face. Heat glittered in his eyes, then quickly shifted to a cold icy blue. As soon as her toes touched the ground, he released her.

Chance stepped away from Amelia, wondering what he was thinking. Touching her had been a mistake. This trip had wrenched memories from the hidden place of his heart. Memories best forgotten. For both their sakes.

"The marshal is an old friend of mine. He'll know if Billy and Molly came through here today." Chance gestured toward the door of the building.

He followed Amelia through the open doorway. The man behind the scarred desk dropped his feet from the top and jumped up when they entered. Chance stretched out his hand to the man. "Walt, how're things going?" he asked.

"Quiet, Chance. How's life over in Mayfield?" Walt Ritter gave his hand a hard shake. His gaze shifted to Amelia.

"Fine." Chance glanced at Amelia. "Miss Amelia Swanson, Marshal Ritter."

Walt took Amelia's hand and flashed a charming smile. "Are you that lady banker from Mayfield? Nobody told me you were so pretty."

"Yeah, she's the banker," Chance said, slightly annoyed at his flirtatious friend. A bachelor, a few years younger than Chance, Walt had a reputation with the women.

Walt kept hold of Amelia's hand. "What can I do for you? Somebody robbed your bank?"

"We're—"

Chance broke her off before she could finish. "We're looking for Billy. Has he come through here today? He'll be with a pretty young woman, blond."

Amelia tugged her hand free. "She's wearing a white gown."

"Can't say I did. Billy could have come through and I didn't see him." The marshal rubbed his stubbled jaw. "But I think I would have noticed a lady. Not too many pretty blondes show up in town. You might ask around at the livery or the saloons. Somebody might have seen them."

"I'll do that, Walt." He pressed his hand into the small of Amelia's back in a possessive manner. "Thanks anyway."

"Nice meeting you, Miss Amelia. I might decide to do my banking in Mayfield." Walt followed them to the door. "See ya'll around."

Amelia pulled away from Chance and turned to the marshal. "I'll look forward to serving you, Marshal."

Her smile brought a frown to Chance's mouth. He didn't know that Amelia had it in her to flirt. Her reputation in Mayfield was of a rigid, serious spinster whose only recreation was balancing the ledgers in the bank. Chance didn't believe a word of it. He, more than anyone, knew the real woman hidden under the stern façade. Unless she had changed, somewhere inside her was a loving, passionate woman.

Chance shook away the thoughts of the past. In these few short hours, she had gotten under his skin. Again. That was something he couldn't afford. His heart still stung after her betrayal.

On the street, he glanced toward the only hotel in the small town. "Amelia, you go over to the hotel and see if Billy and Molly stopped there. I'll head to the livery and saloons. Meet me at the Homestyle Café."

"I suppose it would save time." Without argument she did as he suggested.

By the time he left the third and last saloon in town, it was fully dark. He hoped Amelia had better luck than he had. So far nobody had seen a couple that resembled Billy and Molly.

He entered the café and spotted Amelia at a table in the corner. The expectant look on her face died when she saw him enter alone. "I suppose you didn't have any better luck than I did," he said, taking the chair across from hers.

"Nobody has seen them, and I asked everyone I saw." On a sigh she dropped her head into her hands. "They must have gone on to San Antonio. Molly has friends there who will help her. I'll send a wire in the morning and find out if Callie has heard from Molly."

"Good idea. By now, Molly could be back home safely in her bed."

She lifted her gaze. Worry wrinkled her forehead. "I doubt that. She took the valise she had packed for her honeymoon."

"Oh," was all he managed to say as bitter memories shoved to the surface of his mind. Memories of another couple with a honeymoon in mind. A honeymoon that lasted only one glorious night. "Let's get something to eat. We'll take rooms at the hotel and start out again early in the morning."

"I think we should go on tonight. No telling how far ahead they are."

"Amelia, I've already stabled the horses. It's dangerous to travel like that at night. Tomorrow is soon enough."

"I suppose you're right."

Surprised at how easily she had given in, he picked up the menu and ordered dinner for both of them.

The meal passed in relative silence, both lost in their own thoughts. The strange events of the day had brought them together for the first time in all those years. Over the years, they had passed each other on the street and barely nodded recognition. On the nights he'd spent at Miss Violet's place, he'd made it his business to leave on Sunday morning in time to see her on the way to church. Chance didn't know why he did it. Whether it was to see her or to let her know he wasn't lonely without her in his life. He wound up only hurting himself and thinking about her for days after.

With time, he'd tried to deceive himself into thinking he had gotten over her. Now he realized he hadn't.

Chance shoved his empty coffee cup aside and tossed some money on the table. "Let's get some shut-eye. We have an early day tomorrow."

Amelia stood. "I'll pay for my own meal, thank you." Opening the silk purse she held by the narrow silver chain, she pulled out some coins.

"That isn't necessary, Duchess. I can afford the meal."

"I never thought otherwise. It is only right that I cover my own expenses."

He caught her fingers and stopped her movement. "Consider it my treat. Let's get back to the hotel. I don't know about you, but I'm beat."

"As you wish. I'll pay for breakfast."

Not wanting to argue, he took her elbow and escorted her into the hotel. At the registration counter, he signaled for the clerk. A middle-aged man wearing an ill-fitting suit set aside his newspaper. "What can I do for you, sir?" he asked.

"Two rooms, please," Amelia answered before he could speak.

The clerk ran a long finger down the ledger in

front of him. "Sorry, we have only one room available." He glanced from Chance to Amelia.

She shoved past Chance. "I'll take it."

"We'll take it," he said, reaching for the registration book.

"You can sleep in the lobby. I'll take the room." She jabbed her elbow into his side.

"I have no intention of sleeping down here. We'll share the room."

"Over my dead body."

"Duchess, that can be arranged."

Three

Chance ignored her tirade. His back ached, and his eyes burned. He whispered to the clerk in a friendly tone. "The little lady's been mad at me all day. Guess I'll have to make up with her tonight."

The clerk winked at Chance and picked up a key. "I understand, sir. Room 201."

Amelia shouldered Chance aside. "Little lady? How degrading. I am not your, nor anyone else's, 'little lady.' Give me that." She snatched the key from the clerk's fingers.

Tired of arguing, Chance bent at the waist and neatly tossed her over his shoulder like a sack of grain. Her head hung to his waist, and her rear perched in the air. His arms locked over her jerking legs, he proceeded up the stairs. She beat her hands against his back.

"Let me down, you oaf," she shouted.

"Calm down, sweetheart, you're making enough noise to wake the dead."

"If you don't put me down, you'll be joining them."

In the hall outside their room, he dropped her to her feet. She let out a loud "Oomph," and staggered into the wall. Quickly, he snatched the key from her fingers and opened the door. Slipping under his arm, she rushed inside the room. She shoved her shoulder against the door to shut him out.

"That trick won't work, Duchess." He flattened his hand on the door to shove it wide open. "I'm staying right here tonight." Once inside, he set the lock.

In the thin stream of moonlight from the window, Amelia glared at the man with his back to the door. She curled her fingers into her palms to keep herself from wiping the self-satisfied grin from his face. Fourteen years before she had kissed a similar grin away. This time it infuriated her. Amelia rarely lost her temper or self-control. But nobody had ever wrenched feelings from her like Chance. Love, hate, anger, joy, happiness and sadness all combined into one explosive emotion. Exasperated, she kicked him squarely in the shin. Her toe hurt, but it was worth it to see him yelp and bend over to clutch his leg.

"What the heck was that for?" he asked, glaring back at her.

"Because you're insufferable."

"At one time you thought I was adorable. Or was that wonderful?"

She gritted her teeth. "I've grown up. And I will not be treated like a 'little lady' without a will of my own." She folded her arms across her chest.

He limped to the narrow bed and sat down on the thin coverlet. "One thing hasn't changed, you're just as stubborn as ever." Bending over, he pulled off one boot, then the other. He stretched out on the bed, hands tucked under his head, feet crossed at the ankles. "Are you just going to stand there and stare at me all night?"

She studied the sparsely furnished room. Besides the bed, the room boasted only a small bureau, a washstand with a cracked pitcher, a single straight-backed chair, and a square bedside table holding a kerosene lamp. Chance struck a match and lit the wick on the lamp. The dull yellow light flooded the room.

"Just where am I supposed to sleep?"

He tossed his hat onto the bureau. "Wherever you please."

Amelia patted her foot on the floor. "I would prefer the bed. You can sleep in the chair."

"I'm too big for the chair. We'll have to share the bed."

At the thought of sharing a bed, her cheeks pinked. "We cannot. It isn't decent."

A crooked smile curved his mouth. "You didn't say that last time."

The memory burned in her chest. "We were married then. We aren't anymore."

"No," he said, his voice soft. "Thanks to your father's interference."

Amelia refused to be baited. She had never forgiven her father for what he had done to her. To them. "There's no use bringing up the past. We'll have to make the best of the situation."

"Okay, Amelia. I'll sleep on top of the covers, and you can sleep under them. That way we'll have a blanket between us, and you'll be perfectly safe from me."

In spite of what he said, Amelia knew she would never be truly safe from Chance. He was her first love, her only love. Since his betrayal, she hadn't allowed herself to trust another man with her heart.

"I don't suppose I have a choice."

Chance slowly got to his feet. "Unless you want to bunk out in the foyer or on the floor. I sure intend to sleep on my side of this bed." Boldly facing her, he loosed the buttons of his shirt.

"What are you doing?" she asked, her voice rising to a squeal.

"Getting ready for bed. I would advise you to do the same if we're to get an early start tomorrow." He tossed the shirt on the chair along with his holster and gun.

Amelia stared at his wide chest. Muscles rippled and flexed with every movement. She dug her hands into her pockets to keep from reaching out to touch him—to test the tautness of his body, the texture of his skin, the heat of his flesh. Tingles fluttered in the pit of her stomach. How was she going to get through the long night sharing a bed with him and not following through with her fantasies? Without living the dreams that had haunted her nightly for years?

He stretched out on the bed. "You planning to sleep standing up and wearing all those clothes?"

"Please turn down the lamp." Perhaps in the dark, she could concentrate on getting some rest. However, she doubted it.

Chance did as she asked. Only a thin thread of moonlight streaked across the floor. Taking advantage of the darkness, she removed her jacket and hat. She washed her face, then removed her silk stockings and shoes. Without a brush, she ran her fingers through her hair and twisted the long tresses into a single braid. If only she could take off her constrictive corset. She listened until she heard Chance's deep, even breathing. Only then did she dare take off her skirt. Slipping under the covers, she removed her blouse, then struggled to unhook her corset. The bed squeaked with every wiggle of her body.

"What the hell are you doing over there?" Chance's sleepy voice startled her.

"I'm trying to make myself comfortable." Finally,

the last hook slipped loose. Amelia took her first really deep breath of the day.

He laughed. "Oh, your corset. Why do women wear those torture devices?"

"Fashion and the proper fit of a garment."

Chance let out a sleepy chuckle. "And to torment men. You might as well take off those petticoats, too. I won't look."

How could he know what she was wearing? Or not wearing? Reaching under the covers, she untied the petticoats and wiggled out of them. The white lawn garment landed on the floor beside her. Left wearing only her thin chemise, she stretched out on her side at the edge of the mattress with the blanket tight to her neck.

Chance shifted and she felt the press of his body against hers on the other side of the blanket. Memories flooded her. A tear slipped from her eyes. Being this close to Chance brought back the night—the one night—they had spent together. Their wedding night—the most wonderful night of her life. An interlude that had brought incredible joy, then later unbelievable heartache.

He had been sweet and gentle in his lovemaking. She had given herself willingly with love and passion. And she had thought he had loved her in return. Fool that she was. She fell asleep with her fingers clutching the gold ring she wore on the chain around her neck. The ring he had given her that day.

A noise woke Chance from a restless sleep. It had taken what seemed like hours before he was able to relax enough to sleep. Even without a lamp, he knew every move Amelia had made. He heard the slip of the buttons when she removed her jacket and blouse. The slide of silk stockings slipping down her legs turned his blood into lava spewing from an active volcano. He would never forget those long sleek legs that had once tangled with his. The rustle of her petticoats as they fell to the floor turned his mind to mush. When she slid under the covers, he thought he would go mad with need.

With Amelia so close, yet so far away, he couldn't shut off the memories of her and the events of the past. He had loved her, truly loved her. And he had thought she loved him. Maybe she had, but not enough to stand up to her father—not enough to trust him.

He propped up on his elbow, wondering what had awakened him. His eyes adjusted to the dimness, and he saw no sign of an intruder. He settled back down when he realized the sound had come from the other side of the bed. Amelia tossed her head on the pillow. A sob wrenched from her throat. The noise brought him fully awake.

"No," she sobbed. "Don't take him away from me." Her arms flailed out as if she were reaching for something. Tears dampened her face.

Gently, Chance grabbed her shoulders. "Wake up, Amelia. It's only a dream." He shook her until her eyes slid open.

"What . . . what happened?" she whispered. Her hands clutched his bare shoulders—her fingers felt like icy talons against his skin.

"You had a bad dream." He brushed the stray wisps of hair from her forehead. "You're okay now." The covers between them had slipped, leaving her lying close at his side.

Another deep, heart-wrenching sob tore from her

throat. Chance wrapped his arms around Amelia, and drew her close into his chest. Her body was soft and warm, her breasts lush and full against him. They fit perfectly together, as they always had. Desire for her, desire that had never fully died over the years gushed to the surface. Right now, she needed comfort, not passion. With a supreme effort, he tamped down his need to help her. "Hush, sweetheart. Go back to sleep. I'm right here with you." He dropped a tiny kiss on her forehead.

On a soft sigh, she snuggled into his embrace. Within moments, her breathing was slow and even. "We'll leave early, before Papa finds us." The soft, barely discernible words pierced his soul like an arrow.

His heart clenched. Too many memories, too much pain lay between them. He'd often wondered what would have happened if her father hadn't located them that day. As he inhaled the sweet flowery scent of her hair, all the memories of young love flooded back to him.

Defying her father, they had run away to get married. The priest in San Antonio had performed the ceremony, then laughing together, they had checked into the Menger Hotel. Both were shy and awkward, but so much in love that nothing mattered but each other. They had made love all night, and lay together to watch the sun come up in the morning. Chance pulled Amelia closer into this chest. She came as willingly as she had fourteen years ago.

Their idyllic interlude lasted until noon, when her father burst into the room with the local sheriff. They tore Amelia from his arms, and sent the crying young woman away. Chance was rudely dragged off to jail under the threat of kidnapping and rape charges.

The next thing he knew, she was on her way to Europe and her father was waving annulment papers and a lot of money under his nose. Papers he refused to sign. Money he would not take. Fortunately, Mr. Swanson dropped the criminal charges, allowing Chance to return home. But by then Amelia was gone. He'd supposed she would come back to him someday. It had never happened. He hated to admit her father was right. It had been a mistake. She didn't want him. It had all been just a game to her, a way to defy her father. By the time she returned to Mayfield four years later, whatever love he'd had for her had long since died.

Now, here she was, back in his life and in his arms. If he had half the sense God gave a fence post, he would have ridden back out on the range the minute he spotted her in his yard. But he hadn't. He twisted his fingers in the long silky braid that hung down her back. A vise tightened in his chest. For a strong, determined woman, Amelia had revealed a fragile and vulnerable side tonight. Chance was too confused by their entire relationship to think. Remembering the pain of rejection, he locked his bittersweet memories back into the shadows of his heart. It would do neither of them any good to dig up the pain of the past.

As sleep drifted away, Amelia slowly became aware of the warmth pressed against her side. It felt good, better than good. On a soft moan, she snuggled closer. Rough fingertips brushed across her cheek. Her legs tangled with soft denim. She reached out a hand and encountered hard, warm flesh. The fingers on her face splayed into her hair. What a delightful dream. Amelia seldom awoke with a smile. Today she felt the grin slide across her lips.

If this was a dream, she didn't want to wake up. Sweet sensations skidded up her spine. She had only awakened like this once before—the night she had spent in Chance's arms. The most glorious night of her life. She had relived it so many times in her dreams, it was almost real. She could almost feel his hard flesh under her fingertips, smell the clean fragrance of soap and leather, hear his steady breath near her ear. Not wanting the dream to end, she squeezed her eyes shut tight.

"Amelia." The voice drifted on the clouds of her mind.

She wasn't ready to give up her fantasy "Go away, Callie."

Warmth tickled her ear. "It isn't Callie, sweetheart."

This time the sound penetrated the fog of sleep. If it wasn't Callie getting her up for breakfast, who . . . ? "Chance!" Her eyes snapped open, bringing her face-to-face with her dream. He flashed that too-familiar half smile she'd always loved. The growth of whiskers couldn't hide that alluring grin. "What . . . where . . . What's going on?" In an instant understanding dawned like the sun bursting from behind a cloud.

She had spent the night in a hotel room—in a bed with Chance Sinclair. Her dream. Her fantasy. Her nightmare.

"Time to get up, if we're going to hit the road," he said, not making an effort to leave her side. "But if you had rather, we can spend the day right here."

"Here?" One downward glance showed that she wore nothing but a batiste chemise. "Oh." Swiftly, she tugged the blanket to her chin.

Chance's grin widened. "Don't be so modest, Duchess. I've seen you in a lot less."

A heated flush crept from her toes to her ears.

"Don't be vulgar." She didn't need to be reminded of their actions of the past. Those memories stayed with her day and night. None of the heroes in her romantic novels could compare with Chance Sinclair. "If you will leave this room, I'll be able to get up and dress."

He stretched out on his back, his hands tucked under his head. "I might just relax for a few minutes and admire the view."

She tried to get up, but found the blanket was trapped under his body. Her gaze dropped to his wide chest tanned by the sun, then down at the white strip of flesh where his tight denims had slipped low on his hips. The pants molded his muscular thighs. His bare toes wiggled as if waving at her. She couldn't deny Chance was a beautifully sculpted man with a body honed by hard work. "You can admire the view from the lobby."

He swung his legs and sat on the edge of the bed. "Okay, Duchess. I'll go down and order up some warm water for you. When you're decent, you can meet me at the café."

Amelia averted her eyes as he slipped into his shirt. Moments later, the door squeaked open. Chance shot a glance at her over his shoulder. "I'd like to get going soon. I want to return home by tonight."

"Thank you. I'm sure I won't be long." As the door clicked shut, Amelia released the breath she had been holding. Self-preservation warned her to be careful. The attraction was still there—at least on her side. If she didn't protect her emotions, she could be right back where she had been all those years ago. Alone with a broken heart.

Four

It was full dark when they returned to Mayfield that night. After visiting every church in San Antonio, they still had no word on Billy and Molly. Together they inquired if the priests had seen anyone matching the young couple's description seeking to get married. No one had admitted to seeing them. Nor were they registered at any of the hotels.

Amelia had visited the homes of Molly's friends, young women with whom she'd gone to school. None would admit having heard from Molly for months. They believed the girls were telling the truth. The young women promised to send a telegram if they heard from Molly.

Chance stopped the wagon in front of the big white house at the edge of town. He tightened the lines between his fingers. He had never been welcome in this house. Only when her father was out of town was Amelia able to invite him in. Mr. Swanson had wanted more for his daughter than the son of a dirt-poor rancher. Amelia had had to sneak away to spend time with Chance. He'd hated every minute of their secrecy. But he and Amelia were too young and scared to stand up to her father.

"All the lights are on downstairs. Maybe Molly came back home." Amelia climbed down from the wagon before Chance was able to assist her. She rushed toward the gate, but stopped with her hand on the latch. "Chance, aren't you coming in? Billy may be here." After another step, she paused again. "Don't forget that gun. I might want to shoot him."

On a tiny laugh, Chance tied off the lines. He pressed his hands to the small of his back to ease some of the tension. Spending so many hours with Amelia had been both heaven and hell. Thank God he had finally made it back without making a complete fool of himself. The night spent with her in his arms had been sheer torture and heavenly bliss all rolled into one. To his delight, she had made the trip well without a mention of dizziness or nausea.

He followed her slowly, staring up at the tall pillars of the wide front porch. The heavy leaded glass door hung open. Tucking his hands into his pockets, Chance entered the house. He stopped in the foyer and whistled between his teeth. The house was even more intimidating than he remembered. As a youth, he was more interested in Amelia than in polished furniture, crystal chandeliers, or Oriental rugs. Voices came from his left. He turned and entered the parlor.

Judging by the silver tea set on a low table, the cookies, and china dishes, he wondered if they had interrupted a tea party. Callie embraced Amelia, while Warren Moneypenny looked on.

"I'm so glad ye're home," the older woman said, the lilt of Ireland in her voice. "Did you find our Molly?"

"No. Have you heard from her?"

"No. I've gotten no word, and Warren went all the way to Castroville. We had hoped you'd have found them by now." She looked up and spotted Chance. "Come in, Chance. Would ye like a cup of tea?"

"No, thank you, ma'am." He removed his hat and

twisted it between his fingers. Callie Moran had always liked Chance. He believed she had purposely turned her back when Amelia sneaked out to be with him. And over the years, she had become a friend. He ignored Moneypenny.

"Callie, I could certainly use a cup," Amelia said. She took the offered cup and perched on the edge of a maroon upholstered chair. "We stopped at La Casa, then we looked all over San Antonio. Nobody will admit to seeing them."

The jilted groom settled on an overstuffed chair. "How could Molly do such a thing to me? I was so embarrassed, left waiting there in the church. Everybody is talking about it. I can hardly hold my head up in public." The pompous ass took a sip of tea then whined, "It's all Sinclair's fault. I think we should notify the authorities. The Texas Rangers should be able to track them down before he hurts her."

"Billy won't hurt Molly," Chance declared. "They'll come back when they're ready."

Moneypenny jumped to his feet. "That is preposterous. We don't know what that irresponsible ruffian will do to a innocent young woman like Molly."

Chance was sick to death of his family being maligned. First him, now his younger brother. "Billy won't hurt Molly," he ground out between his teeth.

"Of course you'll defend your brother, Sinclair. You aren't any better. I've seen you coming out of that . . . that house of ill repute on Sunday mornings when decent people are going to church."

He took one step toward the bank teller. Chance resisted the urge to smash his fist into the man's pretty face and mess up his perfectly pressed suit. "What I do is my business. And you aren't sending any lawmen after my brother."

240 *Jean Wilson*

"You can't protect a criminal. He committed a crime when he abducted my bride. I'll see that he pays."

Amelia moved to stand between the men. "Stop this bickering. You aren't helping anyone by arguing. Molly is a respectable young woman. She's eighteen, and I have to believe she knows what she's doing. We'll have to trust her to take care of herself."

Moneypenny backed away from her, as if intimidated by his employer. "It's that criminal I don't trust. What if he, well, I don't want to mention what he could do to her. As soon as he sets his feet in town, I'll see he's arrested."

Chance stepped around Amelia before she could stop him. Sick of the tirade, he grabbed the shorter man by the front of his shirt and hauled him to his toes. "On what charges? Helping Molly escape from a marriage she clearly didn't want?"

"What if he . . . ?"

"Billy would never force himself on Molly. He's crazy about her."

"Chance, please." Amelia caught his arm. "Let him go. He didn't mean anything."

"Like hell he didn't." He released the bank teller and shoved the man onto the davenport. "Remember this, Pennypincher, to get to my brother you'll have to go through me. And you just ain't big enough."

Showing a surprising bravado, the other man straightened his wrinkled necktie. "I don't have to be big. The law can handle you and your no-good brother."

Again Amelia stepped between them. "Chance, you had best go. I'll take care of Warren."

Chance picked up his hat, which he had dropped when he'd grabbed Moneypenny. "I don't blame

Molly for running away. Hell, you're lucky she didn't shoot you first."

Amelia caught his arms and steered him to the door. The hint of a smile touched her mouth. "I'll get in touch if I hear from Molly or Billy. And I will not allow the law to get involved."

"Okay. I asked Walt to send a wire if he hears anything."

She escorted him to the door. "Chance, thanks."

"For what, Amelia?" On the porch, he turned to face her.

"For everything. For helping me, for caring."

He brushed one finger along her jaw. He cared a lot more than he was willing to admit even to himself. "I do care about Billy and Molly." *And about you,* he added to himself. "But tell me something. How did you let a sweet thing like Molly get herself engaged to a jerk like Pennypincher?"

"Moneypenny. And Warren isn't that bad. He's very ambitious and hardworking. And a lot of it is Billy's fault." She glanced over her shoulder. "After Billy left Molly last year, she was devastated. I think she let Warren court her to get even with your brother."

"I can't say I blame my brother for stopping the wedding. But he should never have run away with your niece. He could have come to me."

"We'll have to wait until they return to hear their side. I only pray they come home soon."

Whether due to exhaustion, delicious dreams, or anxiety over Molly, Amelia awoke later than usual the next morning. Mostly, it was thoughts of the past, of Chance, that fluttered across her mind. Now she had new memories to add to the others. The night spent with Chance had refueled the love that had been only dying embers. His touch, his caring, had left her uncertain and vulnerable. She shoved the thoughts of Chance aside and prepared to face Warren at the bank.

By now the gossips would have gotten the full story of Molly and Billy, plus some speculation thrown in for good measure. If only she would hear something. The longer they stayed away together, the worse the gossip would become. Amelia didn't look forward to the day.

Callie was in the kitchen with breakfast waiting for Amelia on the small informal table. "Come in and eat." Her aunt poured two fresh cups of tea and set a plate of scrambled eggs in front of Amelia. "Then ye can tell me all about yer adventures with Chance Sinclair."

Amelia paused with the cup to her lips. There was little about her that Callie did not know. When Amelia's mother had died, Callie had stepped in to raise Amelia. At the time, her own sister, Louise, had recently married, and was living in Dallas. After her elopement with Chance, her father had banished her to Europe, and had sent Callie with her. Only her aunt knew her deepest, most intimate secrets. But Amelia was unable to voice her renewed feelings for Chance. The emotions were too new and raw to admit even to herself.

"We had no adventures. We only looked for Molly and Billy." Carefully, she took a bite of the eggs.

"Ye spent the night together. In the same room. And ye did not have a proper nightdress or change of clothes." Callie propped her elbows on the table and stared at Amelia over her folded hands.

Amelia's eyes grew wide. "How did you know?" she asked, her voice a husky whisper.

The older woman laughed. "I guessed."

"It was all innocent and proper. The hotel in La Casa had only one room, so we were forced to share."

"Of course. Chance forced you."

Before she could form a response, the clock in the hall chimed nine times. Amelia jumped. "Nine o'clock. I'm late. I always open the bank at nine."

Callie caught her wrist. "Warren can open today. I want to know all about Chance . . . and you."

"There is no Chance and me. That was over years ago." Amelia dropped her napkin on the table. "My father bought and paid for an annulment. When Chance took Father's money, it was all over between us."

"Amelia, are ye sure it's over? I saw the way he looked at you last night. Not to mention the way you looked at him."

"How did I look at him?"

Callie laughed. "As if he were birthday cake, chocolate candy, and strawberry ice cream all rolled into one luscious package. And ye couldn't wait to take a big bite. That Chance Sinclair is a fine-looking man."

Amelia couldn't deny what was all too true. But she would deny her desire to her dying day. "I did no such thing. Chance was only concerned for his brother and Molly. He isn't interested in me."

"He's never married or courted any of the local women."

"But he seems to spend his share of time at Miss Violet's whorehouse." The words burned coming out of her mouth.

"Amelia Swanson, what a way for a lady to talk." Callie flashed a knowing smile. The woman saw and knew more than anybody she'd ever met. "Ye seem to be keeping close track of him." She released Amelia's wrist with a gentle pat.

"I can't avoid him when he steps out of that place into my path on Sunday mornings. You're always with me. You see for yourself."

"Not every Sunday."

She had to admit the truth. "No. Just occasionally."

"He is a virile young man, you know. And as handsome as any hero in those romantic novels you keep hidden under your pillow."

"How do you . . . Never mind." Amelia stepped away from the table. "I really don't want to discuss Chance Sinclair's personal affairs. And I must get to the bank."

"Before ye go, I have a confession."

"Confession? Other than sneaking my books and reading them yourself?"

The older woman didn't look at all ashamed or penitent. "On my way to the wedding, I saw Billy sneak into the house. I showed him the back stairs to Molly's room."

The disclosure shocked Amelia. "You helped Billy abduct Molly?"

"I didn't think he would hurt her. I believe she went with him freely. Like ye did with Chance. I hoped somebody would stop that wedding. And Billy did."

Amelia glared at her aunt—the woman who was both mother and confidante to her and Molly. "Why? I thought you wanted this marriage."

"I only agreed to help because I thought it was what Molly wanted. But I could see she was miserable. She loves Billy, not Warren. She was only trying to make him jealous. Then I believe she was afraid to hurt you by calling off the wedding. After all the trouble you'd gone through, and the money you spent."

Amelia sank back into the chair. "She hurt me more by running away. I was scared to death. I still am. And Warren was humiliated by being left at the altar. I don't know how I'm going to face him day after day."

"Simple. You can fire him. Then you'll never have to see him at all."

"I can't do that. It wouldn't be fair. Warren is a very good banker."

Callie shrugged. "I suppose he is. Warren loves money. Anybody's money. I wonder if he loves Molly's inheritance more than he loves her."

"You've never told me any of that before. I thought you liked Warren."

"I do. But not for Molly. Like you said, the man is very ambitious. You made him assistant manager because of Molly. If I were the bank president, I'd keep an eye on him."

"I had to give him the promotion. Molly is part owner of the bank. Her husband should share the responsibility of management."

"Now it looks as if he isn't going to be her husband."

Amelia shook her head. "She changed her mind once, she might change it back again."

"I surely hope not. If Billy Sinclair is half the man his brother is, Molly is lucky to have him."

"If Billy is half the deceiver his brother is, he'll break her heart into a million pieces. And we'll have to pick up the pieces."

"Amelia, are you blaming Billy for Chance's past sins?"

"Of course not."

"Are ye so sure Chance is guilty?"

"Papa said he paid Chance for the annulment. I know that Mr. Sinclair had a huge mortgage on their land. Chance paid off the mortgage after we . . . after I left. It had to be Papa's money. Where else would he get those kind of funds?"

"Have ye ever talked to Chance about it? Isn't it time ye cleared the air? Isn't it time he found out about what happened in Ireland?"

Amelia jumped to her feet. "I can't. I won't. He wanted the annulment and the money more than he wanted me. I'll never forgive him or Papa for that." She hurried to the parlor. At the mirror in the hallway, she set her hat on her upswept hair. "I've tried for years to forget him. It's too late now."

"Amelia, don't you think that it's ironic that both ye and Molly were Saturday brides? And both were terribly unlucky?"

That was something Amelia did not want to remember. Leaving Callie at the door staring after her, Amelia rushed down the street to the bank. At least there she knew what was what. Numbers and figures were black and white. It was a lot easier than dealing with her emotions or trying to figure out how she felt about Chance.

Amelia worked late that evening. Every time someone entered the bank, she looked for a telegram from Molly. Word had spread through town like the plague about Molly running away with Billy. More than a few people tried to drag details out of Amelia. She refused to fuel the gossip fires. Warren on the other hand, elicited sympathy from every woman who walked into the bank. The unmarried women were the most damning toward Molly. She was glad when Warren and the tellers left and she was alone in her office.

Thoughts of Chance, her father, and the annulment haunted Amelia all day. She didn't remember ever seeing the papers that had ended her short—one-night—marriage. Since her office had once belonged to her father, she assumed the documents must be filed away somewhere. Up until now, she hadn't bothered to look for them. It had never mattered before. Now, she wanted to see Chance's signature on the annulment papers. To have some kind of closure to their relationship.

After searching for an hour, she located a small portfolio of personal papers hidden in the back of the desk drawer. She pulled out the documents one by one. In the folder was her baptismal certificate, her parent's marriage papers from St. Louis Cathedral in New Orleans, her mother's death record here in Mayfield, and several faded photographs of the family. Carefully, she replaced all of the documents into the folder. The photographs she kept out for Molly.

As she returned the folder to the drawer, she spotted another envelope stuck in the corner. She tugged it out and set it on the desk. Inside the envelope was a legal document. She unfolded the paper and smoothed it out. Her breath caught. The annulment agreement. She followed the words with her finger. Chance's name and hers were inked in along with the agreement to annul their marriage. Further down were lines for their signatures. However, these lines were blank. Neither she nor Chance had signed the document. Could it be legal, if neither of the participants had agreed to the dissolution of the marriage?

Was it possible that she and Chance were still married?

Five

At eleven the next morning Amelia and Shamus McNab rode into the county seat. In spite of her aversion to travel, she had to learn the truth about her annulment. Again she'd hired the wagon from the livery owner. It was no surprise she'd been woozy during the entire journey.

Her father's attorney, who had handled his legal affairs for years, was now the local judge. As a personal friend of her father, Judge Morrison would know the particulars of the case. She'd told Callie she had banking business to see to, and asked her aunt to inform Warren at the bank that she would be gone all day.

At the courthouse, she entered the judge's office, where his assistant escorted her into the private chambers. She clenched her handbag and the envelope that held her past as well as her future.

The older gentleman greeted her warmly. "Amelia, my dear. What brings you to town today? Got some documents to file at the courthouse?"

She sat on the chair beside his desk and forced a smile. Though a shrewd lawyer and a stern judge, he had always been gentle and kind to Amelia. "No, sir. This is personal." She glanced at the door to make sure it was closed. "And confidential."

He leaned back in his chair. Hands folded over his rounded stomach, he watched her over the rims of his eyeglasses. "Is this about Molly? I heard she left her groom standing at the altar." A hint of humor glittered in his eyes.

"Word certainly travels fast."

"That fellow, Moneypenny, the groom. He raced all over town looking for Molly and that bandit, as he called the man. He was plenty angry. Not that I could blame him. I'd be upset, too, if somebody stole my bride right from under my nose."

"Yes, Warren is very upset. But this is something else entirely." Reaching into her handbag, she pulled out the envelope. "It's about this."

The judge reached out across the wide oak desk. He took the document from her trembling fingers. His eyes widened as he studied the words he had written years earlier. "The annulment. It was . . ." He glanced at the date. "Fourteen years ago. Your father came to me in a fury. He said you had run away with this young cowboy and gotten yourself married. He wanted the marriage annulled. So I drew up the papers."

A lump formed in Amelia's throat. "I found this yesterday. I want to know if this is just a copy or what. As you can see, neither Chance Sinclair nor I signed it."

Again he studied the agreement. "I usually make three copies. One for each of the parties and one to file in the courthouse records. All the copies should be signed and sealed."

Her heart thumped wildly in her chest. "I'm quite certain I didn't sign anything. Could my father have forged my name?"

"Amelia, I'm trying to remember what happened. It seems that after I gave him the papers, he never brought them back to me to be filed." He held up a hand as if to stop her. "That doesn't mean he didn't get another lawyer to help him. Why don't we let my clerk check the records and we'll find out if the annulment was recorded?" Pulling out a gold watch from his vest pocket, he sighed. "I'm due in court in five minutes. I'll give this to my clerk, and by the time I call a recess, we should have the answer."

"Judge Morrison, I really don't want this to get around. Only a few people know Chance and I were ever married."

"Don't worry, my dear. Mr. Hall is the soul of discretion." He stood and reached for a long black robe. "You can wait here, if you wish. Since it's close to dinnertime, I'll make this session as short as possible."

"Thank you." From her chair, she watched the judge speak to the assistant. The young man nodded, and scurried off.

Worry had Amelia pacing the judge's chambers. Was she still married to Chance or not? What if the annulment had never been signed and legalized? What if they were still legally man and wife? The biggest question of all: What did she intend to do about it?

Her stomach in a flutter, she jumped when the door to the office again opened. Still clad in his black robe, Judge Morrison entered. Amelia spun to face him. His grim expression brought a new worry. "Amelia, please sit down."

She did as he instructed. "What did you learn?" she asked, her voice trembling.

The judge took the chair next to hers. He caught her small, cold hand in his large, warm grip. "My clerk searched the records and came up empty. Now, the papers could have been filed in San Antonio, or another county. As a favor, I had him wire the Bexar County courthouse. We're waiting for their answer."

His eyes met hers. "I would like to ask you a rather personal question. Was the marriage consummated?"

Her eyes widened and her mouth went dry. "What do you mean?"

He cleared his throat as if searching for the right words. "Amelia, were you and Sinclair intimate? I'm asking because if you were, an annulment was not an option."

Amelia nodded, not able to lie. Even her father knew the truth. That she and Chance had more than consummated their marriage. "Yes, yes, we were . . . intimate."

The judge sighed. "Then if the annulment was filed, it isn't legal. In my opinion, you and Sinclair are still married."

The road back home was long and bumpy. She supposed Shamus McNab hit every chuckhole in the road. Amelia spent the miles with her face buried in her skirt to stop the dreaded nausea that threatened. Not only was she physically ill, her emotions were in a turmoil.

The judge's words rang over and over in her mind. "You and Sinclair are still married."

Amelia couldn't understand how that had happened. Her father had clearly told her he had gotten the annulment that ended the marriage. At the time, she had been too sick, physically and emotionally, to question him.

The fact remained. She and Chance were man and wife. The only way out of the situation was a divorce. Divorce and scandal were synonymous in Mayfield. Would Chance be willing to keep quiet about their problem and sign the papers when Judge Morrison drew them up? The real dilemma was, did she want to end the marriage?

Another thought struck her. Had Chance taken her father's money, and not carried through with his part of the bargain? Had he duped her father as he had fooled her? There was only one way to find out. She had to settle this once and for all.

"Shamus, turn off when we get near the Sinclair place."

"Yes, ma'am, we'll be there soon."

Chance jabbed the shovel into another pile of muck. After a hard day on the range, this was the job he hated most. However, it had to be done. Since he had chosen to leave most of the hands out with the cattle, he was elected to do the chore. He wanted to stay close to the house in case word came about Billy and Molly.

Late afternoon sunlight slanted through the open barn doors, casting long shadows on the hay-strewn floor. He looked up when he saw one of the shadows move. A woman stood silhouetted in the doorway, her face hidden under her wide hat. "Amelia." Her name slipped from his lips, and his heart skipped a beat. He tossed away the shovel. "Have you heard from Molly?"

She stepped into the darkened barn. "No. But I have something else to discuss with you."

He closed the distance between them. Now that he was able to see her face clearly, he caught the tight expression on her face. Her mouth pulled into a thin line, and fire burned in her eyes. Amelia was out for blood. But why his? Chance had thought they were getting along rather well, considering the circumstances.

"Well, what is it?"

Pulling a sheet of paper from her handbag, she shoved it toward his chest. "This. Our annulment. What do you know about it?"

After perusing it for a minute, he handed it back to Amelia. "Not much. I suppose your father took care of it."

"Did you, or did you not sign it?" Her voice dropped to an angry growl.

Not sure what her point was, he told the truth. "No, I did not."

"You mean you took his money, then refused to sign the document?"

"Amelia, you don't know what you're talking about."

She punched a finger into his chest. Her futile efforts didn't move him an inch. "I'm talking about my father giving you a large sum of money to sign this annulment—to be rid of me, once and for all. I'm talking about how you betrayed me for your thirty pieces of silver."

Her outburst shocked him to the core. Pain settled deep in his chest. "First of all, you're right. I did not sign the papers." This time he poked her in the chest with the finger of a dirty leather glove. He didn't care how many smudges he put on her sparkling white blouse. "And I did not take his money."

She narrowed her eyes. If looks could kill, he'd be a goner. "My father said you did. How else could you pay off the mortgage on this place? Blood money. Like Judas."

He clutched her shoulders in his big hands. "Are you calling me a liar?"

"If the shoe fits . . ." Her hands braced against his chest, she shoved.

Caught off guard, Chance stumbled back a step and tripped over the discarded shovel. He landed on his rump in a pile of hay and manure. She brushed her hands together. "I'll have my attorney get in touch with you. This time I expect you to sign the papers, nice and proper."

He didn't understand a word of it. "What papers?"

"Our divorce papers. It seems we are still legally married." On a huff, she spun on her heel and marched toward the door.

Chance threw off his initial shock. In a flash he was on his feet and at Amelia's heels. He caught her before she reached the door of the barn. "Hold it there, lady. I need more of an explanation." Her struggles to free herself threw them both off balance. She landed on her back, with Chance prone on top of her.

"Get off me, you oaf." Her struggles did little good under his superior weight and strength.

"Not until we get this straight. How can we still be married? Your father told me he had taken care of everything. He said you didn't want anything to do with me, that you wanted me out of your life."

"And he paid you well for it."

She wiggled, pressing her full, soft breasts against his chest. Her movement brought back memories of the night they had spent in the same bed. Since then he'd thought about her constantly. But now wasn't the time or place to give in to his needs.

"I did not take his money. But, hell, you won't believe me."

"You're right about that. Now let me go or I'll scream for help."

"Who do you expect to hear? My men aren't going to interfere." To still her flailing arms, he gripped her wrists and pulled her hands above her head. "And if we're married . . ." As she let out a loud shriek, Chance did what he'd wanted to do since she'd come back into his life. What he'd wanted to do for years. He lowered his head and covered her lips with his. Her eyes grew wide. She twisted her head from side to side. But he was determined to teach her a lesson. The kiss was hard and demanding. Chance took of the sweetness stolen from him years ago. What he'd just learned still belonged to him. His tongue slipped past her teeth and tangled with hers in a battle of wills.

Amelia stopped fighting. Her strength was no match for his. Desire ignited in him. Needs long buried sprung back to life. His mouth teased and caressed. He inhaled the fragrance of her over the animal smells that surrounded them. Married. If that was true, he had every right to claim his wife, here, now. Wanting to feel more of her, he released her wrists. She twined her hands around his neck, her fingers stroked his nape. Surrender was a breath away.

"Miss Amelia." The raspy voice intruded on his lust-dazed brain. "It's near to dark. You ready to go on to town?"

Chance lifted his head and spied Shamus standing in the open door. "Go away, Shamus. I'll see that Miss Amelia gets home safely."

The old man removed his top hat and scratched his bald head. "Is she sick or something? She like to lost her dinner on the way over here."

"No, I'm not all right, Shamus." Amelia pressed her hands against Chance's chest. "I tripped, and Chance was helping me up. Wait just a minute, and I'll be ready to leave."

"I said I would drive you home."

"And I said I'm leaving with Shamus."

Not wanting to argue, Chance rolled to his feet. He reached out a hand to assist Amelia. She slapped his hand away, getting to her feet on her own power. Standing, she attempted to brush some of the hay and dirt from her skirt. Her hat lay crushed on the ground. When she bent over to retrieve it, Chance spied the rear of her skirt.

"Miss Amelia." She slanted a glance at him as she plopped the hat back on her curls. "I believe you're wearing a large cow patty for a bustle." He grinned. Totally disheveled, covered with grime, she was the prettiest thing he had seen in a long time.

She twisted her head to look. "Ooh. It's smelly and disgusting. How could you do this to me?"

"You blaming me because you're clumsy?"

"I'm blaming you for everything." She shook the dress; the mess plopped to the ground. Then, to his utter surprise, she reached down and scooped up a handful of the goop. "Take this, it belongs to you." Her perfect aim caught him in the middle of the chest.

His mouth gaping open, he stared at her through narrowed eyes. "So you want to play dirty, do you?" He reached down into the pile he'd shoveled earlier, packed the manure, mud, and straw together like a snowball, and hurled it in her direction. Amelia leaped aside, and the goop landed squarely on Shamus's extended stomach. She took off on a run.

The old man let out a string of curses that would curl a horse's mane. "What was that for?"

"For getting in the way." Chance darted past Shamus, hot on Amelia's tail. Near the wagon, he caught her around the waist. He lifted her off her feet and hauled her into his chest.

She let out a loud squeal. "Let go of me, you brute." In spite of both of their filth and stink, he enjoyed the feel of her pressed against him. His mouth at her ear, he whispered, "As my wife, this is where you belong."

"I won't be your wife much longer. I'm going to rectify that mistake."

"We'll see about that, little lady." Abruptly, he let her go.

Free of his hold, she tried without success to remove some of the debris from her dress. "And don't call me 'little lady' again." With a swish of her skirts and her nose in the air, she continued to the wagon and climbed up. "Shamus. Are you coming to drive me home?"

The old man took his time meandering to the wagon. "Reckon I'm ready," he grumbled. "Not even Saturday, and the old lady will make me take a bath before I can go into the house."

"Be quiet. I'll pay you extra if you get me home in a hurry."

Chance stared at Amelia. "I'll be in town tomorrow so we can settle our little problem."

"Good. I'll expect you at the bank at four."

Chance let her have the last word, but he planned to show up at his own good time, not hers.

Six

Amelia remained at the bank until five o'clock. After waiting all day, she hadn't heard a word about Molly. She had sent telegrams to every one of her niece's friends from school, but so far not a word had come as to Molly's whereabouts. To top off a perfectly dreadful day, Chance hadn't shown up as per her instructions. It was now obvious he intended to ignore her.

Like a fool, she had spent the day thinking about him and that kiss they had shared. Their situation haunted her constantly.

Since Warren and the tellers had already left, she had nothing to do but lock up and go home. As she secured the door, she glanced up and down the dusty street. With the approach of twilight, pale yellow light spilled from the various windows of the businesses on Main and the homes on the side streets. Loud music came from the two saloons in town while several men made their way toward Miss Violet's House of Pleasure—or sin, as Amelia referred to the establishment.

She halfway expected to see Chance saunter out the doorway, hitching up his trousers. She released her clenched teeth. The man slipping into the alley toward the rear entrance bore no resemblance to

Chance. Slender, dressed in a smart gray suit, he seemed all too familiar. Even the bowler hat looked like one she should recognize. Her footsteps slowed. When a glow from the doorway touched his face, she spotted Warren Moneypenny sneaking into the house of ill repute. That hypocrite. After he had berated Chance, he was guilty of the same sin.

Amelia picked up her pace. Warren had a right to his indiscretions. He wasn't married. Thank God and Billy Sinclair.

Chance was nowhere in sight. Her father had been right all along. Chance really didn't want anything to do with her. He'd taken the money and didn't even bother to honor his part of the agreement. Walking swiftly toward the big house at the edge of town, she had pondered the predicament in which she found herself. The only decent thing for Chance to do was to quietly give her the divorce. He clearly didn't want to be married to her—he had proved that years ago. If he would go along with her, they could end the marriage quietly and without any hint of a scandal. After all, only Callie knew they had ever been married.

Her stomach sank. All night she had dreamed about Chance, about being his wife in every sense of the word. That kiss—that devastating kiss—still lingered on her lips. There they were, covered with muck, rolling on the ground, lost in passion. At least she was. Amelia couldn't say the same for Chance. It was probably just lust for a woman, and any woman would do. She ignored the tightening in her throat and wished for the sanctuary of her home.

Inside the large house where she had been born and had always lived, few lights glowed behind the lace curtains. Usually by this time of evening, Callie had every lamp glowing brightly.

Amelia had shocked her aunt the night before when she had returned home covered with filth. Callie had ordered her into the storage room to remove the ruined clothes. Then, the older woman had laughed uproariously at Chance's part in the whole affair. The only part Amelia left out was that kiss. It was too personal to share even with the woman who knew her deepest, darkest secret. Callie's reaction to the news that Chance and Amelia were still married had been a soft, "Oh," and a speculative gleam in her eyes.

Amelia entered through the darkened parlor, stopping in the foyer to remove her hat. "Callie," she called out, "I'm home."

No answer. She turned toward the kitchen, as this was where she usually found Callie preparing their dinner. Only a single lamp burned on the worktable, and luscious aromas wafted in the air. The table was set for two, but there was no sign of Callie. Lifting the lid on a covered platter, she spied her favorite meal— fried chicken. Other bowls contained mashed potatoes and green peas.

"Smells good, doesn't it?" The deep, masculine voice startled her. A shadow slipped into the kitchen.

She clutched her chest. "Chance? How did you get in here?"

He walked into the light. Tonight he wore his usual chambray shirt and tight denims. His hair was slicked back and his jaw freshly shaved. Chance was more appealing than any man had a right to be.

"Callie let me in."

"You were supposed to meet me at the bank over an hour ago." She stiffened her spine and set her resolve. Thankfully, he couldn't see how her heart pounded wildly at the sight of him.

"That was your idea. Mine was to meet you here at five o'clock. This way, we can have a nice, sociable, civilized meal together. Isn't that what husbands and wives usually do?" He gestured to one of the straight-backed oak chairs. "Among other things."

Heat surfaced to her face at his brash innuendo. "Where's Callie?"

"She said to tell you she had to go to some kind of meeting at the church. Ladies' Aid, Missionary Society, something or other. That we should enjoy our supper together."

Amelia patted her foot on the floor. She knew Callie's schedule well, and there was no meeting planned for tonight. Not at the church, anyway. No doubt Callie had set everything up to leave them alone. "I see. I'm not hungry. I believe we should settle our business, then you can be on your way."

His hands on the back of a chair, he waited for her to sit. "I'm starved. And you know fried chicken is my favorite dish." When she remained standing, he leaned over to uncover the various dishes. "Remember when we were kids in school—we must have been about ten or twelve—and you would sneak extra pieces of chicken into your lunch pail? Then we would sit together and eat all but the bones." He inhaled deeply, sniffing the mouth-watering aroma. "Your Aunt Callie made the best fried chicken in the world."

"I don't remember," she lied. She hadn't forgotten one minute of the time she'd spent with Chance, always against her father's wishes. They had been schoolmates together, sitting side by side since their names began with the same letter of the alphabet.

Callie knew Amelia couldn't eat all that chicken, but she went along with the ruse.

His smile told her he knew the truth. "Sit down, Amelia, you're making me nervous."

"I did not invite you to dinner."

"Callie did." Ignoring manners, he dropped into the chair. He filled his plate and picked up a drumstick. "If you don't want any, that's just more for me."

Her stomach growled. Nerves had kept her from eating a bite at noontime. Not that she would be able to enjoy the meal with Chance sitting across from her. She gave in and took the chair opposite his.

"You know, Duchess, if we weren't married, I'd propose to Callie. That woman sure can put a fine meal on the table."

Amelia cringed. "That is exactly what we have to discuss."

"Later." He held up a hand to halt her. "Let's just have a nice peaceful dinner. We can talk later over coffee and that delicious chocolate cake on the counter. Another one of my favorites."

How could Callie do this to her? She'd told her aunt that she had a meeting with Chance for that evening. She didn't expect Callie to betray her by inviting him to eat and then prepare all his favorite foods. On top of that, she had left them alone.

Once Amelia started eating, she realized how hungry she had been. They spoke little, keeping the conversation centered on the food, the weather, and other benign subjects. She steered clear of the reason she had asked him to come. It hadn't been to eat.

After the meal was finished, and Chance had a cup of hot coffee in front of him, he settled back on the chair and patted his stomach. "That was great. Best meal I've had in years. I could get used to eating like this."

"Well, don't. Enjoy your cake. You won't get it again." Amelia folded her arms across her chest. His gaze dropped to the softness he remembered from their encounter on the barn floor.

"What are you talking about? Callie isn't planning to leave you, is she?"

"No. She isn't going anywhere. Neither are you."

"I thought it would be easier for all of us if I move in here. That is, until I build a larger house out on the ranch."

Amelia jumped to her feet. "You'll do no such thing. I thought I explained it yesterday."

Not to be intimidated by her, he stood and met her imperious gaze. "You accused me of lying to you. We didn't settle a thing."

"Then I'll spell it out to you. My father paid you for an annulment. You took his money, but you didn't sign the papers. Now, in order to terminate our marriage, we have to file for a divorce. Name your price. I'm willing to pay it."

"Duchess, you don't know a damn thing. It's about time you learned the truth. After your father found us in that hotel room, he dragged you away and the sheriff threw me into jail."

She paled. "Jail? Nobody told me that."

"Yeah, jail. They refused to tell me where you were. Your father accused me of kidnapping you. And he threatened to charge me with rape. The only reason he didn't was that he didn't want to smudge your reputation. He didn't want a scandal."

"He knew that wasn't true. I told him I went with you because I loved you." Her voice quivered with emotion.

"I was horribly upset and sick to my stomach. My father said you didn't love me, that you only wanted his money."

"His money. Mr. Swanson offered me a lot of money to sign the annulment papers. I tried to tell him we couldn't get an annulment because we were truly married. I had already made you my wife. That's when he threw up the rape charge."

"But you took the money anyway."

He caught her upper arms and shook her. Years of anger and frustration gushed to the surface. "No, Amelia. I did not take the money. He said it was what you wanted—that you were sorry you had married me. That you wanted to be free to marry somebody better. I told your father exactly what he could do with his money."

"Then how did you pay off that mortgage? That was a lot of money."

"For a dirt-poor cowboy, you mean. I'll tell you, Amelia. I was devastated that you didn't love me, that you didn't even send me a note. He said you went to Europe and that I would never see you again. I took off for Arizona. I became a bounty hunter. And I was real good at it because I didn't care if I lived or died. When I came back after Maw died to help Paw with Billy, I had enough to pay off the mortgage and buy stock for the ranch."

Tears rolled down her cheeks. "My father sent me away with Callie to Europe. We stayed there until Louise and Edward were killed in that train wreck. Papa needed us to take care of Molly."

"You see, Amelia, he lied to both of us to keep us apart."

She shrugged out of his hands. "Now it's too late. We've both gone our separate ways. We can keep the divorce quiet and nobody need know we were ever married."

He laughed, the sound bitter to his own ears. "Keep things quiet. Don't start a scandal. Don't let anybody know that Miss Amelia was intimate with Chance Sinclair. What would that do to her spotless reputation?" His voice trembled with unbridled fury. Both of them had been cheated out of so much.

"It isn't like that at all. Just take the money and sign the papers. Then we can go our own ways." Her demands fueled his fury.

He shook his head. "No, ma'am. I won't do it. I didn't take your father's money, and I won't take yours. I didn't sign his annulment, and I won't sign your divorce. We're married, and we'll stay married. What was it that the priest said? Till death do us part?'" Taking her by surprise, he pulled her hard into his chest. "Honey, we ain't dead yet."

She gasped and struggled to pull free. "Let go of me or I'll take care of that problem."

Tired of arguing, he covered her mouth with his. That was one way to shut her up. The kiss was long and deep, full of all the pent-up tension of the last hours. His lips sipped, hers gave. His tongue thrust, hers parried. His hands stroked, hers clutched. His heart swelled with emotion. His woman. His wife. Nobody, not even this stubborn woman was going to take this away from him again.

Abruptly, he released her. "Remember that kiss, Duchess. Keep it in mind tonight in your lonely bed. Fourteen years ago I was too young and scared to stand up to your father. Now I intend to court you properly. I'll be back tomorrow for supper, and the day after that. I'll give you time to get used to the idea before I claim you as my wife." He swiped away her remaining tear with one rough fingertip. "I'm not a patient man, sweetheart. I'll give you until Molly and Billy come back. Then I'm moving in. Into your house. And into your bed."

Chance grabbed his hat from the peg behind the door and jammed it onto his head. His skin burned from her touch; his body ached with need. Yet, it was important to just walk away, to let her think about his demands. She would come around. He didn't doubt that she still had feelings for him. As soon as she realized she couldn't run roughshod over him, they would be able to work through this strange turn of events.

As he reached for the door, her voice came from behind him. "You forgot something." He glanced over his shoulder in time to see her pick up the plate containing the remainder of the chocolate cake. "You said it was your favorite. You can take it with you."

He jumped out of the way as the entire cake, plate, and all smashed against the door. Bits of chocolate and glass splattered over his clothes. With a grin, he reached out a finger and tasted the icing. "Tsk, tsk, it's really too good to waste like this." Before she could find something else to throw, he stepped over the mess and sauntered through the doorway.

Callie found Amelia on her hands and knees cleaning up the mess on the floor and wall. She'd hoped her aunt would stay away until she'd gotten rid of the goop that had missed Chance by an inch. No such luck.

"What happened in here?" she asked.

The truth was too embarrassing to tell. "I tripped and dropped the cake," she lied, averting her gaze.

"Aye, ye've been a mite clumsy lately. First falling at

Chance's place, and now this. Do you think ye should see a doctor?" Callie reached for a dustpan to collect the broken glass.

"No, I just tripped."

"Oh." Callie lifted an eyebrow in question. She clearly did not believe Amelia. "Did Chance get to sample it before you threw, uh, dropped the cake?"

"Yes. And he loved the chicken." She wiped the last of the chocolate from the wall while Callie swept away the glass. Not wanting to discuss what had happened, Amelia decided to put the other woman on the defense. "How was your 'meeting' at the church?"

The Irish woman laughed. "Aye, you know very well there was no meeting at the church. As you suspected, I just wanted to get away and leave you and Chance alone."

"And use it as an excuse to get up a poker game. How much did you win? Or lose?"

Callie huffed. "I never lose. When the customers in Violet's back room see me, they dismiss me as a sweet little lady without a brain in me head. They're always easy pickings."

Callie dumped the glass into the trash bin. "I suppose you and Chance had an interesting evening."

"Very." Amelia glared at her aunt. "You should have been here. But never mind. Chance Sinclair declared that he intends to return tomorrow night for dinner." She shook her finger at Callie. "And I do not want you to cook his meal. You can go to another 'meeting' and I plan to work late at the bank."

"Young lady, do not shake yer finger at me. I diapered you when you were an infant, wiped your mouth when you tried to feed yourself, and held your head all the way across the Atlantic. And I nursed you back to health in Ireland."

Properly chastised, Amelia had the good grace to look ashamed. "I'm sorry. You're more than my aunt. You're my dearest friend and like a mother to me. I won't tell you what to do, but I would prefer you not encourage Chance."

Callie sat across from her and took her hand. "Encourage him in what?"

"You'll find out sooner or later. Chance refuses to agree to a divorce. He wants to court me properly, then take his place as my husband."

She tightened her grip on Amelia's fingers. "What do *you* want?"

"I don't know. He infuriates me. He never asks, he orders. He claims he didn't take Father's money for the annulment. That he risked his life as a bounty hunter to get the money for the mortgage."

"I don't think he would lie about something like that. And what's wrong with having a good-looking man come courting? You aren't getting any younger, you know." Callie stood and moved toward the sink. "I'll clean these dishes, and get to bed."

"I'll help," Amelia offered. "And I'm certainly not in my dotage."

"I didn't say you were. But if a handsome cowboy came courting me, I wouldn't be working late at the bank."

"Callie, I'm just confused. I thought he'd betrayed me for money, and he thought I had rejected him. I'm not sure I can risk loving him again."

"My darling, give him a chance to prove that he still loves you."

"How can I be sure, Callie? How can I know he wants me and not my money? That he isn't just playing with a lonely spinster to protect his brother?"

Callie pulled Amelia into a motherly embrace.

"Follow your heart, *a ghra,*" she said using the Irish endearment. "But if Chance Sinclair deceives you, I'll shoot him meself."

Amelia kissed the older woman's soft cheek. "You'll have to stand in line behind me."

Seven

The next day, Amelia found that if anything could go wrong, it did. And it had nothing to do with Chance Sinclair—not directly. Though he was in her thoughts constantly, Amelia couldn't blame him for the troubles that beset her at the bank. Maybe it was the lack of sleep, or just her jangled nerves. Of course, Molly's disappearance plagued her all day. She couldn't believe her niece could be so irresponsible as to not notify them of her whereabouts. Nor had Billy contacted Chance.

As Chance had predicted, his kiss had lingered on her lips, and his words had haunted her all night. Whatever the cause of her distress, nothing seemed to go right from the moment she had stepped into her office that morning.

Warren greeted her with a scowl. He wanted her to sic the law on Molly and Billy. When she refused, he moped around all morning like a petulant child. One of the tellers dropped a tray full of coins, and it took all of them crawling on their hands and knees to recover the money.

Wanting some time alone, she retreated to her office. There, she again thought of Chance, and his declaration of innocence. When she went to look for the files on the Sinclairs' canceled mortgage, that, too, went wrong. The documents had been so badly misfiled, it took hours to locate the papers. True enough, Chance had paid off the mortgage three years after her father claimed he had.

Shivers raced up her spine at the idea of how he had risked his life so recklessly as a bounty hunter to raise the money.

With her thoughts on Chance and their dilemma, she looked up as Warren marched into her office and closed the door. His actions surprised her. Amelia liked to leave the door open to keep an eye on the happenings in the bank.

Without a by-your-leave, he hovered over her desk. "Amelia," he said, glaring down at her, "I must speak with you."

Rarely did he use her given name, and never during business hours. The sound of it irritated her. She stood and faced him eye to eye. "What is it, Warren, we're both quite busy at this time of day." And with her problem with Chance on her mind, she simply didn't want to deal with Warren's complaints.

"I think you should take time for this."

"Is there a problem?"

"I believe there is," he said, his voice harder than she had ever heard. "It's about Molly and that Sinclair fellow."

Her shoulders sagged. "We've been all through this. I will not send the law after my niece. I'm certain she'll return soon." At least that was her fervent prayer.

"Amelia, I have been in touch with an attorney. He says that I have a legal right to compensation. Molly has broken a promise to marry me, and that I can sue her for breach of contract." His pale blue eyes glittered with greed.

Anger bubbled up in Amelia like a volcano. She forced a calm she didn't feel. "I've already made you assistant manager with a substantial increase in salary. What more do you want?"

"We both know that I cannot marry Molly, even if she comes back. She'll be ruined. After all, she ran off with a man and has been completely unchaperoned. I would be the laughingstock of the town if I married a woman like her."

Amelia picked up a pencil and snapped it in two. "A woman like her? Are you calling Molly a . . . a . . . ?" The word stuck in her throat. "You're the one who spends time with harlots. Don't pretend you don't frequent Miss Violet's place. I saw you going in the side door."

Color inched up his neck to his face. "A man has needs, and since I have been cheated out of a wife to satisfy those needs, I see nothing wrong with taking advantage of the services being provided by other women."

Her stomach roiled at the thought of her sweet Molly being used so poorly by this man. "What do you want, Warren?"

He tugged on the vest of his tailored gray suit. "In marriage, a man is entitled to his wife's estate. Her money is his. Since Molly cheated me, it is only fair that I be compensated. I'm aware of the value of her holdings. I won't be greedy. I want half of everything she has. As her guardian, you have access to the funds."

Unable—unwilling—to control her temper, Amelia stepped from behind her desk. "You're demanding I pay because Molly jilted you?"

"Amelia, my dear, that's a rather crude way to put it, but yes."

"Warren, you haven't seen or heard crude yet. As of this minute, you are fired. You are no longer an employee of this bank. Get out of here." She marched over and flung open the door. "Out," she shouted. "Now."

"You'll be sorry for this. I'll sue you and Molly for everything you've got."

"I'll take my chances in a court of law."

"You heard the lady, Pennypincher." Chance appeared as if out of nowhere. "You had better get out while the getting's good."

"Stay out of this, Chance; This is between Warren and me." Amelia didn't want or need any help from Chance.

"If he doesn't get out of here, he'll be dealing with me." Chance shoved past Amelia and faced down Warren.

The smaller man huffed like a steam engine. "You haven't heard the last of this."

"That does it." Chance grabbed Warren by the back of his coat and seat of his pants. Under the watchful eyes of the bank customers, he hauled the jilted bridegroom to the door and tossed him into the street.

Amelia could hardly believe what had happened. Within minutes word of the confrontation would be spread all over Mayfield. The only thing that could make this day worse was a robbery. That was highly unlikely. Jim Powell, the sheriff, kept track of the strangers in town. The vaults were strong, and there had never been a hint of a holdup. Hoping to avoid a confrontation with Chance, she moved behind the counter and helped several customers. Chance remained at the door, watching the comings and goings on the street. With a glance at the clock, she turned to the teller. "Hiram, as soon as you finish with these customers, please lock the doors."

The teller looked askance. "But, Miss Amelia, it isn't nearly five o'clock."

"The bank is closing early." She marched back to her office and slammed the door shut.

Chance slapped a hand on the door before it clicked closed. "What was that with Pennypincher all about?"

She sighed, wishing she could avoid mention of the man's name. "Moneypenny. And it doesn't concern you." She dropped into her desk chair.

He leaned over the desk with his palms flat on the surface. "If this concerns you, it concerns me. It's about Billy and Molly, isn't it?"

"Yes." From one confrontation to another, she thought. Now she had to deal with Chance. "He threatened to sue me and Molly for breach of contract."

"Because she ran away with Billy?"

"Yes. And you made things worse when you attacked Warren. Those women in the bank will have this all over town within minutes." She spread her arms for emphasis.

"I don't give a damn what those women say. I was just protecting my wife."

"Please hold your voice down. And I do not need your protection."

As Chance took one step around the desk, a bell rang in her office. Women screamed, and loud voices came from the bank lobby. "What the hell is that?"

Amelia paled. "That's the signal my father installed to warn of trouble."

Chance shoved her down under her desk. "Stay here, and don't come out until I return."

"But . . ." she protested.

"Stay," he ordered.

Chance didn't know what was wrong in the bank, but he did know that it was dangerous to rush out there. An innocent person could get hurt. He cracked the door open to see what was happening. The teller, Hiram, was behind the counter, his hands in the air. He could almost hear the man's knees knocking. Three women huddled together against the wall. Two masked men waved pistols back and forth. So far, nobody had been hurt, and he wanted it to stay that way.

The robbers' hands and voices shook as they ordered the women to silence. A nervous gunman was more dangerous than a calm one. Their backs to the office door, they didn't see him slip out and drop behind another desk. With gun in hand, he watched the men gesture to the teller.

"P—put all the m—money in this bag." The taller of the men tossed a feed sack to Hiram. The white-faced teller lifted the money tray and dropped the entire contents on the floor. Paper flew, and coins rolled across the marble floor.

"Pick it up," the robber ordered. He looked around, but so far he had failed to notice the door to Amelia's office.

To Chance's dismay, that door flung open. Amelia appeared, her hands on her hips in that domineering stance she had learned from her father. "What is going on here?" she demanded.

Both robbers swung their guns in her direction. Chance's heart thudded to a stop. For a moment, nobody spoke or moved. Then, the shorter of the outlaws spoke in a shaky voice. "Cain't ya see, we's robbing the bank."

"Not *my* bank, you aren't. Get out of here."

Taking advantage of the distraction, Chance crept behind the teller's cage to the far side. He signaled the women to silence as he sneaked up behind the robbers. Furious that they had threatened Amelia, he resisted the urge to shoot them both in the back. But Chance had never been a cold-blooded killer.

He jammed the barrel of his gun into the closest man's back. "Boys, you'd better do as the lady says. Drop those guns." The man in front of him did as he ordered. His gun clattered to the floor.

The other fellow swung toward Chance. At that instant, an object sailed through the air and caught the bandit square in the back of his head. Startled, he dropped the gun. "Oow," he shouted, reaching up to touch the blood that sprouted from the back of his head. "I'm bleeding. She kilt me." As he looked at the blood on his hand, the man fainted dead away.

Amelia grabbed the discarded gun and pointed it at the injured man's chest. Chance ordered the other man to lie face-flat on the floor. At last he dared take a deep breath. "Hiram, fetch me a rope. There's some on my horse out front. Amelia, you go find the sheriff."

"But . . ." she started to protest.

"Go," he ordered. She handed him the gun and took off at a run. "You ladies can leave," he told the women who still hovered in a corner. They scurried out the door, whispering together as they went. They had enough gossip to last a month. With Hiram's help, he hog-tied both men. Then he picked up a heavy glass paperweight. Amelia's weapon. He cursed under his breath. The woman couldn't take orders to save her own life. The idea that she could have been hurt burned in his stomach and fueled his temper.

Chance was in a state of fury when the sheriff entered the bank, followed by Amelia. Her breath came in heavy gasps. "Here they are, sheriff. These two tried to rob my bank."

Jim Powell stopped short and surveyed the situation. A dozen or so men crowded the door. "Looks like Chance has everything under control. Let's see who these fellows are." He pulled down the kerchiefs covering the lower half of their faces. "The Clinton brothers." Jim shook his head.

The taller of the brothers, Joe Clinton, started to whine. "I need a doctor, I'm going to bleed to death. She shot me in the head."

"What happened to him?" the sheriff asked, turning his attention to Chance.

Amelia spoke up first. "I clobbered him with a paperweight."

Jim's mouth hung open. He hauled both men to their feet. "I thought you boys were satisfied stealing a cow now and then. When did you decide to rob a bank?"

"That fellow said it would be easy. He said we just had to walk in and take what we wanted. He never said nothing about him or her."

"What fellow?" Chance asked.

"I don't know his name. He came into the saloon and asked us if we wanted to make some quick money. He wore a fancy suit and hat. He said we didn't even have to share it with him."

"Moneypenny," Chance and Amelia said in unison. "He sure didn't waste any time."

Jim stared at Amelia. "Isn't Moneypenny the assistant manager? Why would he try to rob his own employer?"

"I fired him this afternoon."

"And he wanted to get even with you. I'll question him as soon as I lock up these two."

"I'll go with you. I'd like to hear what Moneypenny has to say." Chance grabbed one of the robbers and helped the sheriff escort them to the jail. "I'll be back," he warned, over his shoulder.

Amelia rubbed her forehead against the pounding headache. Too much had happened that day. All she wanted was to go home, crawl into bed, and cover up her head. "Come on, Hiram, let's clean up this mess." For the second time that day, they gathered up the money scattered over the floor. After safely locking the vault, she dismissed the teller. As she turned the CLOSED sign in the window, Chance pushed his way back into the bank.

"We're closed," she told him, shoving against the door.

His face set in an angry mask, he marched into the bank. Ignoring her protest, he locked the door behind him.

"Moneypenny was gone. I went to his room, and he had already left town." Chance followed her into her office.

"I can handle Warren."

A thunderous scowl darkened his features. "Like you handled those robbers? Woman, can't you take instructions?"

She picked up her hat, ready to go home after a harrowing day. "What are you complaining about?"

He settled his hands on his hips. "Didn't I tell you to stay in here, under that desk? What did you think you were doing?"

She shot him an angry glance. "First of all, Mr. Sinclair, I do not take orders from you. Second, this is my bank, and I will not allow anybody to rob it. Third, as you saw, I'm quite capable of handling myself."

"You could have gotten yourself shot." He stalked toward her. Amelia took a step forward, facing Chance toe to toe, nose to nose. "What did you think you were doing? Going after armed gunmen with a paperweight. A bullet is a hell of a lot faster, and much more deadly."

"David went after a giant with a slingshot and a few stones. I had the second paperweight in my other hand."

He growled deep in his chest. "I had everything under control. Couldn't you just let me handle it?"

"I don't need you. I can take care of myself." Her voice rose an octave.

"That's just it, isn't it? You've never needed me. You had your father and his money. What was I, Amelia? A diversion for a rich, spoiled girl?"

"You don't know anything, Chance Sinclair. You don't know what it's like to need somebody so badly you ache. You can't understand what it's like to carry a man's child and believe he doesn't want you. To love that baby more than your own life and to know his father wants nothing from you but money." The pain that had festered in her heart for fourteen years spewed forth like a ruptured dam. "I needed you then. I don't need you now."

Eight

The color left Chance's face. He gripped Amelia's shoulders in his hard hands. Only then did she realize that she had poured out her innermost feelings. Emotions that she had squelched for too long. The secret from her heart.

"What are you saying? You had my child?"

Her knees grew weak. Only sheer will kept her upright. "No. I . . . I don't know what I'm saying. Let me go, Chance. I want to go home."

"No, ma'am. Not until we straighten this out. You got pregnant that night. You had my baby and never told me." A muscle ticked in his jaw. His eyes darkened to almost black. He tightened his grip. "Where is it? Where is my child?" The words roared like thunder, dark and dangerous.

Overwrought, Amelia clutched the front of his shirt. Hot tears flowed down her cheek. "He's buried in a cemetery in Ireland," she squeaked out in a thin whisper.

Chance staggered back a step, taking Amelia with him. For a long moment he stared at her, as if unable to comprehend her words. He swallowed hard. "What happened?" he asked through a voice choked with emotion.

Pain sliced through Amelia at the memory of the

darkest days of her life. Her throat tightened, blocking off the words that needed to be said. Through her tears, she saw the moisture gather in Chance's eyes. "I need to know, Amelia."

She nodded. Through the heartbreak that had never gone away, she knew it was time to share her private pain. His hands on her shoulders, he helped her to the long leather sofa against the wall. Chance gently wiped her cheeks with his thumbs.

"That day when my father found us together, he was furious. He dragged me home and locked me in my room. For days I didn't see anybody but Callie. Then he said that you never wanted me, only his money. He said he had paid you for an annulment and that you had gone away. I didn't know you were in jail."

He cradled her closer into his chest. "I didn't take his money."

She sniffed back her tears. "I didn't know that. To keep me from going to you, he sent me to Europe—said I should go visit my mother's family. So he shipped me off to New Orleans, then I boarded a ship to Ireland. He sent Callie with me."

Gently he stroked her back. "Didn't he know about your motion sickness? Didn't he realize how painful a sea voyage would be for you?"

"Yes, but he didn't care. All that mattered was that I get away before anybody found out I had eloped with you. He didn't want a scandal. He didn't want his name sullied by gossip. If I had stayed, I'd have gone looking for you." Chance's body felt so warm and strong against hers. "I was very ill the whole time. I spent the entire trip in my bunk, unable to eat or move." The memory tore at her heart. "Callie was a godsend. She never left my side. When we reached

Ireland, I realized that I was expecting a child. That was the only bright spot in my life. I had a part of you with me, growing inside me."

Chance groaned deep in his chest. His heartbeat kicked up a notch in her ear. "Did your father know that you were having my baby?"

"No. Only Callie knew. I was still weak when I went into labor. But it was too soon for the baby." Unable to help herself, Amelia let the tears flow. The grief in her heart poured out like a flood. "He only lived a few hours. He died in my arms."

"Oh God, oh God," Chance moaned against her hair. "A boy. My son. I should have been with you."

"For a long time I blamed you, but the fault was my father's. If he had left us alone, and not sent me away, everything would have been different." She choked back a sob. "But it's too late now. Too late for us."

He kissed her hair; his hands stroked her back. "It's not too late, Amelia. We can start over. We can have more children, we can have the life together that was stolen from us."

How she wished it was true. "Chance, we were kids who thought we were in love. We're older now. Things are different."

"Amelia, look at me." She lifted her gaze. Through the mist of tears she saw the raw emotion in his eyes. "I've never gotten over you. Or the love we shared. Over the last few days, you're all I've thought about. I'm falling in love with you all over again."

She shoved her shaky fingers through his hair. Somewhere along the way he had removed his hat. "I've never stopped loving you. Every time I see you coming out of Miss Violet's place, I want to shout that you're my husband, and you have no business going to that place."

"Honey, no other woman can compare to you, or what we shared that one night. Or what we can have again." Leaning closer, he gently kissed the tears from her cheeks. His lips stroked her cheeks, licking away the salty wetness. "We can't forget the past, but we can have the future."

Amelia shivered under his touch. She caught his face in her palms and felt the moisture below his eyes. Left empty by the pain of the past, she wanted nothing more than to fill it with love. Not the youthful love they had known, but a love between mature adults, a love that would grow and last a lifetime. Her mouth found his, offering up her heart and body to him.

Tenderness swelled in Chance's chest as he took the gift Amelia offered him. The kiss grew and deepened. Her mouth opened to him, boldly searching his tongue with hers. Heat erupted in his body, a need that only Amelia, his wife, could satisfy. Desire surged through him. Amelia trembled under his touch. He rained rows of kisses over her face and down her neck. She loosed the top buttons of her blouse as an invitation for him to go further.

Chance continued his exploration of her skin. His tongue stroked the flesh above her silky camisole. He ran his fingers along the gold chain around her neck. The gold was warm from her skin. Nestled between her full breasts was what he at first thought was a pendant. Only when he tugged it free, did he realize that the object was a ring. A simple gold ring.

He lifted his gaze and met green eyes that were shimmering like emeralds. "Amelia, is this—?"

She closed her hand around his with the ring in his palm. "Your ring. The one you gave me on our wedding day."

"You kept it, all these years."

"I've worn it near my heart always. I never take it off."

Emotion overwhelmed him. The years he thought she had forgotten him, she'd borne his child and worn his ring. "Lord, we've wasted so much time, so many years."

"Let's not waste any more time. Make love to me, Chance. It's been so long since I've been held and touched. I need you."

He needed no further encouragement. Chance took what Amelia offered, and gave back a hundred-fold. Their kisses grew wild. Within minutes their clothes lay discarded on the floor. Their lovemaking went from sweet and tender to wild and untamed. The glory of having Amelia stole the very breath from him. She was his life, his joy, his passion. When she cried out her pleasure, he spilled into her with a rapture he had never known.

For a long while they lay cradled together on the couch, lost in the wonder of their love. He lifted the chain from her neck. "Duchess, let me put this on your finger the second time. Let's renew our marriage vows. Let's pick up where we left off. We can have that life together."

A shiver raced over Amelia's skin. Could she trust her heart to Chance for the second time? Could she risk loving him again? She swallowed the lump in her throat. Confusion leaped in her heart. "Chance, I don't know. I'm not sure what to do."

Propped on his elbow, he stared into her eyes. "What do you mean, you aren't sure? Hell, you're lying naked in my arms, and you're not sure? Were you lying when you told me you loved me?"

She turned her head, unable to meet his gaze. "I'm

not sure that love is enough anymore. Once I thought it was all we needed, now I think we need more."

"You want more, Amelia." His fingers twisted in her hair. "I'll give you more."

He smothered her protests with his mouth. Her cries were caught in his throat as he bruised her lips with his kiss. The kiss was full of passion and anger. Of need and frustration. Of demands and submission. Of heat and fire. Her body quivered when she quit resisting and melted under his touch. This time the lovemaking was fast and furious. When she cried out her pleasure, he took the sound into his mouth. Moments later, he sagged against her, his back drenched with sweat.

The emotion that surged through Amelia took her breath away. Her heart drummed against her ribs, and her thoughts were a jumble of confusion.

"I'll contact the preacher," Chance said. "We'll renew our vows tomorrow."

"Tomorrow?" She shoved against his chest, rolling him to the floor. Feeling as if she were being rushed, she sat up and snatched up a petticoat to cover her nakedness. "I can't."

He stared at her as if she had grown two heads. "You can't? After what we just shared?"

Angry at herself for what she'd allowed—no, what she'd encouraged—she glared right back at him. "It was sex, Chance. We're adults, and we made love. You've done it before with other women."

His blue eyes grew glacial. "But you haven't done it with another man, have you, Amelia?"

Shame turned her cheeks crimson. "You know you're my only lover."

"And as you recently reminded me, I'm your husband."

"I still want the divorce."

He stood and tugged on his denim trousers. "I don't care what you want, Duchess. I told you I'm not going to sign any papers." Shoving his arms into his shirt, he continued to glare at her. "I'll give you a week to be sure. Then I'm moving into your bed."

Clutching the petticoat to her chest, she leaped to her feet. "I'll have you arrested."

He laughed, and lifted her chin with his finger. "For what? Making love to my wife? I ought to walk out of here and tell everybody I meet that you're my wife, and I just very thoroughly took advantage of my rights as a husband. And won't they be shocked to learn that the lady banker has little pink roses on her unmentionables?"

"You . . . you reprobate," she shouted. Reaching for the closest object, she flung a pillow at his head.

Chance caught it easily in one hand. "Keep practicing, Duchess. We might be able to get you on one of those baseball teams." Leaving her fuming, he sauntered out the door, letting it click shut at his back.

Amelia didn't know how she got through the next two days. The attempted bank robbery had the entire town talking. Between that and word about Molly and Billy, the gossips had a year's worth of news. Everyone she saw wanted to hear about how Chance had saved the bank. Nobody mentioned that Amelia had as much a part as he in capturing the bandits. Word also got around that Chance had saved the lives of Hiram, the customers, and Amelia. She fumed every time the story grew in importance.

Fortunately, Chance stayed away. But she didn't

stop thinking about him, or his threat concerning their marriage.

To make matters worse, she saw him on Sunday morning on her way to church. He swaggered out of Miss Violet's front door, looking handsome, rested, and smug. He touched a finger to his hat and greeted her and Callie as if nothing had ever happened between them or that he had just come from another woman's bed. Lack of sleep had Amelia irritable and with circles under her eyes.

"'Morning, Miss Callie, Miss Amelia." He fell into step beside her. "Should I call you Mrs. Sinclair?"

Of all the nerve—flaunting his indiscretions in her face. Amelia picked up her pace. "Did you have a nice night, Mr. Sinclair?"

He chuckled. "Ask Callie. I lost a bundle to her."

Callie hadn't mentioned a word about seeing Chance the night before. "I suppose you were distracted by some fancy piece."

"Sweetheart, the only fancy piece I'm distracted by is you."

Callie laughed. "Come to dinner tomorrow night, Chance. After we eat, I'll give you the opportunity to get even."

"How can I refuse such a tempting invitation. I'll be there." He again tipped his hat. "See you tomorrow, Miss Callie, Miss Amelia." Chance sauntered away, leaving Amelia glaring at his back. She clutched her handbag in both hands. The urge to pick up a rock and fling it at him almost overrode her good sense. But with his hard head, he probably wouldn't feel a thing.

Amelia had no intention of having dinner with Chance the next evening. Callie had every right to invite whomever she pleased, but Amelia didn't have to be there. She would just work late at the bank until Chance took the hint and went home.

In spite of her resolve not to think about Chance, every time she glanced at the davenport in her office, she remembered how they had made love. Her skin tingled, and she could not concentrate on anything except him. She couldn't deny that she loved him. If only she could get up the courage to trust him, to believe in his love, to take what she wanted more than anything in the world.

At five o'clock, she locked the doors and dimmed the lights in the bank. Alone, she returned to her desk to finish some paperwork. Amelia glanced at the sofa. Her heart lurched. She was being a fool—a complete idiot. What guarantees did anybody have in life? If Chance said he loved her, she would have to just trust and believe him. Truth be told, he had never lied to her. Her father had separated them, not Chance. And she did love Chance. Without him her life had been dull and lackluster. He brought love and sunshine, fun and humor into her world. Now they even shared the pain of their lost child.

She reached into her desk and pulled out the divorce papers she had received that day from Judge Morrison. With a flick of her wrist, she tore them in half then in half again. Grinning, she dropped the shreds into the wastebasket.

Tonight they would sit down to a delicious meal, and afterward she would ask him to join her on the porch. There she would tell Chance she was ready to become his wife in every sense of the word. With the decision made, she felt as if a huge weight had been lifted from her back. She set her hat on her head, and opened the rear door that led to the alley.

Before she could step out, a man shoved her back
into the office. She bit back a smile, certain it was
Chance. When she looked up, she saw not Chance,
but Warren Moneypenny.

Nine

"Warren, what are you doing here?"

With a quick glance over his shoulder, the man closed the door behind him. His disheveled appearance shocked Amelia. His usually neat suit was wrinkled and dusty. A beard shadowed his jaw. In one hand he held a battered valise, in the other a small handgun.

"I've come to get the money you owe me."

Amelia stood her ground. "Warren, I do not owe you a thing. Get out of here."

"I'm not leaving until you give me my money."

"I'm not giving you anything." She swallowed the fear that lumped in her throat. Warren respected authority; she assumed her bank president persona. "Put that gun away before somebody gets hurt."

He laughed, a bitter ugly sound. "Miss Amelia, I know how to use a firearm. I'm not the idiot you take me for. I need money to get away—to go someplace where the women respect a man. Since you refuse to give me Molly's funds, I'll take yours."

Refusing to be intimidated, she clasped her hands at her waist. "You'll never get away with this. The sheriff is already looking for you. He thinks you helped the Clinton brothers try to hold up the bank."

"I did encourage them. But the fools let themselves

get arrested. This time I'll handle you myself. Please open the vault, and fill this valise. I'll take banknotes, certificates, and gold, if you please."

Amelia edged toward her desk. Her heart sank. Where were her paperweights when she needed them? The gun pointed at her chest said it would be fool-hardy to try to argue with him. By the wild look in his eyes, she knew he would kill her without hesitation.

He waved the gun, and Amelia moved toward the main lobby of the bank. "You see, Amelia, if you had given me the combination to the vault, I wouldn't have had to bother you like this. I could have just helped myself to whatever I needed, and left you and Molly alone with those Sinclairs."

"I've been checking the accounts, and it appears you've already been helping yourself to my funds." That, more than the gun in his hand, infuriated her.

"You didn't expect me to survive on that measly lit-tle salary you paid, did you? A man like me has refined tastes, and it takes money to live well."

"I suppose the promotion and raise in salary weren't enough for you."

"My dear, I was about to marry an heiress, the sec-ond wealthiest woman in town—you being the first. I would have had it all if Sinclair hadn't interfered." He waved the gun toward the large iron vault near the rear wall. "Enough socializing. Please open the vault."

"I need light," she said. Striking a match, she lit sev-eral kerosene lamps that sat on the desk in front of the vault. Hopefully, the sheriff or a passerby would see the light and check on Amelia. But that was un-likely. She often worked late and kept the lamps lit into the night.

With trembling fingers, Amelia reached for the

large dial and spun toward the first number. With Warren's wild behavior, she was glad she had refused to give him the combination when he'd asked for it.

Chance spotted the light through the frosted windows of the bank. As he'd expected, Amelia was still inside, doing her best to avoid him. When she didn't show up at home at her appointed time, he'd decided it was time for a showdown.

He knew she loved him. No woman could give herself so completely and passionately without loving a man. Not a woman like Amelia, anyway. She was all he'd thought about for days. Her, and the child she had lost. His son. A child born out of their love. What he couldn't understand was why she was being so stubborn about admitting her love. Why couldn't she trust him and his love? They would have it out tonight. If she still didn't come around, he would sign her damn papers and set them both free. But Chance knew he would never be free of Amelia.

Approaching the rear door that led directly into her office, he tried the knob. To his surprise, it turned, and the door eased open. That was another thing he had to discuss with her. It was foolhardy to work at night and leave the door unlocked.

He stepped into the dimly lit office. Empty. Voices came from the main lobby through the open doorway. A woman's—Amelia's—and a man's. Jealousy, an emotion he rarely experienced, surged up in his chest. Soundlessly, he entered the bank. The pair stood in front of the large iron vault—certainly no place for a romantic encounter.

"Oh, I messed up. I'll have to start again." Amelia's voice trembled.

"Hurry, Amelia. I haven't got all night." Moneypenny. Chance recognized the nasal tones.

Chance ducked behind a desk. Something was wrong. In the lamplight, he caught the glint of metal in the man's hand.

"Well, if you weren't pointing that gun at me, I wouldn't be so nervous. I can hardly remember the combination."

Damn, Moneypenny was forcing her to open the vault at gunpoint. Chance had never thought the man would have the nerve to do something like that. Being careful not to alert them to his presence, he crawled toward the teller's cage. All he had to do was come up at Moneypenny's back and disarm him. Fury and fear mingled in Chance's heart. He didn't want to put Amelia in danger.

Amelia spun the dial on the combination lock. The numbers clicked loud in the silent bank. Hidden in the shadows, he watched.

"There, that should do it." She jiggled the metal lever with both hands. "It won't open."

"Let me see." Moneypenny grabbed the handle, his attention centered on the vault door.

With the man distracted by the possibility of loot, Chance leapt from his hiding place, and smashed his body against the robber. The gun flew from Moneypenny's hand. Amelia stumbled out of harm's way. Bigger and stronger, Chance had his opponent on the floor within seconds. Unable to stop himself, he smashed his fist into the man's face. Moneypenny gazed at him with wide startled eyes. Blood seeped from the cut at the corner of his mouth. "No, no," the man screamed. "I didn't mean any harm."

Chance lifted him to his feet by the front of his shirt. "You held a gun on my woman and tried to rob her bank. That means you stepped on my toes. Now, I'm stepping on yours."

"I was only taking what should have been mine if your no-good brother hadn't kidnapped Molly."

He drew back his fist for another good punch, but Amelia grabbed his forearm. "Take him to jail, Chance. I'll lock up the bank and meet you at the sheriff's office."

He glanced over at her. The woman had nerves of steel. He didn't doubt she would have found a way to handle Moneypenny without his help. She was right. She didn't need him at all.

Her knees and hands shaking, Amelia managed to extinguish the lamps and lock the doors. Her heart had stopped beating when Chance had appeared out of the shadows and taken Warren down. She didn't know what she would have done if he hadn't come. In the back of her mind, she'd prayed he would come looking for her.

By the time she reached the jail, Warren was already locked in a cell. Chance was giving his statement to Sheriff Jim Powell. Warren shouted that he hadn't done anything wrong. He was only looking for what was his. The sheriff ignored his tirade. Within minutes, Amelia gave a full account of the attempted robbery.

The usual onlookers had crowded the door, ready to spread more gossip around town. Amelia decided that it was time to give them something new to talk about. "Chance saved my life," she said, turning toward him. "I don't know what I would have done if you hadn't come along."

His blue eyes widened in surprise. They grew wider when she wrapped her arms around his neck, rose on her toes, and kissed him solidly on the mouth.

Hoots and howls came from the crowd. "Lookie that, Miss Amelia and Chance."

She ended the kiss. "Let's go home. We have something important to discuss."

Jim started to laugh. "I'll be in touch with Judge Morrison over at the courthouse. I'll let you know once the trial is set."

Still shocked by Amelia's actions, Chance wrapped an arm around her waist and led her out the door. Once they were alone on the street, he stopped and gazed down at her. "Ran out of paperweights, Duchess?"

She smiled up at him. "Couldn't find one anywhere."

"Guess you're lucky I came along."

"Mighty lucky."

"About those divorce papers . . ."

She silenced him with a kiss. "I tore them up. If you still want me, I'll wear your ring forever."

His heart thumped wildly. "I've always wanted you. We'll do it right this time. We'll get married so the whole town can see."

"Let's get home. I want to tell Callie." Amelia picked up her pace.

"In all the excitement, I forgot to tell you. Billy and Molly are back."

"Why didn't you tell me sooner?" Lifting her skirt, she ran down the street.

"Slow down, Duchess. They aren't going anywhere."

Chance and Amelia entered the rear door and found Billy and Callie at the kitchen table, sipping coffee with a huge chocolate cake between them. Molly greeted her at the door with open arms and a hug. The young man leaped up when he spotted them. He shifted from foot to foot, looking like a caged fox about to bolt through the open door.

"Molly, are you all right?" she asked, surveying her niece from head to toe. Clad in one of the new gowns from her trousseau, Molly was a welcome sight. Wherever she'd been or whatever she'd done hadn't hurt her at all.

"I'm wonderful, Auntie. I've never had so much fun in my life."

"Fun? Molly, I was worried sick. We looked all over for you."

Molly slanted a glance at Chance, who leaned against the doorway, his arms crossed over his wide chest. A sly grin curved her lips. "Aunt Callie told me how you and Chance went all the way to San Antonio looking for us."

Amelia set her hands on her hips, ready to give her niece a dressing-down. Chance stepped forward and interrupted. "Billy told me they were in New Braunfels all along."

She shifted her gaze to the young man. Billy backed up a step as if afraid she would strike him. "Sit down, Billy. I won't snap your head off," she said. "Yet."

"Miss Amelia, ma'am, I'm real sorry about what happened. We didn't mean for you to worry about Molly. Reckon we should have left a note or something." He jammed his fingers through his already mussed hair. Molly moved to his side.

"You could have spoken to me."

"Yes, ma'am. We could have."

"Why didn't you?"

A blush crept up the young man's cheeks. At twenty-one, Billy was a robust, virile man, but at that moment, he looked like a mischievous boy caught with his hand in the cookie jar. "I reckon we was kind of scared of you."

Billy Sinclair stood nearly six feet tall, and wore a gun in the holster on his hip. Yet he professed to be frightened of a five-foot-six tall woman armed only with her wits. Amelia knew she intimidated people, but it never occurred to her that Molly was afraid of her.

"Molly, why would you be afraid of me?"

Chance chuckled deep in his throat. "They must have heard that you're dangerous with a paperweight and manure."

She shot him a quelling glance. "I'm not dangerous. Molly knows I only want her happiness. I gave in to all her demands about the wedding."

"Too many of them, if you ask me," Callie added.

"Could be that was the problem, Duchess." Chance spread his hands. "Molly might have been afraid you would be angry because you spent so much time and money on the wedding. She didn't want to disappoint you, but she didn't want to go through with marrying Pennypincher."

"Moneypenny."

Molly slipped her arm around Billy's waist. "Chance is right, Auntie. I know how much you like Warren. He's so much like you with the bank and all. Even if Billy hadn't come back, I knew I couldn't go through with it. I love Billy. It wouldn't be fair to Warren to marry him."

Amelia rubbed her temples at the growing headache. "I'd hardly think 'fair' is a word I would use for Warren. You'll hear about this soon enough. Tonight, Warren tried to rob the bank."

Callie gasped. "Holy Mary, Mother of God. Two attempted robberies in a week. What happened?"

"He came in with a gun and demanded that I give him the money from the vault. Seems he's upset that Molly didn't marry him and turn over all her money to him, as he'd expected."

She smiled up at Chance and the smug look on his face. "Thankfully, Chance came along, again, and saved me and the bank."

Billy's face turned red with anger. "All that Moneypenny wanted was Molly's money all along. He didn't deserve a wonderful woman like her."

Amelia stared at the young man. She had no doubt that Billy loved her niece for herself.

"I love Molly, Miss Amelia. I convinced her to go with me so we could be together. I wanted to get married right away, but she said we should get your blessings first." He stared directly, boldly, at Amelia. "I don't want her money. I'll take care of her. I talked to Chance. He said he'll build us a house out on the ranch and we can be partners, like Paw wanted."

"Billy, I love Molly, too. I only want the best for her. But I would like you to wait before you marry." A thought occurred to her that they may not be able to wait. "Unless . . . unless there's a, uh, reason you, uh, have to—"

"Aunt Amelia," Molly said, clearly shocked at her aunt's insinuation.

The young man's mouth gaped. "No, ma'am. It's nothing like that. Molly said we have to wait until after we're married. I wouldn't dishonor her like that."

Amelia slanted a glance at Chance. They had waited until they were married. And they still were husband and wife.

"Thank you, Billy." She kissed the young man's cheek, then her niece's. "You have my blessing. We'll plan a wedding as soon as you want."

"Not yet, you won't." Chance stood behind Amelia with his hands on her shoulders. "Since we're doing this right, the next wedding you plan will be ours. I told you that as soon as Molly and Billy returned I would make you my wife again. I want the whole town to know we're married, and I want them to witness the renewal of our vows."

"Hallelujah," Callie shouted. "I've been waiting fourteen years for this news."

Both Molly and Billy stared with wide shocked eyes. "What are you talking about? Aunt Amelia and Chance—getting married? I didn't even think you liked each other."

Callie laughed. "Honey, I'll tell you the whole story. Amelia and Chance ran away fourteen years ago and got married. Her father, your grandfather, found them, and separated them. Until a week or so ago, they thought they had gotten an annulment. Only they learned they're still married." She slipped an arm around the young girl's shoulders. "When you ran away with Billy, they worked together to find you. Instead, they found each other again."

"About that wedding?" Chance asked, his eyes shining with the love Amelia thought she had lost long ago.

Callie grinned. "Today is the first of June, so we'll miss the woes of May. And this time, it won't be a Saturday."

"That's just Callie's Irish superstitions."

Laughing, Chance drew Amelia up and into his arms. "I don't care what day we get married. As long as you're my wife in every sense of the word."

Callie wiped the tears from her eyes. "Then we'll aim for Wednesday, the best day of all."

DO YOU HAVE THE
HOHL COLLECTION?

Celebrate Romance With
Meryl Sawyer

Stella Cameron

"A premier author of romantic suspense."